THE LAMP OF THE WICKED

by

Marianne Christian

FAMILY PUBLICATIONS

OXFORD

© Family Publications, 2001

ISBN 1-871217-33-4

cover design by
Joanna Pitt

published by
FAMILY PUBLICATIONS
77 Banbury Road, Oxford OX2 6LF
Telephone: 01865 514408

printed in England by
Cromwell Press, Trowbridge

The light of the virtuous shines brightly
but the lamp of the wicked is put out.

Proverbs 13:9

To my grandchildren
Laurie and Rachel
with the prayer that they may
always know that God loves them

Chapter 1

"I thought I'd never see you again"

The two men parted where the track diverged.

The older man hesitated. "It's not too late to change your mind."

"Thank you, but it's better this way. Now *go* – before you burst out of your skin like a lizard!"

Melkiah smiled. He had believed his growing impatience had been hidden from his companion. "Very well, but I shall expect you tomorrow."

He turned, and at long last took the narrow way he had walked in his imagination times without number over the years. He had already forgotten the other man; his eyes were drinking in the view as eagerly as a bee sucking nectar. His feet splashed through puddles, adding further layers of mud to his sandals and torn woollen mantle, but he was unaware of everything but the gleaming lake before him. His eyes roved eagerly from rain-misted hills to the houses clustered near the water's edge; from the trees with their roots in the water to the beginning of his own property – just visible from this point. Dark rain clouds were racing across the sky like a flock of black sheep racing for their sheepfold, but Melkiah laughed aloud in pure joy. Nothing the elements could devise would prevent him reaching journey's end now.

He could see the walls around his house, the winter-bare branches reaching up from enclosed courtyards; could pick out the vineyard, the olive grove, and the surrounding land that made up his property. In this month of Tebet, the fields were a threadbare brown cloak waiting for the seed which would quicken them into a warm covering; but the cloak held a few patches of vivid green where a winter crop of barley, a soft fleece of wheat, and delicate blades of growing flax braved the winter ground.

Even through the falling raindrops, he could tell that his land had been well cared for. He had never doubted Simeon's ability or loyalty, knowing that in his absence his steward would have been tending the property as if it had been his own. It had been one of his few consolations.

The rain became torrential and now the lake was a grey mist where water met water with force and flowered into ripples, only to be absorbed by the wind-whipped waves. Melkiah knew all the moods of this jewel of a lake, and the opal was as dear to him as the sapphire. He strode on towards the house, his feet sliding on the muddy path, his eyes never leaving his goal. Tiberias Caesar could keep his palace. It could not compare with his own home in Galilee.

No one was in sight as he reached the gate into the courtyard and flung himself inside, helped by a sudden gust of wind. His legs were trembling as he skirted the central fountain and made for the arch leading to the winter quarters. Open to rain and sun, friend and stranger, visiting angels and men returning from the grave – it drew him through to the familiar entrance hall. He threw back the hood of his mantle and stood quite still, unaware of the water trickling down his beard and from his rain-saturated clothes.

The vestibule held no furniture but a small table and a couple of stools and was darker than usual because of the overcast sky. He breathed in the almost-forgotten scent of an oil-lamp but the niche in the wall was empty. Then he heard light footsteps and a girl carrying a lamp came from the adjoining room.

She gave a startled glance in his direction.

"You are welcome to shelter, sir," she began, then her eyes, which had dropped shyly, returned to his face in sudden shock. Her uncertainty lasted a few moments only before turning to blazing joy.

"Abba!"

She took a step towards him, remembered the lamp in her hand and thrust it hurriedly into its accustomed place, then ran into his waiting arms.

Melkiah needed all of the self-discipline he had perfected so painfully over the intervening years to hold on to his senses. He chided himself that it was but a homecoming, no different than any of the occasions when he had returned from Jerusalem after the Passover. The time for tears was over.

But, as his arms held her close, he had to fight to control his emotions. It was no longer the child, Tamar, he held in his arms, but a young woman whose head reached up to his shoulders. He rested his chin briefly against the soft coils of her plaited hair before remembering his condition and pushing her away from him gently.

"I'm sorry, Tamar. I'm making you wet."

"As if I cared! Do you know how long I've waited for your return?" Her eyes held the tears he would not permit in his own, and her voice the stored-up passion of years of sorrow. "I thought I'd never see you again. I thought you were dead! Where have you come from? And why, *why*, have you stayed away so long?"

"It was not my choice." He indicated his rough, mud-stained clothes ruefully. "I'm surprised you recognise me!"

She looked into his smiling eyes, and reached up to wipe away the raindrops that were trickling down his forehead. "I would know you, if you had stayed away fifty years, rather than eight . . ." She gave him a swift kiss. "And I'm keeping you standing here like a stranger!"

She went to the inner archway, called "Eglah!", and fetched a stool while waiting for the servant to appear. "Sit here a moment, Abba."

As a plain woman in her middle-age hurried in, Tamar ordered: "Bring water, the foot-washing bowl, and a cup of spiced wine. And tell Nike to prepare some hot water for a bath."

Tamar knelt before her father and slipped the sandals off his muddy feet. "I can scarcely see which is foot and which is leather! How far have you travelled today? So many of the roads are impassable in this rain."

"Nothing could have prevented me for coming home – even if angels had moved our house to the top of Mount Hermon! Throw those sandals away – they're past redemption." He dropped his sodden mantle onto the floor, revealing an equally damp tunic. "I was given these old garments, but I'm hoping you can find me something better."

"All your own clothes are in your room, exactly as you left them," Tamar responded, as Eglah, colouring with nervous excitement, brought in warm water, towels and a cup of wine.

"Leave them here. I'll see to it. Go and tell Keturah to prepare a meal fit for a visiting king!"

Melkiah laughed. "Poor Eglah. She's not quite sure if I'm the Master she once knew, or Nebuchadnezzar after his seven years of being put out to graze!"

Tamar smiled and kissed his rough hands with their torn nails before putting the bowl at her father's feet. Once he had placed his right foot on the special raised ledge, she poured some warm water over it and washed away the first layer of mud.

"This is a servant's job," Melkiah protested, as she cleansed his heel, but the radiance of her smile silenced him, and once again he had to struggle to keep tears from his eyes. More than anything, he wanted to return to the uneventful, peaceful rhythm of his former life.

Tamar used the towel vigorously then poured fresh water over his other foot. She smiled at him when the job was finished. "I'll bring you some sandals, and see if your bath is ready. She passed him the steaming cup and laughed as he breathed in the strong aroma of cinnamon and cloves appreciatively. "Is there anything else you need?"

He shook his head. For eight years he had bathed in rivers and mountain streams and used their water to quench his thirst. If Heaven had been opened and he had been invited inside, it could surely hold no more comforts than he was being offered now.

The rain was still lashing down outside when Tamar returned. "The water is hot now and Nike has added some juniper and bay to refresh you. I've a thousand questions but I'll wait until you're wearing dry clothes. I expect you're exhausted but I don't think I could bear to wait any longer than that. You won't go to sleep, will you?"

Melkiah smiled at the eager young child showing through the form of the lovely young woman. "I won't rest yet," he promised. "I too have a thousand questions. I'll content myself with just one now: is my mother well?"

"Yes, though this damp weather makes her limbs ache. I went to tell her of your arrival, but she is asleep. I thought you might like to wake her?"

"Let her rest until I'm presentable again. I wouldn't want her to see me like this!"

"Oh, but . . ."

"Be patient. In a very short time, we three will have all the time in the world to catch up on all the lost years."

Tamar was in a state of shock as she hurried from one part of the house to another: to her father's old room to choose some clean garments for him; to see Keturah about the celebration meal; to send the boy, Dan, to her father with figs and wine. At one moment she found herself frowning, for this was not the return of a rich merchant after years of successful trading. But at the next she was singing, for nothing in the world mattered now that he was home again.

When she returned to her grandmother's room, she found her sitting drowsily in her favourite chair by the brazier.

Sarah recognised her footsteps. "I've been having the most wonderful dream: Melkiah was here, and Anne was alive again, and you were a young child playing beside them. It was how it might have been . . ."

Tamar spoke quickly. "Sometimes reality can be better than a dream. And dreams can . . ."

She was interrupted by the sound of someone approaching with a firm tread, and a moment later Melkiah was in the room.

"I no longer look like a drowned rat!" His face was deeply lined, and he had lost a lot of weight, but in his own clothes he looked like the adored father Tamar had held in her memory for so many years.

Sarah was leaning forward, tensed into shock. "Say something else," she whispered. "That voice . . ."

"Don't you know me, Mother?" Melkiah bent down and put his arm around the trembling woman.

"It can't be . . ." But she felt the reality of his kiss on her cheek and clung to him fiercely.

"We didn't expect that we'd meet again, but the Most High has been merciful to us. Won't you look at me?"

Sarah raised her head at his words but her eyes, now faded, were unseeing, and suddenly he understood.

"You're blind!" He turned to Tamar. "When did this happen?"

"Only a few months after you went away." Tamar remembered wondering at the time if shedding so many tears had caused her grandmother's blindness.

"All this time! Simeon never said . . ."

Sarah brushed away his words impatiently. "My eyes don't matter. I learnt to live with my condition years ago. What I want to know is how you come to be here, well again." She reached for him. "You *are* cured, aren't you? You sound so strong."

"I am completely well", he agreed. "Mother, I have much to tell you."

Tamar frowned. "I don't understand why you are talking about sickness. You've been travelling as a merchant in far-away lands. That's why you couldn't come home." The silence that greeted her words brought her to the beginnings of realisation. "It wasn't true! . . . Yet you sent me presents for my birthday and on feast days through Simeon. So, where *were* you? Why didn't you come home? I needed you so much. I cried for you . . ."

She spoke with the candour of a child and Melkiah noticed that her mouth was trembling. "Do you really think that I would have stayed away if I could have come to you?" His voice was gentle but he wished fervently that all the explanations were over.

"I couldn't understand," Tamar persisted. "No one would talk about you or tell me when you were coming home. When I asked Granna, it made her cry too . . . Eventually I decided that you must be dead."

Melkiah looked from the passionate young face of his daughter to that of his mother, whose veiled head was turning alertly to follow their voices. He crossed the room and fetched a chair. "I think I can still remember how to use one of these!" He sat next to Sarah, his hand resting on one of hers, while Tamar pulled forward a stool for herself.

"It's over, Mother," he murmured. "Our new life starts today."

Sarah lifted his hand and held it against her cheek. "I will die content now that I know that you are alive."

Melkiah shook his head at her, not yet used to the fact that she could not see him. "We'll have no more talk of death," he decided. "We are all going to *live*."

Tamar's eyes never left her father's face which had always portrayed vitality and irrepressible good-humour. It was the face that had blessed her dreams but now she was too confused to share the comfort of mother and son.

"Where have you *been?*" she demanded. "Simeon told us you were in Alexandria and Cyrene, and then Crete and Macedonia. When you didn't return, we thought maybe you had gone on to Italy, Gaul and Spain, and other faraway dangerous lands. But I could never understand why you didn't return to tell us of your travels . . . Oh, Abba, where *were* you?"

Sarah tightened her grip on Melkiah's hand. "You have to tell her now."

He agreed.   "But how do I begin?"

"You could say that you've been dwelling in the valley of the shadow of death . . ."

Tamar looked from her father to her grandmother, some instinct warning her that their shared knowledge was going to hurt her.

"I don't understand."

"It's very simple," Melkiah said, his voice brisk now.   "For eight long years, I have been a leper."

Chapter 2

"There is only one Person who can cure leprosy"

Tamar stared at her father, her eyes dark with horror. "A *leper?*" Her imagination had suggested many reasons for his long absence but never anything as horrific as this.

Melkiah spoke swiftly, giving her no time to dwell on his statement. "I'm not going to talk about those years. I want to forget them, and the last thing I want is for you to be haunted by hardships which are now behind me. I forbade anyone to tell you the truth when you were a child and, now that it is over, there is certainly no point in you reliving the past."

"But . . . how did it happen?"

"I had a sore which the doctor told me was the first stage of leprosy." In one matter-of-fact statement, Melkiah told of the diagnosis which had been his death sentence. "I don't know how I caught it, though once I found a leper half-dead with starvation in a cave below Chorazin, and I had to go close to him to revive him."

"But why did you go away? You could have stayed here in isolation and we would have tended you ourselves. No one would have known."

"It wouldn't have been possible to keep such a secret. I'd soon have been discovered – and sent on my way with a shower of stones!"

"But no one would have stoned *you!*"

Melkiah inwardly thanked God that his daughter would never know the cruelty to which men are driven by fear. Until the first time a stone had struck him, he too had believed that others would have pity for a man with such a disease. He had never expected anyone to provide shelter for him, but he had hoped to be given scraps of food by compassionate people as he travelled.

"We could have come with you, and looked after you," Tamar persisted. "We would have found some hidden refuge . . ."

"And I would have repaid you by giving you the gift of living death," Melkiah pointed out.

"Where did you go?"

"I headed for Jerusalem. I'd seen the lepers dwelling in the Hinnon Valley often enough."

"Why did you go so far away? Why didn't you stay in Galilee?"

Melkiah sought a way to explain, without betraying the emotion he was determined to avoid. The truth was that he could not have borne to live too close to the members of his family once they were forbidden to him.

"Perhaps because I thought I might walk home in my sleep!"

Tamar saw tears running down her grandmother's cheeks and suddenly realised the reason for all the unexplained distress the old woman had suffered over the years.

"You knew! You knew Father wasn't a merchant but was living among strangers, mortally ill . . ." Tamar knelt and put her arms around her. "You had to bear it all alone."

Melkiah looked helplessly at their mingled tears and again thanked God that the explanations would soon be over and that they would be able to resume their former life. His feet, now in his own comfortable sandals, moved restlessly on the floor. He moved back from the heat of the brazier unable to bear further delay.

"The only other person who knew was Simeon. He brought me news of you twice a year."

"And every time he went to Jerusalem he took money to one of our contacts there and arranged for your father to be given food regularly," Sarah told Tamar. She reached out blindly for her son. "Each time he returned, he told me that you were coping well – and each time I didn't believe him . . ."

"It's over, Mother," Melkiah repeated. "I am completely cured, strong and well. I wish you could see me for yourself. Tell her, Tamar."

Tamar smiled into her father's eyes, more than content with the lean, tanned face and vibrant expression.

"He looks as healthy and happy as a bridegroom on his wedding day. Though he looks as if he's cut his hair with a scythe and his beard with his eyes shut!"

"I admit I'm in need of Imri's skills. Where is he?"

"Asher's using him on the land. He'll be overjoyed to tend to you again."

Sarah was feeling her son's rough hair. "And tell him to bring me some of the best oil."

Tamar approved, knowing how gladly her grandmother would anoint Melkiah's head, lovingly working the sweet-smelling almond, palm and medulla through his neglected hair.

"But first, Abba, tell us how you've done the impossible. Lepers don't usually recover and the few who do, have scarred bodies. You seem to be quite whole."

"I can't believe that you don't know the answer. There is only one person in Israel who can cure leprosy."

He allowed the silence to lengthen until Sarah whispered. "The prophet, Jesus, from Nazareth . . ."

"*He* healed you!" Tamar was both awed and shocked. Her voice became a whisper. "What are we going to do? No one must find out."

The same anxiety tightened Sarah's face. "We must send for Jairus. He will advise us whether to keep this hidden."

Melkiah had listened to their exchange like one doubting the sanity of his companions, looking from one to the other with raised eyebrows.

"Perhaps you will explain your reaction: I have just related how in the space of a few moments I was taken from death to life. If it had been a doctor who had cured me, you would have rejoiced and made many offerings of thanksgiving. But, as my healer is the greatest prophet who has ever lived, why aren't you praising the Most High that I have met his Messiah and been greatly blessed by him?"

"Not everyone believes that he *is* the Messiah," Tamar began, but her eyes fell before her father's penetrating gaze.

He spoke then with his old emphatic frankness. "I heard that Jesus travelled much in this area and I rejoiced, thinking that at least my family would see the one whom I never expected to see. I was sure that you would have heard him, and I thought that you, Mother, having seen his miracles, would have asked him for one for me."

Sarah's fingers plucked at the warm wool of her robe. "I can't walk far nowadays so I didn't go to hear him when he came here. I've heard reports of all that he's been saying and doing – the whole of Israel knows – but there's no way of finding out whether he is good or evil."

"Evil? When all his works are merciful and all his words are love?" Sarah was troubled. "His deeds *seem* to be good, but they say that his miraculous powers are from Satan so that ignorant people may be deceived."

"Who told you that?" Melkiah asked quietly.

"Zelek and Ezra." Tamar named their Pharisee neighbours. "And most of the other learned people of Capernaum, including Ishmael, the husband of my friend, Miriam. And Asher, of course."

"Asher! I can't believe that Simeon's son . . ."

"Can we forget about the prophet and how you were healed?" Sarah pleaded. "You are well again and I shall never stop thanking the Most High for this day. If Jesus' power is not from him, he knows that you acted in ignorance and will forgive you. May he forgive me too, for there were times when I wanted Jesus to work a miracle for you, even if his power *were* from the Evil One."

The light had left Melkiah's eyes and now his deep weariness was clearly visible. "I knew that Jesus of Nazareth has many enemies in Jerusalem but I'm deeply disappointed that he is not loved in Galilee – particularly here."

Melkiah meant Capernaum but his eyes were on Tamar and she knew that she had let him down. Her earliest memories were of walking beside her father along the lakeside while he pointed out the secrets of nature open to those who cared enough to discover them: the grass tangle of a gull's nest lined with sheep's wool; a delicate frond of wild fennel which smelt so strongly on his fingers as he held it out to her; the straight trunk of a palm tree growing so high above her head that she could not see the date fruits she loved so much.

"'Tamar' means palm," he had told her. "You too will grow tall, with your heart in Heaven appreciating all the beauty the Almighty provides for you."

And, having no son, he had given her all his attention and trained her to observe and think things out for herself. Remembering this now, she realised how blindly she had absorbed and accepted the attitudes of her friends and neighbours.

She sought to comfort her father. "I don't know the truth about Jesus from Nazareth or how you can be so sure. Will you read to me from your scrolls, like you used to do, and perhaps they will help me? But, as Granna says, can't we forget it for now? You are *home* and we want to celebrate!"

Melkiah could not help delighting in the enthusiasm of her lilting voice, so different from the child's high piping that had haunted his memory in the intervening years. His daughter's hair was lighter than his own, the colour of oiled olive wood, and the brilliant iris-blue eyes she had inherited from him were gleaming with the mixture of mischief and pleading which he remembered so well.

"Whatever you wish," he agreed. "But, no banquet, please! Soon I will celebrate my return with my neighbours; but, for today, let us be by ourselves."

He walked towards the lattice screen covering the narrow window and peered through the torrential rain.

"Where are all our labourers? I suppose some are on the hills with the sheep, and there's enough work in the barns for the rest. I want to see Simeon the moment he comes in."

He had his back to the two women so did not see their sudden stillness and changed expression until he turned.

"What is it? Is Simeon away, or ill?"

Sarah's lips were trembling so Tamar, her heart filled with anguish and pity for both her father and grandmother, forced herself to speak.

"He's dead, Father."

For a moment Melkiah refused to accept the news. He had not expected the rest of his life to be free from sorrow, but somehow he had believed that this one day at least would be one of unmarred joy. *The Lord gave, and now He has taken away.* The familiar words enfolded him and he raised his chin in acceptance. *So be it. Blessed be the name of the Lord.*

"He wasn't very old. How long ago was his illness?"

At her father's resigned words, Tamar turned from Sarah's distress. "I'll tell you about it, but let's leave Granna in peace for a while."

Melkiah understood, and when they had found Eglah and sent her to minister to her mistress, they walked together down the dark staircase.

"I want to show you something."

Tamar led the way briskly along the covered colonnade and took his arm as they passed the rooms around the central courtyard. Their pace slackened as she told the tale, speaking clearly to be heard over the rain that was falling harder than ever.

"Simeon's accident happened two weeks ago. He fell from up there." She pointed towards the corner of the courtyard where a flight of steep stairs led to the roof. "It was terrible for all of us – particularly Asher. Our neighbours were very kind. They helped make all the arrangements and came each day to mourn with us. Poor Asher: those seven days were the hardest of his life. He continues to grieve, of course, but he was determined to do what his father would have wished: he's taken over all Simeon's tasks and is working so hard we scarcely see him."

Melkiah remembered the newly-ploughed field he had passed and pity mingled with his deep sadness.

"Where is Asher now?"

"He went to the hills to see Elias about the sheep. He'll be back soon."

Melkiah peered through the driving rain, bouncing on the paved stones of the courtyard, and saw the outline of a man coming through the main entrance gate.

"Could this be him now? I haven't seen him since he was a young boy . . ."

The youth's face was hidden under the hood of his mantle, but Tamar recognised him with relief. "He hasn't really changed. You'll know him, Father."

Asher did not see the two watchers until he had crossed the courtyard at a light run and come through the dark archway into the colonnade.

He was breathless, but not weary, exhilerated by his battle with the force of the rain, and he was smiling as he threw off his hood and mantle in one swift movement.

Melkiah looked with interest at the fine-looking lad and recognised the truth of Tamar's words. In spite of his sixteen years, Asher's complexion was still as smooth and delicate as a child's and, although his face held traces of recent suffering, his features had altered little from the boy with striking dark eyes and ready smile.

Melkiah was about to greet him warmly but Asher, having murmured the traditional greeting of peace, suddenly became very still. If the older man had been an angel, demon, or disembodied spirit, Asher could not have reacted with more consternation.

Melkiah saw the blood leave the boy's face, the shock striking his eyes like a flash of lightning, and hastened to reassure him.

"I'm not a ghost, Asher! Perhaps you didn't expect to see me again but the Angel of Death has given me a reprieve!" He covered the few steps between them and embraced the stunned son of his late steward. "Feel! I am real!"

"Melkiah . . . Master." Asher's voice was a scared whisper.

"I'm sorry to have given you such a shock, but I didn't think you knew of my leprosy. Simeon said he had not told you."

"He didn't." Asher, still in the grip of Melkiah's warm arms, was recovering. "But the last time we went to Jerusalem, he seemed to be acting secretively so I followed him and I saw you in the Hinnon colony. We spoke of you then, and he said you would never return home . . ."

Melkiah smoothed the boy's damp hair back gently and released him. "My homecoming is saddened by hearing about your father's death. I wish with all my heart that I could bring him back from Sheol for you. I cannot tell you how much I'm going to miss him. He was a good and loyal friend to me." Meeting Asher's troubled gaze, he continued in his usual forthright way. "I hope that you will be able to take some consolation in my presence. You were like a son to me, and I would be a foster-father to you now. Unless you think you're too old to need my help and guidance?"

"I thank the Most High for your safe return," Asher responded readily. "You were always more than generous to me. You honour me and I promise that I will serve you with the devotion of a faithful servant and son."

"That's enough speeches! Go and find yourself a dry robe. It is my wish that you should dine with us tonight." Seeing Tamar's nod of approval, he promised them both. "Later, we will try and catch up on all the lost years."

But that evening they discovered that if periods of life are not shared at the time, they cannot be retrieved; and that no amount of talk can substitute for weeks, months, years, that have been lived apart.

Nevertheless, the hours sped by in eager conversation and Tamar and Sarah went to bed full of happiness and anticipation of all the joyful days to come in Melkiah's presence.

However, Melkiah could not share their simple joy. To find himself under his own roof was the fulfilment of an impossible dream, the realisation of all his longings. Yet now, lying in a comfortable bed in his own room after three thousand interminable nights on hard ground, he found himself unable to sleep. The three major disappointments of the day stirred up muddy eddies in the clear pool of his gladness: his mother's blindness; the Galilean prejudice against the one who had healed him with a miracle of love; and Simeon's unexpected death. His steward had died so recently. Perhaps if he had returned earlier, the accident would not have happened . . . It was foolish to sow barren seeds in his mind, yet he knew he would not be able to accept Simeon's death until he had learned exactly how he had died.

Eventually the combination of physical and emotional tiredness muffled his troubled thoughts like snowflakes settling on a wind-ruffled pool. Tamar's radiant welcome had restored to him the glowing face of his wife, Anne, who had died so long ago, and he sank into drowsy contentment.

Just before his memories turned into dreams, a final thought came to him: he had forgotten to tell the two women that Joel would be arriving the following day. However, this did not disturb him; his friend would be here in a few hours time and they would see him then. His breathing became slower and he sank into peaceful slumber.

He would not have slept so well if he had known that Joel's coming would lead to sorrow, fear, violence and death.

Chapter 3

"I have brought back a treasure beyond price"

Tamar woke early and dressed quickly in a warm, woollen robe. She went eagerly to her father's room but his bed was empty and his room was as tidy as if it had never been occupied. For one brief moment she wondered if the events of yesterday had been a dream: so many times in the intervening years she had pictured Melkiah's return, living each imaginary detail so vividly that his presence had seemed almost tangible. Yet surely the events of yesterday had been real?

She had banished the foolish thought long before she found him, after a swift but fruitless search of the large house. Through an arch in the courtyard she had seen the sun glinting on the lake and knew instantly where her father would be.

She fetched a warm hooded mantle but in fact the Shebat day was not a cold one. Its sunshine held the promise of spring, although there would be another two months of rain and sunshine before the glorious month of Nisan arrived.

Melkiah was standing on the tiny shingly beach which belonged to their property, his gaze on the misty hills opposite. The sun was well above the horizon and the waves were no longer ruby-tinged but were sparkling like polished diamonds. Melkiah's head was uncovered and his eyes filled with a deep appreciation of his restored kingdom. He turned at Tamar's step and drew her to his side.

"This is where I have lived in my dreams. I didn't expect to see it again." He took a deep breath of cool air, fragrant with sea, fish and wet sand, and murmured. "Paradise itself could not be more beautiful."

Tamar saw his elation and her own joy in the surroundings increased a hundredfold. Although nearby willows had not yet unfolded their new leaves, their shape was graceful and here and there an overhanging branch trailed into the water making rippled circles each time the wind blew. Two gulls swooped joyously over the fresh-water lake, expressing for the watchers their own exultation in being alive on such a day.

"You won't go away again, Abba, will you?" she asked; but she knew well enough what his answer would be.

"Not willingly. They'd have to drag me away!"

As they returned to the house for breakfast, Melkiah smiled at his daughter. "There's something I must tell you. We have a visitor arriving today, and he'll be staying some time."

He could see that Tamar was disconcerted and he squeezed her arm reassuringly. "His name is Joel of Shallum and he's been a good friend for most of the years I've been away. He began by saving my life. He, too, was a leper and the Messiah healed us both at the same time."

"How did Joel save you?"

Melkiah felt again the sharp stone that had struck his forehead but pushed the memory away before she could read it. "That's a story for another day. We believed that we would be healed if ever we met Jesus – though we could not go in search of him and had almost given up hope. However, we used to dream of the impossible happening, and I promised Joel that if it did, he should come and make his home here with us."

"He's going to *live* here!" Tamar could not hide her dismay. She had been looking forward to endless days of her father's exclusive company as they caught up on the lost years. "Has he no family of his own?"

"He has relatives in Bethany. But he cannot go there."

"Why not?"

"Perhaps he will tell you. If not, you must not ask him. It will be hard for him to live here when he belongs in Judea. I know you will help to make him feel truly welcome." His words were part appeal, part command.

"Of course."

Melkiah glanced at her downcast face as they brushed past the wet leaves of a honeysuckle. "There is nothing I'd like better now than to have some breakfast with my grown-up daughter. I haven't tasted Galilean fish for eight years!"

"There's no fresh fish, for the weather has been stormy, but there's plenty of dried. Kenturah is baking some bread and I found a few late figs on one of the trees only yesterday. I didn't know I was picking them for you!"

Tamar walked lightly beside her father, her happiness restored, and she was able to welcome the stranger with genuine warmth when he appeared a few hours later.

As Joel approached the well-designed country house he admired its lakeside position as the last property south of Capernaum. Even a glimpse of the outer walls protecting the many rooms around a central courtyard was enough to confirm that the owner was a wealthy man, and Joel could see that the rich and fertile land surrounding it had been tended with loving care.

He had scarcely taken a step inside the paved courtyard before his friend was striding to meet him, his whole bearing radiating vitality.

The two men embraced warmly and, as he broke away, Joel caught sight of a young girl watching them. Knowing her identity, he smiled and offered her the traditional greeting. "Peace to this house."

"Peace to you, sir," Tamar returned, hiding her surprise at her first sight of Joel of Shallum. She had expected the ex-leper to be a man of her father's age but his friend could not be many years past twenty. His headcovering hid most of the springy black hair but his neatly trimmed beard failed to hide the expressive mouth and his eyes were sparkling with life and humour. Apart from being unusually thin, there was no trace of his recent disease.

Melkiah, too, had taken in his appearance.

"It seems I've lost my bedraggled companion of many years. Perhaps I should add chameleon to your abilities!"

Joel bowed, laughing. "Transformation by courtesy of Jairus – synagogue ruler! He insisted on giving me his best clothes, and making me submit to the drastic administrations of his personal servant. I'm so clean and tidy that my own father would not recognise me!" Both father and daughter noticed the slight hesitation before he continued. "Jairus gave me this ring – and the invitation to stay with him whenever I wish. The people of Capernaum are blessed to have such a wise and generous man to guide them."

Melkiah, knowing now that many of his fellow citizens had not been influenced by Jairus, was impatient to talk to his friend, and urged him towards the archway leading to their winter quarters.

"Come, let us look after you. Tamar has chosen a room for you overlooking the lake and the hills."

"First the desert, then the promised land," Joel murmured. "It's a good thing that all the tribes didn't see Galilee before they shared out the land, or there would have been civil war! Like the psalmist, I can truly say that my lot has fallen in pleasant places."

His appreciation was genuine yet Tamar realised the courage that lay behind his words. She did not want this stranger to live with them but, recognising his longing for his own home, she would make the substitution as easy for him as possible. However, this would not prevent her from trying to discover why he could not return to Bethany.

As it happened, she had little opportunity to observe Joel for, no sooner had the customary courtesies and ministries been observed, than the two men had left the house and were crossing the courtyard to begin a comprehensive tour of the property.

First, they had climbed the outside stairs to the roof terrace, from where Melkiah viewed the familiar lie of the land in deep satisfaction. From his room, Joel had already glimpsed the pebbly shore through the graceful branches of a tamarisk, but now he was able to look southwards to where widely spaced rows of skeleton vines formed an impressive vineyard. They were protected from northerly winds by a line of mature fig trees and, nearer the house, green shoots were already holding their own in the waterlogged vegetable garden.

There was a well in front of the fig screen and Joel remembered passing one in the inner courtyard. "How much water do you have on your property?" he asked.

Melkiah followed his gaze. "That old well is no longer in use. We only need one for our household needs, as there's plenty of rainwater in the cisterns, and there is a spring over there which we channel to the fields in the dry season."

Joel nodded, realising how very different life was here in Galilee from parched Judea where every drop of moisture was precious. Water was life and he could see its benefits here in every sturdy tree and plant; in two plump donkeys standing easily under their loads in the stable courtyard; in the surrounding slopes which he knew would remain verdant throughout the summer's heat.

Melkiah was rejoicing in the growth of the corn and barley. In a week or two, the first careful hoeing would begin, and in the meantime there was plenty of other work for a sunny Shebat day.

As they walked along the terrace towards the southern side of the property, they could see several workers busy in the orchard. Six or seven men were pruning fruit trees, wielding saw and sickle skilfully and tieing the lopped branches into bundles for burning. Others were using dry cane to reinforce the hawthorn hedge that separated the orchard from the seashore.

"When blossom-time comes, it's like standing above a cloud at dawn," Melkiah remembered aloud. He took a deep breath, nostalgic for the scent of a Galilean Spring as they descended the nearest stairs into the courtyard, went through the main gate and headed for the orchard.

A young man was supervising the planting of a new apple tree, arranging the roots carefully in the base of a deeply-dug circle.

"Come and meet Asher."

When Melkiah called a greeting, the good-looking youth gave a swift command to the older man assisting him, and sprang up agilely to greet his master.

"Joel, this is Asher, son of Simeon, whom you have seen more than once." He remembered he had not told his friend of the calamity that had occurred so recently, and continued swiftly. "Asher, this is Joel of Shallum, a guest of this house."

"Peace to you, sir." Asher bowed, but not before Joel had met a swift, assessing glance from the vibrant, dark eyes.

Humility doesn't come easily to the lad, Joel thought, amused. Perhaps his looks win him so much admiration that others are only too willing to obey his wishes.

"Since Simeon's death, Asher has temporarily taken over his father's duties," Melkiah explained.

Joel read a revealing flash in the boy's eyes at the word "temporary" before the meaning of the sentence registered. "Your steward is dead?" He felt pity for his friend, knowing all that the loyal servant had meant to him, and how much he had been looking forward to astounding him with his miraculously restored health.

"Come with us, Asher," Melkiah ordered, and he followed them towards an old walnut tree. Joel noticed Asher's backward glance

24

after signing to his subordinate to complete the tree planting, and smiled inwardly. The acting steward was a perfectionist who did not trust anyone to do a job properly without his guidance.

His amusement died as Melkiah asked the youngster to tell of his father's death. Asher stood quite still, gazing towards the house, then pointed to the roof terrace at the right of the main gate. "Father and I were repairing the balustrade. I was on the terrace and he was climbing the stairs bringing up some more stone. Just as he reached the top, he overbalanced." Asher's eyelids were flickering nervously as he relived the recent tragedy. "He fell backwards before I could reach him. He hit the ground heavily . . ."

The inner staircase could not be seen from where they stood but they could picture the scene all too clearly: Simeon losing his balance and unable to save himself because of the load he carried; the son watching helplessly as his father fell to his death.

There was remembered horror in Asher's eyes as he relived the event he had been trying desperately to forget, and Melkiah and Joel were filled with helpless pity, not knowing how to offer comfort for the recent tragedy.

Their long silence was accompanied by a distant hammering from a servant who was mending the wooden door of a shed; nearer to them, the rythmical sawing of an unproductive branch of an apple tree measured the moments of their silent sympathy, which lasted until the bough fell heavily to the ground.

"I share your loss," Melkiah said at last. "Return to your work now, but I want your promise that you will come to me whenever you need any help."

Asher saw his chance. "There is one thing I would like: to be steward in my father's place, so that I may serve you as he did."

Melkiah was taken aback. "You are very young. I had in mind to appoint a temporary steward to oversee the property until you are experienced enough to take over."

Asher's eyes blazed with sudden vitality. "It isn't necessary. I've worked alongside my father all my life, and his knowledge is mine. Also, I have learned much from other landowners. Although I'm only sixteen years of age, the other workers have accepted me as my father's son and have followed all my instructions without complaint. They respect . . ."

Melkiah smiled at the lively enthusiasm in Asher's voice, but held up his hand to silence him. "Enough! For your father's sake – and for your own too – I will leave things as they are at present. We'll see how the property shapes up in your hands for the next few months, and then I'll let you know my decision." He looked at the young man's radiant face. "Are you satisfied?"

"Yes, Master."

"And remember that I am here now to give you all the advice you need."

"Thank you."

But as Asher turned back to his work in the orchard the two friends laughed quietly.

"That confident young man won't be running to you for decisions!" Joel commented, watching Asher's springy step. "Tell me, if you had never returned here, what would have happened to your property?"

"I have a daughter."

"A beautiful daughter, and a wealthy property that many people would covet. Her marriage would have given it a new owner . . ."

Melkiah nodded. "I'm sure I would have had many offers, if anyone had known where to contact me. Doubtless they were waiting for news of my return – or of my death. Simeon had promised to seek a suitable husband and bring me word of Tamar's wishes on his next visit."

Sadness returned, but as the friends walked alongside a field, already drying in the breeze and sunshine, they were met by a well-dressed servant.

"From Zelek, my neighbour," Melkiah murmured, as the man reached them and bowed.

"My master, Zelek ben Ananias, greets you on your return from your long voyage. He begs you to honour him with your presence at a feast this evening, in thanksgiving for your safe return."

Melkiah gave in to the inevitable. "Thank your master for the invitation, which I shall be honoured to accept. Tell him I shall be bringing my guest, Joel ben Shallum, with me."

The servant bowed again, hiding his disappointment at the over-swift acceptance – not customary in the best society; he would have preferred to have had the opportunity to deliver all the persuasive messages he had memorized.

Melkiah pointed towards the property adjoining his own. "Zelek lives there, with his wife Azubah, and his six sons. The eldest, Ezra, was nearly twenty years old when I left. It will be interesting to see what the years have done to him. He had many good qualities but showed signs of becoming as fanatical a Pharisee as his father. I have already heard from Tamar that they do not accept Jesus as the Messiah, or even as a prophet."

Joel nodded. "Jairus has told me of the disappointing response in this area. Even worse, of the hostility against Jesus of Nazareth. It is not what we expected when we heard how much time he has spent in Galilee."

They climbed a path in reflective silence until they were almost as high above the lake as they had been on their approach on the previous day. Now the amethyst hills across the inland sea were splashed with gold and Joel could see several green valleys leading to the water's edge. The lake itself was like an ice-blue sapphire sprinkled with illusionary ashes by a multi-fingered breeze.

Melkiah glanced at his friend's thoughtful face. "Our synagogue leader is a just man. In the past we spoke much about the coming Messiah, and I have been rejoicing, imagining all the opportunities he has had to listen to him." He frowned. "Jairus is so greatly respected that I don't understand why our people have not let themselves be guided by him."

"They say that Jairus is prejudiced. His daughter was gravely ill and had died before Jesus could reach her. However, the Messiah took her by the hand and *raised her from the dead.*" Joel was reliving the wonder he had shared with the grateful synagogue leader. "It was such a great miracle that many people came to believe in Jesus because of it."

"And the others?"

"They say that it was a planned deception, or that she wasn't really dead and would have recovered without the prophet's prayers. And some say what is said about all his undeniable miracles – that he achieved it through the power of Satan." Joel narrowed his eyes to follow the flight of a hawk but his own vision was as single-minded as the bird of prey. "We must speak of our experiences and tell others of all the good things we have heard about him in Judea."

Melkiah knew that Joel found it hard to speak of himself and to share his faith with unsympathetic or apathetic people so appreciated the courage behind his resolution.

"We can start tonight, at Zelek's house. He will have gathered all his like-minded friends around him. I doubt if Jairus will have been invited."

However, Melkiah was wrong. He and his guest were greeted with genuine warmth by Zelek and his sons, and the air was heavy with the scent of the spiced olive oil used in the welcoming ceremonies. As the banquet began he was led to the highest position as the most honoured guest and he found Jairus on the adjacent dining-couch. His host was on his right hand, and Joel opposite him, next to Ishmael of whom Melkiah had but slight acquaintance.

As they sipped honeyed wine, and tasted expensive delicacies arranged artistically on shallow baskets decorated with greenery, Joel glanced discreetly around the sumptuous dining-hall. In the soft clear light of multi-wicked lamps and a central chandelier, he noted several rich tapestries, curtains with a striking design, and exquisitely-worked carpets. This was very different from the house interiors of strictly-observant Judean Pharisees. Their homes were as austere as their owners: furnished with heavy, functional furniture, plain curtaining, and without ornaments of any kind. Not even simple vases were permitted, for flowers themselves were forbidden, and there was nothing to lighten the deliberately plain decor. In contrast, Zelek's room held beautiful elegant furniture inlaid with ivory in leaf patterns, embroidered tablecloths, and an array of costly dishes, chalices and amphorae.

Roast meats were brought to the tables by a procession of well-trained servants, and the aroma tantalized the nostrils of the impatient guests as Zelek broke off a piece of new bread, dipped it into the sauce, and handed the token meal to Melkiah with a smile. Then the richly-attired men helped themselves with enthusiasm – and not a little greed – to the various courses provided for their pleasure.

The two ex-lepers exchanged glances more than once, reading the other's memory of their lepers' fare – on the occasions when there *had* been something to eat.

When the meal was over, and the satisfied guests were reclining with amphorae of wine within easy reach of their chalices, Zelek turned to Melkiah. "And now, my friend, tell us of your adventures. I understand that you have travelled to the four corners of the world, and have brought back many treasures?"

"I have been no further than Judea, but I *have* brought back a treasure: something which is beyond price."

The Pharisees within earshot leaned forward eagerly, belying their professed scorn for the Saducees' excessive love of riches. Ezra's eyes asked very clearly, *what have you brought?* but he knew better than to speak aloud with older men present.

The room was now silent, and even the occupants of the lower tables were listening intently, although they could not hope to hear any but the loudest utterances.

Melkiah raised his voice deliberately and spoke clearly. "I left here eight years ago – when I realised that I had become a leper. I travelled around Judea, living in caves and woods and valleys, and became progressively weaker. I lost the ends of three fingers."

All eyes flew to his hands, but they were clenched and they could see nothing.

"My friend, Joel," – he indicated the man from Bethany who appeared to be relaxed but was listening intently – "was also a leper, and we have spent the past few years together. Death was ahead of us, yet we lived in hope from the time we learned of the existence of Jesus of Nazareth. I don't need to tell *you* who he is, for he began his ministry here, and you know of his concern for those who are poor and sick. We could not move among men to seek him, so could do nothing but wait and hope that one day he would pass by.

"Then, on the eve of the Dedication of the Temple, we were in a sepulchre in the Hinnom valley in Jerusalem when we heard a voice calling us. We went out and were greeted by two of Jesus' disciples, who had brought us some food. They told us that he was near, and would cure us if we believed in him."

As Melkiah spoke, the listeners realised that he had travelled far from them, and was again reliving the encounter that had changed his life.

One moment he and Joel were biting hungrily into the rare fresh bread, the next their appetite was forgotten for He was there before them.

As one, they had fallen at his feet, asking him to use his power to cure their leprosy, yet all the while knowing that their words were not really necessary. This man, the Messiah, said by some to be the Son of God, knew everything about them. He smiled and greeted them as warmly as if they were his dearest friends, and their hearts beat their hope almost audibly.

He spoke to Melkiah first. "Why do you want your health again?"

"Master, I have a daughter far from here who is growing up without mother or father. And my own mother is breaking her heart over me."

Jesus stepped forward and put his hand gently on the older man's diseased head. "Go home to your family – and tell what I have done for you."

Then Melkiah felt a strange sensation, as if someone was pouring warm oil into his body and it was spreading through every vein.

Melkiah returned to the present, speaking with the conviction he had felt at the touch of Jesus' hand. "I knew then that I was whole again." He looked intently at his neighbours. "The treasure beyond price that I have brought back with me is this: the knowledge that, at long last, the Messiah has come to us." He raised his arms towards the circle of candles suspended from the ceiling. "Praise the Most High with me for his mercy."

Ishmael, a swarthy man with piercing eyes, was staring mesmerized at the whole fingers of Melkiah's upraised hands. He murmured something to his host, who turned to Joel.

"We should be honoured if you too would tell us of your encounter with Jesus the Nazarene."

The words were courteous and Joel rose to his feet readily but, as he looked from one bearded face to the next, he wondered why he was suddenly reminded of an occasion when he had come face to face with a pack of hungry jackals.

Chapter 4

"Tell me that nothing has changed between us"

"I had been a leper for four years," Joel began, as he looked at the circle of attentive faces. "A short time out of a man's life – but an eternity for the one who is living it. However, my banishment was lightened by the companionship of your neighbour, Melkiah of Capernaum."

The friends exchanged a warm glance, and the older man knew that Joel's pure accent, so different from the Galilean speech, combined with the easy way he wore his rich borrowed robes, were making a good impression on the assembled men.

"When Jesus came, I asked him for healing – and it happened instantly at his touch. I had limped towards him, but as I rose to my feet I found that all my diseased flesh had been restored."

"What did the prophet say to you?"

"I told him that I could not go home, and he told me to go with my friend and to use the Light that he had given me." Joel hesitated, wondering whether to repeat Jesus' other words to him, then decided that it could not harm his mission. "He said to use the Light – 'for the lamp of the wicked shall be put out.'"

Most of the listeners recognised the quotation from the Proverbs of Solomon and had no quarrel with the words themselves. Was not the Law light to a man's soul, and extinction the fitting end for those who did not know it; or, knowing it, refused to obey it to the letter?

As if to refute their definition of the Light, whom Joel had seen as a Person, he returned to his narrative. "There were other lepers with us and Jesus said to them: "Because of your faith, you are cured and forgiven. Take this food and oil, and tomorrow my disciples will bring you some clothes."

Joel too was reliving the rapture of his encounter with the Messiah. "I wish you could have seen the joy in his eyes as he made us whole again."

Several of the listeners were eager to question the Judean, but Zelek's voice rose above them as he pressed a restraining hand on Ezra's arm.

"Once you were purified . . ." He paused, waiting for the slight nod that confirmed that the ex-lepers had fulfilled their obligation in this respect. "Why did you not return to your family, Joel ben Shallum? Have you no wife to rejoice at your return from the living dead?"

For an unguarded moment, Joel remembered the way Rhoda's eyes had kindled when he had returned to her after a short absence. However, that battle had been fought and won soon after disaster had befallen him, so now he was able to answer his host with composure.

"I have no wife and, as far as the rest of my family are concerned, I am dead – and shall remain so."

Zelek's eyes were not the only pair to show curiosity, but he would not overstep the bounds of courtesy by asking further personal questions. Also, there was a more important issue to discuss, as impatient signals from his friends reminded him, and he proceeded to open the debate.

"We too have seen Jesus of Nazareth, but we are yet to be convinced of his identity as the promised Messiah. We do not deny that he is an eloquent – or should we say popular? – speaker, and that he has the power to work the kind of wonders that dazzle unlearned people. Beyond this, there are no signs that he is the one we have been expecting for so many centuries."

"What more can you expect than perfect goodness?" Melkiah protested, adding, "do not mistake his kindness and mercy for weakness."

Ishmael was scornful. "The real Messiah would not have time to woo the common people, to concern himself with trivial miracles. He will make Israel glorious, and the first thing he will do is use his power to give us revenge on the Romans who have occupied our country for so long. Then, when they are utterly defeated, our Messiah King will continue to conquer until Israel is the glory of the world."

"Are you saying that the Most High does not concern himself with unlearned people?" Joel challenged.

Ezra leaned forward eagerly. "He has commanded all his people to know his Law and keep it perfectly. If they choose to remain ignorant, they are no better than pagans and have put themselves beyond his mercy. The Lord keeps his blessings and guidance for those who are faithful to him through the Law that he has given us. And, one day, he will choose a leader from among us and he will be the true Messiah of our God."

The leader of the synagogue spoke quietly. "There is only one Messiah and I believe he is already on the earth. If you study the prophets, you will see that there is not one that is speaking of anyone other than Jesus of Nazareth."

"Jesus healed your daughter." The statement was not so much a commendation as a reason why Jairus' words should not be taken seriously.

The correction came swiftly. "Mirjiam was *dead*. Jesus brought her back to life."

Melkiah looked from the trustworthy face of the synagogue leader to the stubborn faces of his peers under their ornate head-dresses. "From where do you imagine Jesus the prophet gets his power, if not from Heaven?"

"From Satan." Uzziel, a man whom Melkiah recognised as an elder of the Capernaum synagogue, spat the words with hatred. "Jesus is possessed by evil spirits and is a deceiver, a seducer, and a blasphemer. The Devil is using him to lead our nation astray spiritually and morally – and if too many follow him, the Romans will fall on us and destroy us completely."

Zelek saw the exchange of glances between Melkiah and Joel and spoke almost apologetically. "You must realise that the Jesus who healed and deceived you does not keep the Law. If he *were* the Messiah, would he not keep the Law of the one whom he claims to be his Father?"

"In what way does he infringe it?" Joel demanded.

"He does not keep the Sabbath. Oh, he comes to the synagogue, but he heals people on the way out – and sometimes even inside!"

"Jesus usually heals by the power of his word. Since when is speaking counted as forbidden work? I've yet to attend a silent synagogue service!"

"Being cured of leprosy has blinded you to the main issues." Sadoc, an arrogant elder, told Joel. "The Most High has healed people of grave diseases in the past. He does not need the help of Jesus – self-styled Rabbi."

"The Lord God does work such miracles occasionally," Melkiah agreed. "And some of us have met men who have been cured of leprosy. But, although they are no longer infectious, their bodies have remained deformed. But when Jesus . . ."

"We're not disputing his power to work miracles," Ishmael interrupted. "All that matters is his identity. As you know, we look to Jerusalem for guidance in all things . . ." Melkiah and Jairus exchanged an amused glance, remembering many occasions when the Capernaum elders had turned a blind eye to guidance that had not suited them. "And they have directed that Jesus the Nazarene is a false prophet. They have forbidden him to speak in the Temple, or synagogues, and have ordered that anyone who follows him should be expelled from the Jewish community." Ishmael's hands were clenched in frustrated anger against the absent prophet who had brought division to the land. "He has criticized our priests and leaders and made the people despise them."

"Or see them for what they are?"

Ishmael ignored the interruption. "How can he be 'holy' if he does not reverence the High Priest and Doctors of the Law? He tells his followers that they do not need to study the Law of Moses to be saved! He seduces them with some nonsense about a Law of Love. His naïvety would have made him a laughing stock long ago if he had not allied himself with Satan to gain evil powers from him." Ishmael returned to his original contention. "The true Messiah will not be concerned with the ailments of common people, but he will call down fire from Heaven to destroy all our enemies. He will set Israel free."

"The Messiah has come to bring us a far greater freedom," Jairus told a roomful of closed minds. "He has come to save us from the slavery of sin. His Kingdom is a spiritual one which will spread throughout the earth."

Several voices protested excitedly, and the argument was still continuing later as the company divided into small groups making their way home.

Ishmael pulled at Ezra's sleeve, as the latter turned back towards his house. "How can we find out more about Joel of Shallum?"

Ezra's gaze was on the dim shape of Joel as he held a lantern to light the path for Melkiah. "First, we must discover where he comes from." A smile lifted his neat moustache. "You may leave that to me."

Tamar was still awake when her father entered the house. She heard the sound of Imri's voice as he ministered to the two men, and felt comforted as she heard the familiar timbre of her father's in reply. Her thoughts returned to the events of her own evening, to the incident which had unsettled her and was preventing peaceful sleep.

After the evening meal, her grandmother had gone to her own room, where a brazier burned day and night to ease aching limbs caused by a damp winter. Feeling restless, Tamar had taken a lamp and gone to check the contents of the room where the house wine was stored. If she could not be with her father, she would plan the menu for their own feast.

She had just decided that there was sufficient good wine, without transferring some from the underground store, when she heard a sandal strike the floor behind her.

"It seems we had the same idea."

Asher indicated the wineskins and set his lamp beside hers in the stone niche.

Tamar smiled. "We must have the very best of everything to celebrate. Isn't it wonderful to have my father home again, Asher?"

"It is an unexpected joy," he agreed, but the tone of his voice was formal rather than convincing.

Tamar realised then that Asher's own father could never return and regretted the insensitivity of her words. She put a hand on his arm and looked up into the good-looking face. She could not see his eyes clearly in the lamp-light, but had looked into them often enough to recognise the intensity they held.

"Asher . . ." But she did not know what to say to him.

He put his hand over hers. "Tell me that nothing has changed between us."

His hand seemed to burn hers, but brought her no comfort. He was too close to her.

Her compassion gave her words. "How could anything ever change between us, Asher? You have been a brother and a friend to me ever since the day of my birth."

"Is there not love as well?"

"Of course there is love." But her voice betrayed her disquiet. Asher's companionship had made her childhood rich with interest and laughter;

they had shared everything, as if they had truly been brother and sister, rather than the daughter of the house and the steward's son. And when the young boy had turned into a youth with such striking looks that women of all ages had been unable to keep their eyes off him, she had been proud to be his friend. He had a good singing voice which, to his relief, had not been lost as his vocal chords had mellowed into the deeper tones of a man, and he was a talented musician. As he sang the psalms and other sacred songs requested by Sarah during the long winter evenings, he plucked the strings of a kinnor so skilfully that the instrument hummed in duet with him like a second voice. But, Tamar remembered, Sarah had not been present in the orchard last summer when he had sung the love songs of Solomon to her, with his dark eyes speaking a passion she did not understand.

Since that occasion, their relationship had undergone an indefinable change. There was still friendly conversation between them but it seemed to Tamar that too often there was an unspoken plea in Asher's eyes to which she did not know how to respond. He treated her with the courtesy and reverence due to the heiress of a wealthy property, yet he claimed too the rights of an adopted brother. He would reach out to tuck strands of her hair back under her veil on windy days, or kneel to remove a stone from her sandals and fasten the leather thong around her slender foot with a swift caress.

Once he had heard Simeon telling her that she must marry, and had waylaid her before his father had disappeared from view. "Do you really want to marry and leave the home you love so well? If you marry me, you could stay here for ever . . ."

He had laughed to indicate that he had not meant his words to be taken seriously, but they had remained there between them ever since. Simeon had suggested the names of several of the wealthy Capernaum families, including Ezra, eldest son of their neighbour Zelek, and Tamar knew that one day one of these men would be chosen for her.

"There will always be love between us," she said now, yet knowing that her words would not satisfy him. She did not know what he was asking of her and it was foolish to feel afraid. *This is Asher, the friend who has shared my life with me*, she reminded herself. However, this headstrong youth was no longer the light-hearted companion of her earlier years. She realised that she had not heard him sing for many months, nor did he laugh or enjoy life as he used to do. His father's recent death would have been reason enough, of course, but the change had occurred long before the tragedy.

She picked up her lamp. "I must return to my grandmother."

Asher did not move. "Tell me about Joel of Shallum."

She was surprised by the sudden change of subject. "I've scarcely spoken a word to him. Father has told me nothing, except that they were lepers together, and that he has invited him to stay with us."

"Where does he come from?"

"Bethany, I believe."

"Then, when Passover comes, he will probably return there after our pilgrimage to Jerusalem?"

Tamar did not disabuse him. She did not want the stranger to live with them, but if she were to speak of her father's intention it would somehow make it more definite.

"It will probably happen that way," she agreed. After all, several months must pass before the spring pilgrimage. There was plenty of time to find out what was preventing Joel from being reunited with his family – and to remove the obstacle if at all possible.

She lay awake long after she heard her father's return with Joel, but she was not considering the problem of the stranger. Thoughts of Asher continued to trouble her, thoughts which she now realised had been fermenting at the back of her mind for some months. When her father had come back after so many years' absence, she had naturally been overjoyed to see him, yet her rapture had included an overpowering relief that she had not understood. She wondered now if it had been connected with Asher. His eyes had smouldered with an urgency and fire that seemed to demand a response – and yet he was fired with the same enthusiasm when he spoke of his plans for her father's land.

Well, her father was back now, and it was up to him to discover Asher's desires and to satisfy them, if it were right to do so. She fell asleep thinking of Melkiah, reminding herself that she must remember to call him "Father" rather than the childish "Abba".

The sun shone again the following morning but there were clouds over the lake that spoke of rain to come later in the day. Melkiah and Joel set off for the village early to visit Jairus, having refused breakfast.

"We have eaten simply for so long, it will be a while before we can cope with banquets," her father had explained, though in fact neither of them had done more than taste the rich food the previous evening. The friends set off contentedly, each rejoicing in the other's newly-restored strength.

May we never stop thanking the Most High for his mercy and goodness to us, Melkiah thought, while Joel gazed at the mirrored forget-me-not pink and blue flashes on the still lake, sharing his companion's deep gratitude.

Tamar looked at the food they had refused and packed it quickly into a woven basket. She instructed Keturah to add some cheese, honey and newly-baked loaves, and went to fetch her mantle.

She set off in the same direction that the others had taken but instead of following them into the village, she took the narrow path that went to the lakeside. A pied kingfisher flew into its nest in the bank as she turned onto the path that ran between the shore and the fishermen's homes.

She made directly for a dwelling so close to the water that the wall nearest the shore was discoloured from the spray of storm waves.

As the door was open, Tamar stepped inside calling swiftly, "Abital? Susanna?"

"Tamar!" A colourful young figure rushed across the dark room and hugged the visitor enthusiastically. "I've been longing to see you."

"You'd see me better if you released me!" Tamar pointed out breathlessly, but her heart lifted at the warmth of her friend's greeting.

She looked round. "Is your mother-in-law not here?"

"She's gone marketing. She thinks she can get better bargains than I can! I am to make the bread."

Tamar saw no trace of resentment in Susanna's lively eyes. She shook her head ruefully, indicating the grain that she had scarcely begun to grind, and her home-made shell ear-rings swung each side of her olive face. Her cedar-brown hair had been gathered back so carelessly that tendrils were already escaping, and were pushed back off her smooth forehead with the automatic gesture that Tamar had come to know so well. Each time her bracelets slipped down her arm, jingling a cheerful accompaniment to the constant movement of a woman who wanted to be everywhere at once.

Tamar knew it would be some time before the flour mixture reached the kneading trough and held out her woven basket. "There are some loaves in here. Tell Abital that you're a quick worker!"

Susanna accepted the gifts gratefully as from a friend. There was no rich/poor barrier between the two young women, though both knew that the wheat bread Tamar had brought was considerably more palatable than the barley loaves that Susanna would have made. The young wife lifted a small pottery jar from the basket. "Just wait until Eliza sees this honey!"

A glance towards the corner had shown Tamar that the sleeping mats had been rolled up neatly and that the simply-furnished dwelling held no one but themselves. "Where is your daughter?"

"She's gone to the market with Abital. She became very restless during all these rainy days. She wanted to know if ducks go on enjoying themselves whatever the weather, why couldn't she?" Susanna's wide smile lifted her round cheeks. "I'm inclined to agree with her! However, she had a wonderful day yesterday 'helping' Tobit mend his nets."

"Is he fishing today?"

"Just for a short while. He says the rain will have returned by afternoon."

Tamar noted the poverty of her surroundings and knew that this fishing family, like all the others, was almost entirely dependent on how co-operative the fish were to being caught. Tobit had a single fig tree and vine on the small patch of land where he grew the vegetables which kept them alive when there were no fish to sell. Tamar would gladly have filled the poor house with sufficient gifts to take away the anxiety of living from hand to mouth, but had long since learned that such an action would have incurred the resentment of Abital and Tobit, and changed the basis of her own friendship with Susanna.

The fisherman's young wife pulled Tamar down beside her onto the wooden bench which Tobit had made. "Now, tell me! Are the rumours true? Has your father returned, and is it true that he doubled his fortune in Alexandria, and brought you home a head-dress made entirely of pearls?"

Tamar laughed. "Yes, he has returned, but no, he has not been to Alexandria, and the pearl head-dress only exists in the mind of the person who invented the story!" She smiled radiantly at her friend.

"Susanna, he's come back to us. You can't imagine how much joy there is in our household now."

"It will make up for your recent sorrow over Simeon. And how happy Sarah must be."

"Yes, she looks ten years younger, and the life has come back into her voice. I hadn't realised how much she'd changed until I saw her revive. Of course, she had known the truth about my father all along."

"What truth?"

"That he has been a leper all these years . . ."

Tamar went on to tell her all that she had learned about her father's absence, realising as she did so how very little that was.

After the first startled exclamation and appalled realisation of the truth, Susanna interrupted frequently. "How much of your father's body was affected by the disease? . . . Where did he shelter when the weather was bitterly cold? . . . How did he survive without warm clothes and bedding?"

"I cannot bear to think of all his suffering," Tamar admitted. "I want to forget it ever happened and it would be more difficult if I questioned him about those years." She knew Susanna was not satisfied and sought a way to divert her. "He has brought a friend home with him, Joel of Shallum."

However, this diversion proved to be unhelpful as she could not answer Susanna's questions about him either.

"I don't want him to stay with us permanently," she told her friend. "I'm determined to find out why he cannot go home to his family – but how, when my father has forbidden me to ask him directly?"

"By asking him indirectly, of course! Talk to him as often as you can, and you will gradually glean all the information you need."

"I'll try." Tamar heard the doubt in her own voice and looked at her friend ruefully. She knew that Susanna's warm friendliness and genuine interest in everyone she met drew their life stories from them in less time than it took to land a netted fish.

Her hazel eyes were sparkling now with a new idea. "Perhaps your father has brought Joel to Galilee to marry you!"

Chapter 5

"She disappeared two weeks ago"

Tamar was appalled at Susanna's words. She realised that her friend was teasing her about Joel, yet there was a possibility that her suggestion might be true. Once her father would not have considered a man who was not wealthy for his only child, but he had returned with changed values. Melkiah and Joel had become close friends during the years of their suffering, and perhaps he would see such a marriage as the solution to Joel's own problem: the younger man's longing for his lost home would be alleviated were he to become heir to a prosperous estate in Galilee.

She remembered the urgency in Asher's voice last night as he had trapped her hand beneath his own, seeking her confirmation that nothing had changed between them.

Susanna was looking at her expectantly, but Tamar was not able to share her friend's amusement.

"Why does everyone keep talking about marriage? Now that my father is home, I am perfectly content. Why does anything have to change?"

Susanna wondered who else had been discussing marriage with Tamar but realised that the younger girl was genuinely distressed and regretted her own light-hearted remark. When a child's voice called nearby, she turned to the diversion with relief.

The three-year-old came in beaming. "Look what I've found!" Her smile widened as she caught sight of Tamar and she veered towards the visitor with her treasure.

Tamar knelt beside the eager girl and gently touched the object in her small hand. "What a beautiful feather! Did a seagull give it to you?"

Eliza's laughter acknowledged the teasing but her star-lashed round eyes met Tamar's confidently. "No, but he left it beside the door, specially for me . . ."

"Perhaps it was meant for your Granny?"

Eliza considered. "No, because it would blow away before she could see it. She's walking very slowly."

"Everyone walks very slowly, compared with you," her mother pointed out. "Look what Tamar has brought us!"

"Honey and raisin cakes?" Eliza suggested hopefully.

"You shall help me make some," Susanna promised, picking up her daughter and swinging her high above her head.

Their laughter mingled, their round faces and mischievous, sparkling eyes so alike that Tamar was smiling as she made her way homeward.

When she rejoined the main track that led from the village to her own house, Ezra suddenly stepped in front of her. They were on the borders of Zelek's property, and she had encountered him in this spot more than once.

They exchanged greetings but, after the first glance, Tamar kept her eyes lowered. No woman of Israel would look boldly into a man's face, and she was glad of the custom for of late there had been a new, ardent gleam in Ezra's eyes. She had liked him well enough as a youth but in the intervening years his conversation had come to hold less and less interest for her. For friendship's sake, she had tried to hide her boredom – and had succeeded all too well for the young Pharisee had no idea that their encounters gave her no pleasure.

"You will make many sacrifices of thanksgiving for your father's safe return," he began.

Was it an order or a question?

"I cannot thank the Most High sufficiently," she agreed. "I . . ."

"Melkiah tells a strange story of his healing from leprosy," he cut in abruptly. "It must cause you great distress."

"I cannot be distressed to see my father in such good health. I am deeply grateful to the prophet Jesus for such a miracle."

"He is not accepted as a prophet by the holy priests of the Temple!"

Tamar suppressed a sigh. Ezra was quite capable of discussing the controversial subject for hours, particularly if she told him the scandulous truth: that she did not care from where Jesus had acquired the miraculous power that had cured her father. She admired Ezra's zeal but had no wish to experience its evidence by suffering a passionate torrent of words that would leave her dazed.

However, Ezra had a more urgent reason for way-laying his young neighbour.

"Your house is honoured by a visit from Joel of Shallum. He is a man of good education, and has obviously been much in the Temple. He is familiar with the teachings of Gamaliel and Hillel, and yet he doesn't come from Jerusalem, does he?"

Tamar was silent, realising that Ezra was not asking out of casual interest and wondering why he was so interested in their guest.

Ezra admired the curve of Tamar's dark eyebrows and the black fringes of long eyelashes against her pale cheeks but wished he could read the secrets in her lowered eyes.

"Joel is a good man," he urged. "I believe that he has been misled but that will be put right when the deceiver has been revealed for what he is. In the meantime, we who are his friends must help Joel of Shallum. He told us that he is dead to his family but if we knew where he came from we could make some discreet enquiries about his circumstances. Once we know the situation, we will be able to work out the best way to help him. The Most High would bless us for such an act of charity."

Tamar was not interested in heavenly rewards but responded warmly to Ezra's suggestion. "You are a good man to concern yourself with the problems of a stranger. I, too, would like to help Father's friend." Her brow furrowed in thought. "I have been warned not to distress Joel with questions about his past, so I know nothing. Except that he comes from Bethany."

Ezra smiled. "That is enough." He made a restless movement. "I will not detain you any further. You have the Sabbath preparations to supervise."

He bowed to her, but even as she inclined her own head in farewell, she looked up again startled at his parting words: "You will make a good help-mate. My father will come to see yours soon." He strode along the track away from the lake, without a backward glance.

Tamar watched the retreating figure in exasperation, hoping that she had misunderstood. "I shall see my father first," she murmured. "He will not find a husband for me against my will."

A sudden gust of wind blew her veil across her face and she saw that clouds were beginning to skim across the sky like thistledown racing boats. She watched them absently, her ear-rings swinging gaily as she moved her head; but her joy in the bracing morning had vanished.

Her father had not forbidden her to tell anyone that Joel came from Bethany. Why then did she feel as if she had betrayed their guest?

✡   ✡   ✡

Tamar's momentary regret about discussing Joel with Ezra vanished during the festive Sabbath meal. Sarah was positively sparkling with the rapture of an event she had never expected to happen again – the weekly celebration being led by her son, now back in his own place. Tamar too was so deeply thankful to see her father taking his part in the traditional ceremonies that she gave little attention to the food and drink set before her. However, seeing Joel, dressed in one of Melkiah's best robes, eating and conversing with apparent contentment, she could not help resenting the presence of someone who did not belong in their household.

The two men were speaking of their visit to Jairus, with whom they had discussed the needs of the poorer people of Capernaum. In thanksgiving for his restored life, Melkiah had given a generous offering to the synagogue leader for them, but he wanted to do more.

"I wish I too could make a gift," Joel said. His words were quiet but Tamar realised suddenly the pain behind them and felt unexpected pity for the exiled man.

"Perhaps you could give time?" Melkiah suggested. "There may be some work you can do for Jairus. Jonathan too may know of ways to use us."

"Who is Jonathan?" Sarah asked.

"He is Chuza's steward, in Tiberias," her son told her. "He is also one of Jesus' disciples and one of his most loyal friends."

"But Chuza is Herod's man! Surely he doesn't permit Jonathan to openly profess his faith in a man whom some people would put as king in Herod's place?"

"Haven't you heard? Chuza himself is a supporter of Jesus – from the time Jesus cured his wife Johanna of a mortal sickness. Now the whole household is friendly to him."

Tamar shared Sarah's amazement. Neither of them had ever been to Tiberias, although it was but a few miles from their home. The wealthy Roman city was a by-word for worldliness and decadence among the Jews. Pagan gods were worshipped in the bathing-places of the healing springs and in the luxurious villas at the water's edge, while in the corrupt market-places Greeks, Romans, and people of all nationalities mingled, outbidding each other for luxury goods and slaves to serve their depraved lives. It seemed an unlikely place to find followers of a man who preached that happiness came to those who lived humbly and were content with few possessions.

"You're not going there, Father?" Tamar asked.

He nodded. "We shall go to Tiberias once the Sabbath is over."

Tamar knew "we" meant her father and Joel, knew too that he would never take her there. She had sailed past Tiberias frequently and admired the Roman villas with their magnificent gardens leading down to the lake and the purple-canopied pleasure craft moored to their private piers. The white houses dotted up the hillside were built far from the quayside of the hard-working fishermen. A grove of trees concealed the famous healing springs, but she had been able to make out the distant forms of sick people making their way up the wide avenue to the sulphurous waters where they hoped to receive relief.

Sarah felt for her wine but the movement sent a pain shooting through her shoulder and she gave a stifled cry.

Tamar smiled at her father reassuringly and put the chalice in Sarah's stiff fingers. "I'll get Asher to mix up one of your rheumatism remedies."

"Wait until after the Sabbath," Sarah reminded her quietly.

Tamar knew better than to argue with the blind woman and respected her reverence for the prescribed day of rest.

"My mother is very knowledgable about herbs," Melkiah told Joel. "She has a cure for every complaint – except the taste of her remedies!"

Sarah smiled at the old joke. "I can no longer see to mix and measure. Tamar and Asher are the experts now. They gather the herbs and know all their uses."

"Adina used to help you search for them on the hillsides," Melkiah remembered. "Where is she? I haven't seen her since my return." He saw Sarah's mouth tighten and Tamar's anxious glance at her, but his question was not answered.

"You were very fond of her," he reminded his mother. "I still see her as a young girl but I suppose she must be about sixteen years of age by now. She was such a lively child. I expected her to be one of the first to welcome me!"

Tamar stood up. "You cannot see her, Father. She's gone away." Her voice was steady but Joel noticed that her hands were trembling. "I'll go and tell Kenturah to bring in the special desert she's prepared for you."

As her footsteps died away, Sarah turned in her son's direction. "She's very upset. I gave Adina to Tamar to be her personal maid many years ago and they became good friends as well as mistress and servant. They always went together to the market-place, and to visit the fisherman's family, and helped each other learn how to spin and weave. They have both been very good to me, and, once I could no longer see, they sought out strongly-perfumed flowers for me to enjoy. They . . ."

Melkiah could hear Tamar returning. "Where is Adina now? Tell me quickly, Mother."

"We don't know where she is. She ran away."

Tamar had heard her grandmother's bewildered words and touched her shoulder consolingly. "You don't believe that any more than I do."

"But she was missing, and Asher said . . . "

"I know what Asher said, but he is mistaken. Adina had no reason to run away. She was happy with us – and she certainly isn't a thief!"

Kenturah brought in the desert and placed it in front of Melkiah proudly, but left the room puzzled by his lack of response.

Melkiah turned to his daughter. "When did this happen?"

"Just over two weeks ago. It must have been the day after Simeon died. We were all so stricken by his sudden death that it was only gradually we realised that none of us had seen Adina for hours. The servants searched everywhere, but she had completely disappeared."

"Surely you looked further afield?"

"Of course. We sent men into all the surrounding villages, and along the shores of the lake." She could not hide her distress. "I haven't given up, Father. I *know* that she will come back to me."

Sarah's head was bowed as she murmured. "She cannot come back, if it is as Asher says . . ." She lifted a shaking hand helplessly. "A large sum of money disappeared with Adina."

"She would no more have stolen from us than Asher would!" Tamar cried passionately. "She often said that everything she wanted was here. She never wanted to live anywhere else – and why should she need money? We fed her and gave her warm clothes, and I even gave her some of my jewellery."

Joel was frowning over his cup of wine. Although the mystery was a domestic one, there was a chance that it could be connected with the mission that had brought him here.

"What did Adina take with her?" he asked Tamar.

She knew he was not referring to the missing money. "Everything she possessed – all her clothes, and the earrings and bracelets I gave her."

"Did she take any food or drink?"

"I asked Keturah but she doesn't think so."

"Runaway slaves or servants usually take provisions for several days," Joel pointed out. "After all, they don't know where they are going, or when they will be able to eat again."

All the anxiety Tamar had felt on the day of Adina's disappearance returned. "How can she have survived without food or shelter in this cold season?"

Her father reassured her. "She must have known where she was going, to have taken all her possessions."

"But she doesn't *know* anywhere – or anyone. She's spent her whole life with us, and she's never left Capernaum."

The three looked at each other helplessly and Melkiah saw tears in his mother's unseeing eyes.

"We'll talk no more of this now, but I promise you that we will widen the search until we get news of her. Tell me one last thing: was Adina depressed or anxious during the few days before her disappearance?"

"No!" Both of the women answered simultaneously and emphatically. Tamar went on. "On the contrary, we'd never seen her happier. She was always in good spirits, but a week or two ago she seemed to be brimming over with joy, almost as if she had some marvellous secret hidden inside her. She sang from morning 'til night."

"And the day she went away?"

"Simeon had just died so we were all stunned with grief and shock – Adina too. If only I'd been able to give her my attention . . ."

After the meal, Melkiah went in search of Asher. "Tell me about Adina. Where do *you* think she is?"

Asher, who had greeted Melkiah with the assurance of a steward in complete control of all his Master's affairs, was momentarily disconcerted.

"I've no idea where she is, but it may be my fault that she has gone." The handsome face flushed under Melkiah's keen gaze. "I should have taken better care of your money. It was locked in a chest, but Adina knew where I kept the key."

"Do all my workers know?"

"No, but when Tamar came to my father for money, Adina was usually with her. They both knew where we kept the key. I had no idea that Adina would be tempted. Forgive me for my carelessness."

"You were not to blame. Tamar tells me that it was totally unexpected as the girl seemed happy in our household."

"She did seem happy," Asher agreed. "It was a very great shock to us all. Master, as it is my fault, I will repay the money to you gradually if you will be patient."

"You were not to blame," Melkiah repeated. "And I have no concern for the money. But Adina must be found."

"She had enough money to go far from here," Asher pointed out. "Perhaps it would be better to leave her to the new life she has chosen."

"Tamar won't be content until we know what has happened to her. But when we find her, we won't bring her back unless she wishes it."

"She is a thief," Asher muttered.

"Perhaps. But my mother and daughter do not believe it. However, if she did take the money through some momentary foolishness, the poor child must have suffered very much ever since. I must find her, to show her that she is forgiven, and give her a new chance."

"You would trust her after this!"

"There are none so faithful as those who have been forgiven and trusted."

Asher's face was no longer the smooth, untroubled one of youth, but furrowed in anxiety.

Melkiah put a reassuring hand on his shoulder. "You're not alone now. Take care of the land, and leave the problem of Adina to me. Don't worry. I'll find her."

Asher looked far from reassured but Melkiah knew that young men were inclined to take all the responsibilities of the world upon their own shoulders. He could not free Asher from his imagined guilt, but time would restore his peace of mind.

He found Joel in the library, eagerly examining shelves of scrolls. Melkiah understood, having been deprived of his treasury – his sacred scrolls – all the years of his exile. They had shared with each other the passages they had memorised from the writings of Moses and the prophets, but now they could read the familiar, precious words for themselves. They smiled at each other without speaking, and read contentedly until the flickering lamps reminded them that the night was far advanced.

Melkiah had decided to put the problem of Adina from his mind until the Sabbath was over. He approached the synagogue the following morning with Joel, Tamar and Sarah, who had declared that she would not miss this joyful occasion even if she had to walk there at her own slow, painful pace. However, she had been more than satisfied to cover the half-mile in a wagon, and was unaware of the pity and interest of her old acquaintances as she and Tamar took the separate entrance that led to the women's section of the synagogue. Melkiah knew that she would find the steps up to their gallery difficult and was relieved to look up and see his mother sitting near the front, smiling as old friends congratulated her on her son's return from the dead.

The service went by in a daze of happiness for Tamar. It was not new for her attention to wander during the set prayers, the recited psalms, the reading from the scroll and commentary by one of the elders. For so many years she had gazed at the body of men on the ground floor of the synagogue, imagining her father amongst them, and now it had happened and he was really here.

He sat in his old place on the platform, with the other leading men of Capernaum, and Tamar murmured her own radiant prayers of thanksgiving, her eyes on her father's alert face. She saw no one but him, and held her grandmother's hand tightly, sharing her joy and pride. They were a family again, and all was well.

✡   ✡   ✡

After the rain on the eve of the Sabbath the clouds cleared leaving the sun unchallenged as Melkiah and Joel set off for Tiberias. There was no need to tackle the muddy roads when the smooth highway of the shining lake beckoned. Asher prepared the small sailing boat for the two passengers, launched it, and watched as the sail caught the cool northerly breeze. Melkiah was dealing with the ropes and tiller competently, and laughed as he caught Asher's worried look.

"Don't worry about me, son. *I* taught *you!*"

Asher smiled and waved an acknowledgment, but his face was grim as he turned away. However, his anxiety had nothing to do with Melkiah's sailing ability.

Chapter 6

"I can never return"

Joel had never been sailing before and obeyed Melkiah's instructions readily. He looked back over the crystal wake of the small craft and saw Mount Hermon in the far distance, beyond the shore where the river Jordan flowed into the lake. His gaze returned to the land they were passing and seeing its wooded slopes and verdant pastures, and the houses where man could be king of his own small kingdom, he nodded in deep appreciation.

"There is nowhere on earth I would rather be," he said aloud.

They were leaving Melkiah's estate far behind and Asher was now a blurred splash of colour against an evergreen tree.

"You're good to that boy."

"He's like a son to me," Melkiah told his friend. "His mother died when he was a few weeks old, just after Anne had died in childbirth with Tamar. So my child and Simeon's shared a wet-nurse, and they were brought up together like brother and sister."

Joel knew better than to dwell on the double tragedy of the past and gave his attention to the two half-orphans. "Such a situation could have created problems."

Melkiah understood. "Simeon made sure that Asher knew his true role in our household."

But, as the boat skimmed across the shining waves, he remembered how he had been tempted to give Asher the same attention and education he would have given his own son. He remembered his pride on the day of Asher's Shearing of the Son ceremony, when the newly-shorn small boy had gravely welcomed other children to the party celebrating his readiness for schooling. He had had such hopes for the intelligent youngster, and had looked forward to the day when he would present him to the Temple in Jerusalem as a true Son of the Law. He had not known that before that day came he himself would have been exiled from his own home, and that the child's true father,

Simeon, would have gently led his son in a different, humbler, direction.

Perhaps his leprosy had prevented him from making a grave mistake, yet he would never have any other son.

Anne . . . His longing fell uselessly into the gulf between the worlds of the living and the dead, his loss as constant as the waves slapping against the side of the boat.

Joel, sitting obediently on the side of the boat to balance it against the strong breeze in the sails, was very much aware of being in the land of the living. The cool wind penetrated his mantle and filled his tunic so that it flapped like an imprisoned sail, but he held his head high. After so many years of sickness with all the fetid smells of ulcerating bodies around him, he could never have too much of the pure, fresh air of Galilee.

Gulls flew overhead, making for the amethyst hills on the eastern side of the freshwater lake; the water sparkled in the sun like shoals of diamond fish leaping to the surface, and water-fowl bobbed up and down on the waves like tiny jewelled boats.

They reached Tiberias all too soon for him. The fine walled town spread along the shore and up the hillside and was dominated by the summer palace of Herod Antipas. The wealthiest properties adjoined the lake and many had their own small jetty, but Melkiah steered for the main harbour.

"We'll have to find out where Chuza lives."

Once they had moored their boat and begun to explore, they could not help admiring the well-planned town. Everything had been designed to withstand both winter rain and fierce summer heat, and the straight roads and avenues which channelled away surplus water even on the wettest days, were firm and dry. Several people were crossing a wide square and women were filling water jugs from a marble-based fountain in the centre.

Joel looked with interest at the Roman houses with their columned arcades and caught glimpses of marble-paved courtyards where fountains were surrounded by ornate flower containers awaiting the touch of spring to burst into colour.

"I haven't seen more beautiful houses in Jerusalem."

They made for the market square and stopped beside a stall selling ornamental oil-lamps. The owner was shouting the merits of the double-flamed one he was holding up, but his voice was lost in the noise from a seller of farm implements. This vendor struck scythes, axes, and ploughshares repeatedly to show their strength, and, not to be outdone, a copper-smith struck his wares with such enthusiasm that the cymbal-like sounds drowned the monotonous appeals of beggars moving from one likely benefactor to another. It was surprisingly busy for a winter market: the poorer women were shopping for food while elegant Roman and Greek ladies wandered unhurriedly from stall to stall, accompanied by idle men; to them the market was but a diversion from the tedium of a rainy winter. Everyone was glad of the weak sunshine, though the gusts of wind caused them to wrap their cloaks around themselves more tightly.

An old woman was holding the hands of two young children and she was taken by surprise when the boy pulled away from her suddenly. Joel heard the old servant's cry of alarm and, as the child could not have been more than five years old, was quick to follow the darting boy. It was a short chase as the youngster had stopped beside a donkey and was pulling ineffectually on its reins.

"He's eating your vegetables!" he told the stall-keeper, and again used his light strength to tug at the leather strips.

At that moment the donkey's owner returned and a fierce argument began, with the vegetable-seller demanding compensation, and the other contending that the vendor should have been more watchful.

Joel took the opportunity to lift the child into his arms and turned to seek the old servant.

"She's over there." A small hand pointed, and Joel met the breathless old woman hurrying towards them.

"Thank you, sir." She took back the richly-clad boy gratefully but could not refrain from reproaching her charge. "You promised you would stay close to me."

"I will, Esther. I only went to stop that bad donkey stealing."

Joel smiled at the old nurse. "You needn't worry about a child with such a keen sense of justice." He saw the Roman-style garments of the two children, now whispering to each other with dancing eyes.

"Perhaps you can help us." He indicated Melkiah who had come to join them. "We're looking for the house of Chuza, steward of King Herod."

"That's our house!" the little girl cried, her brother echoing the cry. Two young faces gazed up at Joel wonderingly.

"These are the adopted children of Chuza and Johanna, my master and mistress," Esther explained. "Would you like us to take you there?"

Joel could see that the children were torn between wanting to explore the market further and retracing their steps with two interesting strangers.

"Just tell us how to find it," he suggested.

At the same moment that she began her explanation, a young woman who had been passing through the market, caught sight of Melkiah and gave a loud cry.

Her eyes were wide with shock, and her arms made a strange movement, as if she were feeling for support that was not there.

"Master!"

The word was enough to bring recognition to Melkiah and he stepped forward thankfully. "You've changed from the child I left behind, but I'm so glad to meet you again, Adina."

The girl did not respond in any way to Melkiah's reassuring words. She shrank back at his approach, staring at him as if he were a visitor from Hades.

He stopped, finding it hard to identify this tense young woman with the open-faced lively child he remembered. Her eyes which used to sparkle like the sun on raindrops were now dull and fearful.

"Did you think I was dead? I could have died from leprosy but the Messiah healed me." But even as he spoke, he wondered how Adina could have known something that had been hidden from his own daughter.

"He said you had died." She was speaking more to herself than her former master and Melkiah scarcely heard the shocked words over the clamour of the market.

He held out a hand. "Come. Let us talk where it is quieter. Tamar will be overjoyed to know that we have found you."

Adina followed Melkiah and Joel to a sheltered spot where the branches of two palm trees formed a canopy over the corner of the square, but her face did not lose its stunned expression.

Melkiah tried to alleviate her fear. "My mother and daughter have been very anxious about you. Adina, why did you run away?"

"I didn't!" Her bewilderment was unmistakeable. "They knew why I was going. They gave me money . . ."

The men exchanged glances but Melkiah kept his voice gentle. "Who gave you money?"

"It was from Tamar. Asher said . . ." Colour drew across her face like a crimson curtain as realisation came to her. "Whose money was it? You don't believe . . . ?"

"Some money was missing the day you went," Melkiah said evenly, "but Tamar does not believe you took it."

Adina's legs were trembling so much that Joel hurried to her side and led her to a low wall nearby. She sank onto it and covered her face with shaking hands.

"The money doesn't matter," Melkiah told her quietly. "But you do. We care about you and we want you back where you belong. Will you come with us today, when we've finished our business in Tiberias?"

Adina did not lift her head. "I can never return." Before Melkiah could frame another question, she had risen, slipped past him, and darted through a nearby archway.

Joel wasted no time in following. "Don't worry. I'll find her." Just before he disappeared, he called back. "Go on to Chuza's. I'll meet you there."

It should have been easy for Adina to lose Joel in the town she now knew so well, but the roads of the new Roman town were wide and straight and not designed for evading pursuit. By the time she had admitted defeat, she had led him on to a hill road high above the harbour. It was one of the much-travelled avenues leading to the healing springs and was set at intervals with wooden seats for weary travellers.

As Adina collapsed onto one breathlessly, Joel was careful to keep his distance. "Don't be afraid of me. I'm staying with Melkiah. He's a generous man and I owe him much. If you will let me help you, I'll be doing him a favour."

Adina shook her head. "It's too late. I needed help when I first came to Tiberias."

"Tell me why you came here. It was because of Asher, wasn't it?"

Adina looked up startled, then shrugged. "It doesn't matter now, does it? The money has gone, and I've cut myself off from everyone that matters to me."

"Truth always matters. Tell me what Asher said when he gave you the money."

In fact, Joel had already guessed what the girl would tell him and her words, spoken without emotion, confirmed it.

"We loved each other – or perhaps it was only I who loved him. I thought we would marry. The very day Simeon died, he told me we must put our plans in action if we were to be together in future. He said that the Master had died of leprosy, and now that his own father too was dead, there would be changes. Tamar would marry Ezra, who would bring his own steward to manage his new land."

"Couldn't you have waited to see what the future would bring? I'm sure there would always have been a place in the household for you."

"I wanted to be with Asher. He told me that Valerius, a wealthy Roman here in Tiberias, had offered him the position of steward of his estate. He said he was a good man, who had not only agreed to our marriage, but had promised that I could be his wife's personal attendant." She smiled wryly. "I thought it was too good to be true ..."

"Why didn't you discuss it with Sarah or Tamar?"

"There wasn't time. Asher told me that a servant from Valerius' household had come with a wagon to collect me. Apparently, the mistress needed me immediately as her child's nurse had just died. I wanted to go to Tamar, to ask her to forgive me for leaving her so suddenly, but Asher told me that both she and Sarah were too upset about Simeon to see anyone. I felt I couldn't argue with him – not when he was so shocked by his father's death. He said that Tamar wished me well and had sent some money as a farewell gift.

"I didn't want to leave without saying goodbye, but the man was waiting, so I collected my clothes quickly and went with him. Asher said he would come to join me as soon as his period of mourning was over ... "

"What happened when you reached Tiberias?" Joel saw that there were several Roman pleasure boats sailing in the strong, northerly wind but he couldn't rejoice in the colourful sight with an age-old human tragedy being relived before him.

"The driver was dumb, so I couldn't ask him anything. When we reached the outskirts of Tiberias, he indicated that I should step down onto the road. But as he drove away I realised that the only buildings in sight were boating sheds and fisheries. It was getting dark by then and there were few people about. No one knew where Valerius lived and I was so cold. A fisherman's wife took pity on me and let me stay in her house overnight." Seeing Joel's compassionate gaze, she was impatient suddenly. "You don't need me to go on. I asked day after day for Valerius, but never found him."

"At least you had some money."

She shook her head. "It was stolen the second day."

"What did you do?"

She made no answer but Joel could see that in spite of her drawn, unhappy expression, she did not have the look of hunger. Her mantle was thick and warm and he had caught several glimpses of a richly-embroidered robe as she had fled from him. He did not press her to admit to what he now suspected and returned to the original mystery.

"You've had a long time to think about this. Tell me, why do you think Asher sent you away?"

She shook her head. "I don't know."

But there were secrets in her eyes – secrets she had no intention of telling a stranger.

Joel was reluctant to question her further but felt instinctively that the truth she was concealing was more important than the story of a romantic betrayal.

"Tell me, if Asher had told you that he had no intention of marrying you, would you have remained in Capernaum?"

The girl's colour deepened, but once again she made no reply.

"Tamar misses you very much and Sarah too is deeply concerned about you. They will not be content until they have seen you again."

A sudden gust of wind whipped a lock of glossy hair into her face. She did not seem to notice, and perhaps it accounted for the sudden tears in her eyes, yet Joel had seen the moment that hopelessness had replaced the yearning in them.

"I *cannot* come back. How could I? Ever since the moment I saw Simeon fall to his death, my life changed. There is no going back."

"No one will force you to do anything against your will," Joel promised, "but at least come with me to speak to your master."

Adina sprang up. "I have a new master now!"

For the second time within the hour, she rushed away, this time down the steep road towards the lake, her mantle following her on a cushion of air like the wings of a fallen angel.

Joel allowed her to go without pursuit and went soberly on his way towards Chuza's house. Adina was too young to pay such a high price for her unwise loving. He felt a wave of anger against Asher and, although he had no right to question another man's servant, resolved to speak to him on his return.

There was plenty of time for conversation as he and Melkiah tacked slowly back to Capernaum. Knowing his friend's fondness for the steward's son, Joel chose his words carefully as he spoke of Asher's part in Adina's departure for Tiberias.

As he had anticipated, Melkiah was inclined to take his part.

"He's a handsome boy. Any young girl would let attention from him go to her head. Who's to know where the fault lies?"

"And the money?"

"There seems no doubt that she went off with it. I will never believe that Asher gave it to her, and then allowed her to be suspected of theft."

Melkiah's hand was steady on the tiller but Joel could see that his thoughts were far from the challenging waves, the wind trying to blow his garments back to Tiberias, and the falling sun which was beginning to define the horizon with shining gold.

Joel was wondering if Sarah too had the same blind trust in Asher when, as if reading his thoughts, Melkiah said, "My mother will have taught Asher absolute honesty. And his own mother, Helah, was a fine woman, a merchant's daughter. When my wife died, she cared for our baby, Tamar, with great tenderness and when Asher was born shortly afterwards, she fed the two babies together as if they were twins. If only Helah had lived . . ."

A bird sped past, mocking the occupants of the small boat for their slow progress, but Melkiah did not notice. However, he straightened his back and faced the cold wind squarely. "But my mother gave Asher the love and care she'd have given her own grandson, and you have seen for yourself how devoted he is to her."

"Asher was fortunate to have her guidance. Your mother has a kind and loving disposition."

Melkiah read his friend's reservations accurately. "Perhaps my mother was too indulgent with him, but Simeon was too wise not to guide his son aright. It seems to me that Asher fulfils his unique role in our household with grace and assurance."

"He has unusual confidence."

Melkiah smiled. "You mean his ambition to be my steward? There's no fault in that. He's unusually intelligent and his education will equip him to deal well with landowners and merchants."

Joel gazed at distant Capernaum, which seemed to come no nearer. "Will you tell Tamar that we've seen Adina?"

Melkiah considered, then shook his head. "Say nothing to her yet. The next time I go to Tiberias I'll ask Jonathan to find out under whose protection Adina is living. We'll keep an eye on her but from what you've told me she seems to have chosen a new life. I doubt if we'll learn the truth now and I'm inclined to leave things as they are. As for Asher, I don't want him troubled over this. He has enough to cope with, bearing the pain of his bereavement."

The boat heeled in a sudden gust of wind and the conversation came to an abrupt end. Joel obeyed Melkiah's crisp instructions with dawning understanding and he decided that he would learn to sail on this shining gem of a sea.

Another part of his brain was registering the information that he had only dimly perceived at the time of his encounter with Adina. The girl was undoubtedly pregnant.

Chapter 7

"There is something wrong in that household"

Joel spoke of Adina's secret to no one. At the back of his mind, there were several things troubling him about her story, but until he could clarify them, there was no action he could take.

His determination to tackle Asher, which had sprung from the pity he had felt for the servant girl, had faded into uncertainty. The days that came after their journey to Tiberias had been wet and windy so they had seen plenty of the young would-be steward. Melkiah had urged Joel to join them in their planning for the year ahead on the fertile land of his property, and the three men had exchanged ideas and knowledge like a well-matched team of oxen. Far from wanting sole control, Asher had showed himself eager to learn anything that could be of use to enhance the land and increase its productiveness. He listened intently as Joel spoke of the methods used for crop and fruit growing on his parents' property in Bethany and the three debated how appropriate they would be for the warmer climate of Galilee.

Asher was a likeable youth and the sorrow of his mourning fell from him as he spoke with enthusiasm on his favourite subject. Neither Melkiah nor Joel could imagine Asher suggesting any plan that would involve him leaving the property he cared about so much.

Why didn't he simply marry Adina here? Joel wondered. He had noticed that Asher paid no particular attention to any of the woman servants, in spite of their inviting glances and eager response to his least request.

The only girl he treated with warmth and interest was Tamar herself. Once, as Joel was taking the shortcut through the covered colonnade to Melkiah's scroll room, he came upon them unexpectedly. They were arguing in low voices and Asher's hand was gripping Tamar's arm as if to prevent her leaving him.

"I don't want to think about it now," she was saying. "I don't *have* to decide . . ."

At that moment Asher had caught sight of Joel and released Tamar abruptly. He plunged through the archway into the courtyard and disappeared.

Tamar had gone away as swiftly, as if to avoid a second unwanted encounter, but Joel had followed her into the small room where jars of dried herbs were stored.

She was reaching for a pottery container with an unusually awkward movement and Joel knew that her mind was not on her task.

"Is Sarah suffering? Does this rain make her bones ache?"

Tamar frowned at the jar in her hands as if she could not remember why she needed the remedy. "Grandmother? She's always worse in the winter, but she hasn't complained once since my father returned. She says happiness is the best medicine of all."

"A cure for everything? Enough to counteract every anxiety, every irritation?"

"How could it be?" Tamar knew that they were no longer talking about Sarah. "But little trials don't matter in the slightest when something wonderful happens – like my father coming back to us."

"And big trials? Such as an unexpected permanent visitor?" He saw her colour rise and knew he had been unfair. "I know you don't want me here, Tamar, but I promise you that I shan't stay for ever."

She looked up quickly, genuinely upset. "Forgive me, if I have been less than welcoming . . . I have given orders for every comfort for you . . . I beg your pardon if I have said or done . . ."

Joel rushed to reassure her. "You've done nothing, and it is I who should apologise. My brother was forever chiding me for presuming to read his thoughts – and invariably getting them wrong! You have received me as graciously as if I had been an angel in disguise."

She smiled then. "I never imagined Raphael to look like you!"

He laughed and his usual good-humour dispelled the earlier tension between them. "I wish I *were* Raphael so that I could use the gall of the giant fish to restore your grandmother's sight."

"Like Tobias cured his blind father," Tamar remembered. "I love that story." She sighed. "Why don't archangels come visiting now?"

Joel tried to hide his sudden exasperation. "Tamar, you've had someone greater than an archangel visiting your town. Jesus of Nazareth has performed so many miracles that the whole country is talking about him! Why didn't you ask him to heal Sarah's blindness?"

Tamar stared at Joel, trying to remember the events of the previous year when the prophet had visited Capernaum on at least three occasions. "We never knew when he would be coming . . . My grandmother couldn't have walked so far . . . They all told me to have nothing to do with him."

"They?"

"Zelek, Ezra, Ishmael, Asher . . ."

"And Jairus? Simeon? Sarah herself?"

Tamar shook her head. She knew that the old steward and his son had had more than one argument about the man who was said to be the long-awaited Messiah. And Sarah had longed to hear him and had listened eagerly to all the reports of his stirring words and compassionate actions. Tamar had, in fact, seen Jesus for herself but did not dare admit it to Joel. The events that had followed immediately afterwards had confused and frightened her and she still did not know the truth of all that had happened that day.

She sought to divert Joel from the past. "The very next time Jesus comes, I will have my grandmother taken to him. He will probably come here again in the spring."

Joel approved. "We will all go together. His disciples have told us many of his words but your father and I long to hear him for ourselves."

He thought back to the names Tamar had quoted and wondered what connection she could have with the over-zealous Pharisee, Ishmael. He must have murmured the name out loud for she spoke of him as they left the herb store.

"He's married to my friend, Miriam. They live on the other side of Capernaum, where the rich merchants trade."

Joel, remembering that Ishmael was about fifty years of age, wondered what Tamar could have in common with a middle-aged Pharisee's wife.

"She's very creative. She designs carpets for Ishmael's business. I met her a couple of years ago when I went to choose a rug for my grandmother. Granna cannot see how beautiful it is, but its warmth helps protect her from the winter damp."

Joel had noticed the striking design of Sarah's treasured rug and his interest was aroused. "I would like to meet Miriam."

"Go past the synagogue and through the street of the Spring Well. Their carpet shop is just where the road begins to climb up the hillside."

"Won't you come with me?"

Tamar hesitated, then responded to the friendly invitation. "It would be better to wait until the weather improves. It can be dark in the buildings where the girls work and you wouldn't be able to see the colours properly."

"You shall choose the day."

It was a week before the sun shone again. Birds were singing loudly pretending that it was spring and steam was rising from the waterlogged fields as Tamar and Joel headed towards the centre of Capernaum. The hills on the other side of the lake were waves of violet beneath a blue sky where white feather clouds swirled together.

Tamar glanced at her companion and, seeing his deep appreciation of the beauty that was Galilee, forgave him for being a stranger. This foretaste of spring gave her a feeling of well-being and she felt at ease with Joel for the first time.

"You spoke of your brother, the other day," she reminded him. "Will you tell me about him?"

"His name is Daniel. He's younger than I am."

Joel had answered readily enough but the wariness in his voice warned her not to ask any further direct questions about his family.

"I would have liked a brother or a sister," Tamar reflected. "It must be wonderful to have a permanent companion and friend."

Her words did not evoke any more information from him, as she had hoped. Instead, her own words lingered on the air like a complaint of past loneliness. She changed the subject quickly.

"Miriam's mother is a pagan but her father is a Jew. The whole family are involved in a carpet business in Ashkelon. Ishmael was a merchant then and met Miriam while purchasing some rugs from her father. It was the talk of Capernaum when he returned from his travels with a Philistine bride."

"An unlikely alliance for a strict Pharisee. How long ago was this?"

"Twelve years. They say her Jewish father was enough to make Ishmael overlook her mother's nationality." She knew as well as Joel the Pharisees' horror of mixed marriages and reflected. "Or perhaps Miriam's beauty and creative talents were irresistible assets to him."

Joel realised from her tone that Tamar disliked Ishmael and was pleased that she was not lacking in good judgement. It made him even more eager to meet her unusual friend.

Tamar saw Susanna and Eliza nearby as she and Joel passed the Spring Well. She smiled at them and was about to retrace her steps when she caught sight of Abital just behind them. The morning was too glorious to be marred by a meeting with Susanna's carping and talkative mother-in-law so she contented herself with blowing a kiss to Eliza. However, the little girl did not see her as her vision was partially obscured by the large empty jug she had insisted on carrying.

"Susanna, wife of Tobit, the fisherman," Tamar explained briefly. "With her daughter and Tobit's mother."

Joel liked the look of Tamar's friend and realised that he had not as yet met many of the poorer inhabitants of Capernaum. He decided that once the spring came he would wander along the shore and meet the fishermen who drew their living from the gleaming lake.

"This way." Tamar knocked lightly on the entrance gate of a wealthy house and, after greeting the maidservant who opened it, asked if her mistress were at home.

The servant smiled her recognition and glanced curiously at Tamar's companion. "She's in the workshop." She pointed through the courtyard to an inner square beyond a jasmin-covered arch.

Following the two women, Joel saw that rooms led off three sides of the yard and soon discovered that all of them were filled with looms and workers.

As his eyes widened at the size of the business, there was a cry and a woman came towards them, holding out her hands to Tamar.

"I should have known you would come with the first sunshine!" She gave Tamar a brief but fierce hug. "I want your opinion on my new designs." She smiled a friendly welcome to Joel. "Have you bought me a buyer?"

Before Joel had time to be embarrassed about his poverty, Tamar had introduced him as her father's guest and Miriam was greeting him with interest.

"Where do you come from?"

"Another world, compared with this corner of paradise. I'd be very interested to see your looms – if it wouldn't disrupt the work too much."

"Come." Miriam accepted his evasion without rancour and led the way into the first room.

Joel estimated her age to be about thirty years. No man could have helped responding to such radiant vitality and the life sparkling in her dark eyes. Her husky speech was vigorous, reinforced with the contours of her face moving as constantly as the waves of the sea, and her smile was as natural as sunshine spreading over a meadow. Her attraction was far greater than beauty and Joel no longer wondered that the strict Ishmael had overlooked her parentage.

She explained the working of a loom concisely and confidently while, under the focus of three pairs of eyes, the girl weaver continued her careful work with heightened colour.

Joel and Tamar followed their guide from loom to loom, showing their delight in the beauty being created before their eyes, and the vivid colours of the finished products were like a glowing pathway of precious stones spread at their feet. Joel had never taken much notice of the furnishings of his parents' house and had little knowledge of the value of such carpeting, yet knew enough to realise that these creations were for the wealthiest purchasers only. Tamar was feeling the softness of a rug which represented blazing poppies on an emerald meadow and he wondered if Ishmael truly appreciated his wife's unique artistry. He did not regret the Pharisee's absence.

They went from room to room and Joel noticed that Miriam was treated everywhere with great respect and affection by the young women who worked for her. As she admired their work and made tactful suggestions, her easy relationship was that of a mother to a brood of much-loved daughters.

When they came to the last room, Joel thanked Miriam. "I have no money now, but I have promised myself that one day I shall buy one of these very fine creations from you." Momentarily he imagined himself presenting a rug to his mother but pushed the thought away determinedly. He turned to Tamar. "Perhaps you will help me choose one?"

"Wives like to choose their own," Miriam suggested, not without guile.

"I have no wife," Joel returned easily. It was true so why did a sudden image of Rhoda's face reproach him?

Miriam's far-seeing eyes saw the shadow in Joel's, and she was glad of the diversion of her husband's presence as she led them into a large reception room.

Ishmael greeted Joel and Tamar courteously, and ordered refreshments immediately from one of the servants. He spoke to Miriam with the same smooth affability, but Joel noticed that the expression in his eyes did not match his gracious words.

Joel attempted to add warmth to the atmosphere. "Your wife is very talented. I have not seen work like this, even in Jerusalem."

"You have not then been to Ashkelon?"

Joel's surprise at the mention of something he would have imagined the older man would have tried to keep hidden, changed into realisation that the reference had been made to wound his wife. It made no sense for he could not believe that Miriam was ashamed of her family. Yet her expression had become wary and Tamar too had reacted to Ishmael's malice.

She turned away from him and reached for Miriam's hand. "Have you any plans to visit your parents?" She knew that Miriam had not returned to the port on the Great Sea since her marriage, and knew too how much the older woman missed her close and loving family. "You could show them your new designs." But even as she spoke, she realised that Ishmael would not be in favour of such an idea.

Miriam did not look at her husband. "One day, perhaps. My sisters are more talented than I. I would like to see their latest work."

Servants brought in wine, fruit and almonds, but Ishmael stayed no longer than it took to drink the first courtesy cup with them.

"He has no love for any of us," Tamar thought. "Joel, because he favours the prophet Jesus; me, because I do not practise my religion with fanatical zeal and am not, therefore, the best influence on his wife; but Miriam . . . ?" She simply did not know what could have caused his change of attitude. She had never understood why someone as vital and free as Miriam should have wanted to marry the strict and humourless Ishmael. It was true that until now she had seen genuine affection between husband and wife, and she had believed that marriage to Miriam would gradually soften the narrow-viewed Pharisee.

Her friend had seemed contented enough and Tamar, while regretting her friend's choice, had accepted Ishmael for Miriam's sake.

"There is something wrong in that household," Joel said, as they walked home.

He had not meant to speak out loud and saw Tamar's surprise and displeasure that he should presume to judge the relationship between those who were after all near strangers to him.

Tamar remembered something that Susanna had once said. "There is conflict between husband and wife in every marriage," she quoted, and Joel knew that her words were intended to end the conversation.

He smiled, knowing that she had no personal experience of any close relationship, but his mind was uneasy. Words he had once heard came back to him: *"If you look for sunshine, you will see it even on the river bed on a cloudy day; if you look for evil, you will see it everywhere."* Was his mission making him see evil where there was none to be found? Miriam was a good person, and Ishmael no worse than any other Pharisee who missed holiness by a mile in his fanatical search for righteousness.

There was no real wickedness here, yet an oppressiveness seemed to hang over the household. He had never had a foreboding in his life, yet now he felt that some unknown calamity threatened. If evil had not yet entered the house, it was approaching, and would soon be knocking at the door.

Chapter 8

"Anyone who follows the prophet, will be following him to death"

Melkiah went to Simeon's grave on more than one occasion to pray. He knew that he would never cease to miss the practical wisdom of his faithful steward, and prayed that the Most High would give him his eternal reward. Those who were sleeping the centuries away would not have to wait long now before the Messiah opened the gates of Heaven for them.

He never saw Asher go to his father's grave but assumed that he, too, visited the burial place beyond the village when he could be sure of being alone. Yet, as the days went by, the cloud of mourning for Simeon, which had subdued the full joy of Melkiah's return, dispersed gradually.

A diversion came when Zelek approached him on his son Ezra's behalf.

It took Melkiah a while to understand the purpose of the visit, for some shepherd disciples of Jesus the Messiah had been staying with him for two days and he fully expected that his neighbour had come to find out all that had been said behind closed doors. Believing this, he waited expectantly while they exchanged the customary courtesies and drank wine together.

After a lengthy discussion about the crops on their adjoining lands, Zelek spoke of Tamar. "It must have been a great blessing for you to discover such a lovely daughter on your return."

Melkiah nodded, still waiting alertly for the other to introduce the subject he had expected, but Zelek had reached his desired topic.

He sighed, pulling at his grizzled beard with a strong, square hand. "Naturally, it is also an anxiety for you to decide where to bestow such a virtuous treasure – particularly when you have lost so much time. If you had been here, Tamar would have been a wife by now. Doubtless you are giving the matter much thought?"

Melkiah's smile was carefree. "I will give it my attention when it is time. There is no urgency, but I appreciate your neighbourly concern for my daughter's future."

"I too am a father." Seeing Melkiah's eyebrows rise in the amused way he remembered, Zelek hurried on. "Ezra is everything a son should be. His brothers are dutiful too, but Ezra surpasses them in his knowledge of the Torah and his zeal for keeping every tenet of the Law. You could safely trust your daughter to such a man."

Melkiah nodded. "I remember Ezra's keen interest in the Torah as a young boy. I do not doubt his piety or that he possesses the qualities necessary in a husband. However, you are not the first to approach me on the subject of Tamar's eventual marriage." He saw the other register the word 'eventual' and went on evenly. "As I have no son – no other children – it seems that the far-seeing men of Capernaum are looking beyond an immediate dowry, to the future. Several fathers have claimed that their sons are as virtuous as Tobit – possibly remembering that Tobit had inherited all his wife's parents' property!"

Zelek managed a smile. "An excellent prospect for any man, of course, though a consideration that would scarcely occur to a friend. May the Lord God grant you many years before you join your ancestors." He returned doggedly to the suggestion he had come to make. "I repeat, that your real treasure is Tamar herself, and I urge you not to bestow her hand lightly."

He drained his chalice and accepted another, though his flowing words scarcely needed a stimulant. "As you know, I am a wealthy man and have no need of your property, now or in the future, but Ezra and Tamar are fond of each other, and it would be an excellent match."

"Has Ezra spoken to Tamar?"

"He would not presume to do so, without your permission. But he loves her as deeply as Jacob loved Rachel and he has set his heart on marrying her."

Melkiah's keen blue eyes were thoughtful but he gave no indication of his response to this declaration. Silently he put his empty chalice next to the amphora of wine, rose to his feet, and strode across to the window. He looked towards the winter-bare branches of the vineyard but his eyes were unfocused until he saw his young steward and two of his workers walking in the direction of the old well.

He turned back to his old friend with the suppressed energy of one who could not bear to sit idly another moment. "Let us leave the conversation here. I thank you for your candour and your concern for Tamar's future. I will remember all you have said and, when the time comes, I will consider Ezra's claim."

"But surely the time is now?"

Melkiah held Zelek's gaze. "When I left here, Tamar was a young child. I saw nothing of her until, a week or two ago, I met a young woman whom I would not have known but for her resemblance to Anne. I have missed so many years of my daughter's company. I owe it to Tamar to be a father to her before I send her from me to a husband's protection."

Zelek admitted inwardly that if he were in Melkiah's place he too would not be in a hurry to give away such a pearl – unless there were great financial gain, of course – and nodded his reluctant agreement.

"I will tell Ezra to be patient. However, I promise you that if you will trust Tamar to him, you will be able to see her as often as you wish." He rose, then hesitated. "As we are old friends, tell me: is there another man that you are considering as a husband for your daughter?"

There were in fact two other men, one of whom would scandalize Zelek, but Melkiah's clear expression betrayed nothing. He avoided the question neatly. "When the time comes, Tamar herself will make the decision."

Once Zelek had left him, Melkiah went thankfully into the winter sunshine and strode in the opposite direction to his neighbour's property. Tamar's marriage was a problem for the future. Today he would inspect his fields of growing flax. A school of sparrows flew into the air at his approach, scolding him noisily for disturbing their meeting, and he smiled at them. His restored life was too new to be taken for granted. Like Tamar, he was utterly content with the present, and saw no need for change. There was no reason why he should not keep his daughter in his own house for a year or two yet.

He had reckoned without his mother. That evening, no sooner had he settled beside her for his customary visit, than she spoke the thoughts that had been dominating her mind all day.

"They tell me that Zelek was here this morning. Did he come to speak on Ezra's behalf?"

Melkiah was amused. When his mother had had vision, she had always known everything that had taken place in her household; it seemed that her loss of sight had not impaired this ability.

"Were you expecting such an offer?" he countered.

"Zelek approached Simeon before the Feast of Lights and Simeon discussed it with me. We decided that he should talk it over with you the next time he came to see you. But of course he died . . ."

Melkiah saw the tears in her faded eyes and realised how much his mother continued to miss the steward whom she had known since the days of her early marriage. "Talk *it* over?" he queried. "Do you mean Ezra's wish to become betrothed to Tamar?"

Sarah straightened. "No. I mean the whole question of her marriage. The truth is, we have no need to look for a husband for her. There is only one man she should marry."

"Asher?"

"Yes." She sounded surprised. "Has she spoken to you of his love for her?"

"Not a word. But I have seen the way he looks at her, and I know she has a great fondness for him."

"Are you not opposed to the idea of your daughter marrying a steward's son?"

"I would have been once. But traditional values don't seem so important to me since my encounter with Jesus of Nazareth. In any case, we both know that Asher is no ordinary servant. He's more like the son of the house."

"It would ensure the continuing care of your property," Sarah urged. "Asher really loves the land. You wouldn't find another man in the whole of Israel who would dedicate himself to it as totally."

"It's almost an obsession," Melkiah agreed. "He works too many hours and seems to resent the enforced rest of the Sabbath."

"If you had had no daughter, perhaps you would have made Asher your heir . . ."

"It's very likely. But as I do have a daughter, my only concern is to do what is best for her. As I recall, she liked Ezra well enough once."

"When they were young children. Melkiah, have you thought what

Asher's future would be if Ezra marries Tamar? After your death – which I pray will be many years in the future – he would take over this property, and perhaps put his own steward in Asher's place."

"If Tamar marries Ezra – and it's a big if – I would put something in the contract to ensure Asher's future. But my only real concern is to find out where Tamar's happiness lies. With Asher or with Ezra? Or with one of the other men whose names have been suggested to me?"

"I've nothing against Ezra," Sarah said. "I can tell from his voice that he is sincere and he certainly has a great devotion to the Torah. Yet, he cannot be unaware of the material riches he would acquire by marrying Tamar."

"As would Asher. And *he* possesses nothing."

"Through no fault of his own. Son, between us we have guided Asher and made him into the person Tamar, and the estate, need. What is the point of looking elsewhere?"

Melkiah was glad of the interruption when the curtain was pushed aside and Nike carried in a jug of warm water.

He stood up thankfully. "I will leave you to prepare for the evening meal." The aroma of perfumed oils filled the room as Nike poured the warm water into a bowl, and he touched his mother's hand to gain her attention. "Promise me that you will say nothing to Tamar. It is my wish that we take no action for the time being."

Sarah nodded, already shrugging off her warm shawl and offering it to Nike in their practised evening routine. She would say nothing but the Most High would hear her petition on behalf of her granddaughter and the youth she looked upon as a dearly-beloved grandson.

Joel too had taken advantage of the day's sunshine, not even regretting its lack of real warmth. After four years of enforced outdoor living, he found the brazier-heated rooms stifling, and left the house at the slightest suggestion of a fine day. Even when lashing rain made the tracks impassible, he threw on a borrowed sheepskin and paced the roof terrace, watching the lake drinking in the raindrops with eager gulping circles.

Soon it would be Nisan and he would witness spring in one of the loveliest places on the earth. Today's sunshine was only a foretaste but it drew him along the shingly shore towards the fishermen's dwellings. There was more than one boat on the glinting water and not far away a man in a half-beached boat was throwing a line as far as he could reach. At first Joel thought that his line was incredibly long until, as he drew nearer, he realised that a leaded rope had been used to extend the fishing range.

A tiny girl ran out of the nearest house straight to the water's edge where a young man was working on a net draped over his boat. Joel recognised the slight figure at the door of the dwelling as Susanna whom Tamar had greeted in the market-place, so guessed the identity of the fisherman bending down to listen to the little girl.

By the time Joel reached the pair, Tobit had returned to his work of mending the net while his daughter was grasping a nearby section and pulling at the wet knots with small but determined fingers.

"I see you have a good helper."

"I couldn't catch any fish without Eliza's help." Tobit smiled courteously at the stranger but his hands continued their practised work.

Joel knelt beside the tiny girl. "Tell me what you are doing."

"I find the holes – and Abba mends them." She pulled at the heavy net importantly. "See. Here is a very big one."

"Perhaps a whale took a bite?"

The suggestion won a delighted laugh and a boast. "My Abba could catch a whale."

"It's more likely that the whale would catch me," Tobit murmured.

"You could live inside him – like Jonah," Eliza agreed. She turned to Joel. "What is the biggest fish you've ever seen?"

Joel considered. "I saw a tadpole once. It grew bigger and bigger until it hopped right away."

The three-year-old responded to the joke joyfully, but whirled away suddenly as she caught sight of Susanna. "Mummy's collecting firewood. I'm going to help her."

She danced away, her small sandals making scarcely an imprint on the sand among the beach-stones, and had soon pounced on her first find at the water's edge.

Tobit worked on steadily, undisturbed by the stranger's silence, but his curiosity was aroused by the other's thoughtful gaze. "What do you see out there on the lake?"

Joel turned to the fisherman. "I was trying to imagine a man walking over the waves."

Tobit laughed. "You mean Jesus of Nazareth? His disciples say that he ran over the sea as easily as if it were a Roman road, but there's no end to the wonders they claim for him. They'll be saying that he flew through the air next!"

"Why not? – if he's who he claims to be? Angels fly, and a heavenly chariot was provided for Elijah. Prophets can do anything – if the Most High wishes it."

"Are you one of his disciples?"

"I am Joel, a leper cured by him. By the time I was purified, he had disappeared, but perhaps I will become a disciple one day." He looked thoughtfully at the strong young fisherman. "Did you see him when he came here?"

"I heard him when he spoke in the synagogue."

"Do you think he is the promised Messiah?"

Tobit shrugged. "Time will tell. He is a prophet, and speaks better than any man I've ever heard – but John spoke powerfully too."

"John, whom they called the Baptist?"

Both men relived the shock that had spread through the land at the news of his execution by King Herod. There was pain in the fisherman's eyes and Joel guessed the reason.

"You knew him."

"I was his disciple. He convinced me that a new age of God's favour had begun. I would have followed John anywhere."

"Did he not say that Jesus of Nazareth was the Messiah?"

"And if he is? He's certainly a holy man, and I'm glad if he's leading sinners to repentance, but a sensible man will keep well away from him. He speaks out too fearlessly and makes powerful enemies everywhere he goes. He's heading for destruction and anyone who decides to follow him will be following him to death."

Joel knew that there was truth in Tobit's words and felt the wave of helplessness that good men always feel when evil approaches like on oncoming tide that cannot be checked. And yet, he consoled himself, if Jesus was truly the Son of God, no evil *could* overcome him.

Joel was seeking an answer for the man who had found the cost of following a prophet too high, when a small hand slipped into his.

"My granny says to bring you to our house." Eliza pointed towards the small house on the shore where Susanna and an older woman were waiting.

"I'd like to come," Joel assured his new young friend, then turned to her father impulsively. "I know nothing of fishing but I would like to learn. Will you teach me?"

Tobit was taken by surprise but had no time to question the stranger from Judea for his daughter was tugging impatiently at Joel's hand.

He nodded. "Come out in the boat with me one day."

"Granny has made you some scones." Eliza announced. Her round eyes were alight with anticipation and, as they drew nearer the waiting women, the aroma of fresh baking confirmed her words.

On this fine day the women had not used the indoor stone oven but the portable inverted cone that could be used with fuel in the winter and as a sun-griddle in hot weather. Today the scent of burning wood mingled pleasantly with the cooked flour-cakes.

The older woman stepped forward and introduced herself and her daughter-in-law. "I am Abital and this is Susanna. Come inside."

Joel gave them his name as he followed them into the dark dwelling, although he had no doubt that they not only knew his identity but also his connection with Melkiah.

As he sat down, Susanna gave him a scone and a cup of pomegranate wine. He thanked her, warming to the small young wife whose alert yet innocent eyes reminded him of a friendly robin.

The brief exchange was all that Abital allowed them. "Take a scone to your father" she ordered Eliza, then turned to Joel. "I saw you talking to my son. He's the best fisherman on the lake and no one can handle a boat better than he can." Her face was long and stern in repose, but her eyes gleamed as she praised her son. "There are races in the spring – time-wasting foolishness, of course – but it does show who are the strongest and most skilful. My son proved to be the best single oarsman."

"Because Simon of Jonah was away . . ." murmured Susanna.

Abital turned on her daughter-in-law fiercely. "Don't speak of him. Tobit has been too influenced by that man and his prophet already." To Joel she explained. "Simon of Jonah was an excellent fisherman too, and he knows as much about boats and the ways of the sea as

Tobit does, but he's thrown it all away for nothing but a dream."

"Is Jesus the prophet not real?"

"He may be a prophet, in which case it is his job to pass on the words of the Most High. But he should not take a man away from his living to follow him."

"Should men not follow when the Most High calls?"

"The Most High wants men to stay at home and work for their wives and families," Abital declared, as his self-appointed spokeswoman. "Prophets should choose their disciples from the Scribes and Levites in the Temple, and from all those rich young men who have nothing to do but wander from one Rabbi to the next."

"But perhaps those men do not believe in a Galilean prophet."

"They are the wise ones. I know Porphirea's mother well – Porphirea is Simon's wife – and she tells me that her son-in-law is hardly ever at home. The amount of fishing he does would scarcely feed a sparrow!"

Abital's voice was loud in her grievance and Joel guessed that she was ensuring that Tobit, at the water's edge, could hear every word.

He tried to calm the old woman. "Tobit has no intention of following Jesus the Messiah," he reminded her.

"Jesus, *said* to be the Messiah."

Joel remembered one of Jairus' stories. "He has done many miracles here. Even helped Simon of Jonah to make a huge catch of fish all at once – perhaps to make up for some of his absences."

"What does a carpenter know of fishing? These things happen naturally. Tobit caught a whole shoal of fish once."

"Your son is skilful," Joel agreed, but as he left the simple shack, he was thoughtful. If rich people would not follow Jesus because he refused to be one of them, and the poor could not afford the cost of following him, then how could his mission succeed? A Kingdom could not exist without leaders.

The number of Jesus' enemies was growing all the time, and anyone who publicly acknowledged him as sent by God would be calling down a share of hatred and violence upon himself.

The lamp of the wicked shall be put out.

Yes, but sometimes the sons of Light had to die to accomplish it.

Chapter 9

"Joel of Shallum is an impostor"

The brilliant sunshine of the month of Adar raised people's spirits and put warmth into the smiling greetings of neighbours. Even Sarah left her room and took a slow turn about the courtyard, only to be coaxed by Tamar through the arch into their lakeside garden.

"Is there blossom on the almond tree?" Sarah asked. She took a deep breath as if the faint perfumes of early spring would bring to her mind's eye the vista she had once known so well.

Tamar pulled the end of a branch towards them. "Feel the buds," she suggested. "They're nearly ready to burst into flower. And can you hear those sparrows squabbling? They've found something among the new grass under the tamarisk. I'm afraid they're flattening the saffron crocus as usual."

"I can hear voices. Is someone coming?"

Tamar looked round. "Asher and Joel are crossing the orchard and Joel is pointing to one of the trees. He's probably asking how to plant an orchard! He's interested in everything. If he'd been a woman, he'd be learning to make a carpet on one of Miriam's looms by now!"

Sarah nodded, smiling, but her thoughts were with the youth who was so dear to her. "Asher too likes to learn. He questions everyone who comes here, in case they can teach him something about the land and animals."

In fact, the two men were learning from each other. Joel had caught Asher's enthusiasm for farming and learned much as they explored the countryside together. In return, he remembered the cultivating methods used in Bethany and offered them to the younger man.

Today, with the grass paths beginning to dry out, they were making for the fold on the hillside where Melkiah's sheep were wintering.

As they approached the stone-walled enclosure surrounding a low arched building, they saw a jackal crouching outside, attracted by the bleating of a host of unwary lambs.

Asher took a corded leather pouch from his belt and bent to pick up a smooth stone. He fitted it into the sling, whirled the cords in the air, and let go. The stone sped unerringly to his target; the jackal yelped in pain and, forgetting his hunger, retreated as far as its injured shoulder would allow.

Joel nodded his approval and held out his hand. "May I?"

He took the sling weapon and chose a stone similar in size to the one Asher had used.

Asher was amused. "It's not as easy as it looks."

Joel looked towards the thorn-topped enclosure wall and saw a rag caught on it, fluttering in the breeze. "This stone's a little muddy. It needs cleaning."

Even while the ropes were still playing the air with a humming vibration, Asher realised that Joel was no novice. The stone sped straight and true to the pierced rag, tore it from the thorns, and disappeared into the depth of the man-made hedge.

Asher laughed. "When were you a shepherd?"

"My uncle has many flocks in Bethlehem. One year my cousins were ill so my brother and I went to help him out for the season. We soon learned how to protect the sheep."

Asher could see him using a shepherd's flint-embedded club as competently and decided there and then not to become involved in a test of strength against this man. From within the fold came a rhythmical lilting sound, accompanied by clapping hands, and he turned to Joel in resignation. "And I suppose you learned to play on a reed pipe too?"

Joel grinned. "Doesn't every young boy? But I'm no musician. Tamar says you can play the kinnor. I'd like to hear you sometime."

"I used to."

Remembering Asher's loss, Joel did not pursue the subject, but his sympathy led to thoughts of the servant girl's accusations. "Has there been any word of Adina's whereabouts?"

The name made Asher start but his step did not falter as they made for the opening of the sheepfold. "I've heard nothing. She must be far away by now."

No doubt Asher would like her to be as distant as Rome, Joel thought. The young steward had made a mistake in leaving her in nearby Tiberias, but of course he had not expected Melkiah to return, and no one else from the household would ever have gone there. Adina had been found once, and could be found again, and there were questions that Joel intended to ask.

It was only long after his encounter with her, that he had realised two things: that Adina had known of Melkiah's leprosy; and that she had witnessed Simeon's death. Therefore, Asher must have told her what Melkiah's own daughter had not known – and gone further, and anticipated his master's demise. Had Asher truly believed that Melkiah was already dead, or had he deliberately lied to Adina? Perhaps he had plans for the masterless estate and had confided them to her. Or, if he had not intended that she should take any part in them, had deliberately removed her from the scene.

And Simeon? Adina had said, "I saw him fall", but was Asher aware that she had witnessed his father's death? If it had truly been an accident, the fact was not important, yet some instinct told him that he should hear Adina's version of the tragedy.

Unaware of Joel's disturbing thoughts, Asher was leading the way through the narrow gap of the sheepfold. "We've scarcely lost a sheep all winter. Our men tend them better than they do their own children, and they're quite fearless when wild animals attack. You won't find better lambs in the whole of Galilee."

Joel was immediately surrounded by a living sea of warm, white waves that parted in alarm at his alien presence. He smiled at their noisy protest, noting that these sheep were very different from the long-legged Egyptian breed his uncle favoured. The new lambs did look exceptionally fine and healthy and he nodded his approval. "Melkiah will have no trouble finding perfect animals to take to Jerusalem for the Passover."

"No." But Asher's voice betrayed the perpetual reluctance of a shepherd asked to sacrifice the creature dearest to him. Joel sympathised, knowing how often a man tried to turn a blind eye to his best animal and persuade his conscience that a different one would be acceptable to the Most High.

Watching Asher moving confidently amongst the herdsmen,

questioning them and examining the lambs gently, Joel wondered why he could not accept him as the dependable youth he appeared to be. Perhaps he had been too influenced by Adina's words, whereas the truth could be that it had been she who had seduced Asher. If this were the case, then this boy was guilty of nothing more than the weakness of any man faced with temptation.

However, Joel could not see Asher as a weak person. His young head was so filled with ambition that he did not believe that any girl, however lovely, could divert him from his chosen path. Asher's private thoughts were as well guarded as a robber's den, but time would reveal what kind of person he really was.

Joel himself was the subject of more than one discussion in Capernaum after Ishmael's contacts in Bethany had brought news. Miriam's husband had wasted no time in contacting Ezra, and the subject revived after the Thursday synagogue meeting where a dozen devout Torah scholars lingered in the hall.

Eli, who was as deaf as a tax-collector to a plea of poverty, elbowed his way to Ishmael's side. "Is it true that Joel of Shallum is an impostor?"

Ishmael edged away slightly. Conversations with Eli required time and patience. "It is possible," he said clearly. "His parents say that their son is dead."

"Could they be referring to one of their other sons?" Uzziel, one of the elders, asked.

"According to Aaron, who lives near the family, there were but two sons. The older, Joel, became a leper and died; the younger, Daniel, a married man, lives with his parents and has taken over the main burden of running the estate."

"A wealthy one?"

"A small place of no consequence. There's scarcely enough land to support the family."

"What proof is there of Joel's death?"

"The parents sent one of their servants to the lepers regularly, and one day he brought back the news that Joel had died. The body was buried by the other lepers, of course, but they never doubted the truth of the report. They still mourn him, even though their other son, Daniel, has married recently."

Zelek was thinking back to the evening of the celebration feast he had given for Melkiah when he and Joel had first returned. "Joel did say that as far as his family were concerned, he was dead," he pointed out.

"A convenient cover for someone taking on a dead man's identity! If Joel were who he says he is, can you think of any possible reason that would prevent him from going straight home to his parents?"

"Honour your father and mother," Joachim murmured censoriously. Joachim, known for his excessive care never to infringe the slightest precept of the very demanding Pharisaic laws, prided himself on the cold material help he gave his own parents. "A true son of the Law would not break the third commandment so blatantly."

Even the listeners who had not conditioned their consciences to speak only if they were in agreement with their owner's wishes, were unable to think of any circumstances to justify a son who had acted as Joel of Shallum.

Eli, who had heard only some of the exchanges, returned to his original question impatiently. "Tell me! *Is* that young man an impostor?"

He saw the slow nods of his companions and pursued. "Then, why has he come here?"

"Melkiah has no son," Ishmael pointed out. "To whom should he leave his property but to the young man who befriended him when he was in need?"

"Melkiah has a daughter . . ."

"Who is in need of a husband. Perhaps Joel of Shallum would be son-in-law as well as adopted son."

"The man who *calls* himself Joel of Shallum," Ezra corrected sharply. Tamar was to be his own bride, not bestowed on a Judean without even a shekel to his borrowed name.

Joachim could scarcely contain his impatience. "You talk of trivialities and miss the major issue. Have you forgotten Joel's own explanation of his presence in Galilee? He admits that the Nazarene sent him here."

"Yes. There was some nonsense about bringing the light."

Joachim was triumphant. "This is yet another instance of the falseness of the so-called Messiah. He who claims not only to know all truth, but to *be* the truth, was not able to recognise a deceiver!"

"He recognised him as a kindred spirit!"

Ezra, who had no love for his rival, felt compelled to be fair. "Joel may be genuinely deceived in Jesus' identity. He does not strike me as a wicked man."

The others turned on him with words that he was not displeased to hear.

"A man who leaves his parents in torment – if he *is* Joel of Shallum – or a common man of unknown parentage who tricks a wealthy man into accepting him as a friend . . . a cheat and a liar who dares to attend the synagogue . . . a man who follows Jesus, the leader of a rabble of the most worthless people in the land . . . Perhaps Joel is a murderer fleeing from justice."

"What action should we take? How should we deal with him?"

Eli pulled at Joachim's sleeve. "Do you mean the young man, Joel, or Jesus the prophet?"

Joachim pulled his mantle closer around him, dislodging the eager hand. "Jesus will be dealt with, as we dealt with his cousin John."

He smiled, remembering how easy it had been to ensure that King Herod's wife had been told all the derogatory words John the Baptist had said about her; as they had anticipated, this had led to his arrest and eventual execution.

"The Nazarene too is condemning himself with every word that he says, and is going towards his own death like a lamb to the slaughter. He'll have every chance to practise the meekness he preaches then!"

"He's caused enough disruption and division," Uzziel agreed. "We need the people back on our side, ready to follow the true Messiah when he appears."

"The real Messiah will be a Rabbi of great wealth and power. We will make him High Priest and then King," Eli pronounced.

"But what of Joel, the ex-leper?"

"We should warn Melkiah . . ."

Zelek thought of his neighbour and shook his head. "I doubt if he'd listen. He'd take his friend's word against ours."

"We could tell the impostor that we've discovered that the real Joel is dead."

"He will deny it, and we cannot prove otherwise – any more than he can."

"Bethany is so far away. If only we could confront him with his parents."

Zelek's eyes kindled. "We'll do just that. We'll bide our time until Passover is near. Then, when it is time for the pilgrimage, I'll invite the whole family to stay in my town house there. I'll devise a way to get Joel on his own and, with your help, persuade him to accompany us to Bethany to the house he claims to be his own."

Ezra scarcely heard the approving voices promising co-operation with his father's plan. The others could bide their time, if they wished, but Passover was still many weeks away. He would make quite sure that Tamar did not remain in ignorance of the impostor beneath her roof for even one more day.

Tamar was returning from visiting Susanna when Ezra caught sight of her on the shore. She was smiling in memory of some of Eliza's conversation, and feeling a strange envy of the completeness of the fisherman's family. They did not discuss outside events or seek changes in their simple life. They existed from day to day, accepting with serene faith whatever befell them: the Most High was watching over them and they were content that he should deal them joy or sorrow, bounty or want, as he saw fit. Tobit and Susanna, no less than Eliza, lived in childlike trust and simplicity and greeted the gift of each dawning day with gladness.

Tamar wished that she could clear her own mind of every cloud and live her life as simply and contentedly. She was overjoyed to have her father back, of course, but he had changed from the attentive father she remembered. He and Joel were obsessed by the prophet Jesus and when they weren't welcoming some of his disciples and questioning them eagerly, they were seeking out those in Capernaum whose lives had been changed by him. Her father had missed so many years of her life; she couldn't understand why he didn't want to give her precedence now. It was true that he urged her to join him in listening to tales of the Messiah from passing guests but, although they were not without interest, she wanted their relationship to be the way it used to be. She longed to walk alone with him, as in childhood, when he had opened her eyes to the secrets of nature and made her world alive and beautiful.

Her grandmother was strangely restless too. She would ask Tamar to tell her what was happening in their olive grove and vineyard and to describe the appearance of every field, and hillside meadow of their property. She would listen intently, nod her approval, and praise Asher's stewardship as warmly as if she were recommending him to a new owner. Then she would go on to discuss their neighbour's property and ask Tamar her opinion of Ezra and his brothers. They had never had such conversations before and Tamar was at a loss to understand what was in the old woman's mind.

Yesterday, Tamar had visited Miriam, and she too had changed. Her welcome had been as cordial as ever but her vitality had been dimmed and Tamar got the impression that her mind was disturbed by anxieties of its own. She had assured Tamar that all was well with her, but the expression in her large dark eyes had belied her words.

Now, with the waves dancing on the shore and the warm breeze tugging at her veil, Tamar decided that she was worrying unnecessarily. She lifted her face to receive the sun's benediction, her thoughts still on the fisher-family she had just left. She too would count her blessings and rejoice.

Ezra approached as she was skirting a clump of bulrushes that thrived in the water-soaked soil. Tamar, reaching out to touch the new leaves of a willow tree, did not see him and was startled when he spoke.

"You are as lovely as a willow. You belong here where the lake reflects the sapphire of your eyes." He had composed and practised the speech with great earnestness and hoped that it did not sound as foolish as it did to his own ears.

Tamar half-smiled and he could not tell whether it was from pleasure or amusement. She continued pressing on the willow branch to make it dip into the water, so she would not have to meet his eyes.

"I have news of Joel of Shallum."

As Ezra had hoped, she swung round at his words. He continued.

"His parents at Bethany say that their son Joel is dead."

Tamar was unimpressed by the dramatic announcement. "Most lepers leave their homes to die. As he hasn't contacted them, they're bound to assume that he is dead."

"They *did* hear – from the other lepers. They say that Joel died and was buried."

Tamar stared at him. "There's some mistake, for Joel is here, very much alive. His parents must be told."

"Why doesn't *he* tell them – if he's truly their son?"

Tamar tried to remember what Melkiah had told her when Joel had first arrived at their house. "I don't know, but there is a good reason. My father says that he cannot go home."

"Your father could be deceived. Joel has brought nothing with him but a name – possibly one he borrowed from another leper who died."

"My father is a good judge of character. He says Joel was a good friend to him while they were both ill."

"But now that Joel is well and free to go wherever he wishes, why should he stay here where he doesn't belong?"

"Do you know why?"

"Perhaps he wants to share not only your father's property but his daughter too."

Tamar was exasperated, remembering Susanna had suggested the same thing some weeks before. "I have no personal interest in any of our guest's plans but he will stay with us as long as my father wishes."

Ezra was only partially satisfied with her reassurance. It was obvious that Joel had not won Tamar's affection, yet the door seemed as firmly closed against his own suit.

Boldly, he put his hand on the willow branch, imprisoning her between the tree and the lake, but dared not let his ringed fingers touch hers. "You know that my father has spoken to yours about our marriage?"

He saw the shock and dismay in her eyes and disappointment filled him. He sought to lessen the shock. "Perhaps you don't wish to leave your father yet but, if you will agree to a betrothal, I'll gladly wait a year for our marriage."

Tamar's hand tightened round the rough branch. "If you truly care about me, you will not ask anything of me for a year."

Ezra's eyes glowed, and now he dared to put his hand over hers. "Tamar, I will prove my love for you by waiting patiently. And, at the end of the time, I may ask you again?"

Tamar was confused, both by his words and his unwanted closeness. All she wanted was to end the conversation.

"Yes," she said. He could *ask*, but she could not imagine herself agreeing to marry him.

Ezra interpreted her reply according to the desire of his heart and, when he left her, he strode with the energy of a man who has been promised half a kingdom.

Neither of them saw Asher, half-concealed behind a terebinth. As he gazed after Ezra, his eyes were dark and he was far from exultant.

Chapter 10

"Asher watched his father fall"

Joel's opportunity to return to Tiberias came when some of Jesus' disciples stopped briefly at Capernaum on their way to Judea. They had stayed overnight with Jairus, but by the time Melkiah and Joel heard of their presence the men were already eager to continue their journey. Knowing that the rain could return at any time, they wanted to take advantage of the good weather and reach Jerusalem as soon as possible.

Melkiah had business elsewhere but Joel offered to accompany the travellers as far as Tiberias. He would enjoy their company and there would be plenty of time to glean new tales of the wonder-working prophet.

As they took the path above the shore, screaming gulls drew their attention to fishermen unloading their catch. Even from a distance, they could hear spirited haggling as they sold the fish to merchants from other villages.

Turning away from the shimmering lake, fringed in blue like a Pharisee's mantle, they headed south and took the narrow footpath. Pools of water checked their way at intervals, spilling from streams rushing down the hillside at a speed Roman charioteers would envy.

Joash, an excitable youth, strode the track at a rapid pace, leaping over obstacles exuberantly. Every step was taking him closer to the Messiah to whom he would offer his homage and his life. Andrew was more cautious yet shared his companion's eagerness to arrive at their destination. Unlike Joash, he had never seen Jesus of Nazareth but fired by his friend's enthusiasm was prepared to listen to the man who had set the whole country ablaze.

They had spent the night before last at the home of Judas and Anne near Lake Merom. "Jesus has visited them twice and all the workers on their estate are filled with praise of him. They say their bountiful harvest was the result of his blessing, and as they were celebrating they saw a further wonder: Jesus was on the terrace, speaking to the estate workers, when a mother carried her son up to him. The child had broken his back, but Jesus healed him instantly and the boy had to lead his mother down the steps she was crying so much!"

"The whole district is filled with admiration of Jesus' power and wisdom," Joash confirmed. "Everywhere we go, we hear of the great love he inspires. Men who wouldn't make a Sabbath day's journey to listen to a Rabbi from Jerusalem, will travel for days on the merest rumour that Jesus is in the area."

"Where is he now?" Joel asked.

"We don't know exactly – but we'll find him! A dazzling star cannot remain hidden."

"You've spoken of Jesus' friends, but what of his enemies?"

"They're easy to identify: jealousy and spite cannot be disguised."

"You don't appear to be worried. Isn't there real danger for Jesus?"

Joash plucked a trailing branch from a dead tree and swished it through the air.

"From his throne in heaven, the Lord laughs and mocks their feeble plans . . . You are my Son. You will shatter them into pieces like a clay pot" he quoted. "If every man in Israel were against him, it would make no difference. He is the Son of the Most High God, and his victory is certain."

"Are you expecting him to use his miraculous power to fell his enemies?"

"He has not told me his immediate plans," Joash admitted, and submitted ruefully to his companions' laughter. "But if he wants an army to fight for him, I shan't put my sword down until his Kingdom has been established."

Joel was stirred. He too wanted to keep walking until he came face to face with the man who possessed all goodness and all power. How gladly he too would kneel before him and offer his service, and fight at his side until all the battles were over and Jesus was the recognised King.

Yet, hadn't he already knelt before Jesus and been given a mission? Or, could it be that he had read meaning into the Messiah's words that had not been intended?

Looking back towards Capernaum, he was compelled to shake his head. No. He must stay until he had played his appointed part and light had overcome darkness in the hostile village.

He parted from his new friends on the road high above Tiberias and walked down towards the lake past the walls of Herod's palace. His bird's eye view had taken in its Greek sculptures, and the layout of all the ornate villas enclosed within the semi-circle of the town walls. Joel knew that there was more than one theatre in the thriving town but his eyes were drawn to the distant amphitheatre where Greeks and Romans frequently gathered to watch battling gladiators and touring theatre companies.

The town was so large that Joel knew he could wander in it for days without meeting Adina, particularly as he did not know the name of her wealthy protector. He decided to go to the house of Chuza and seek out Jonathan who had welcomed Melkiah so warmly on their last visit.

Remembering the way from his earlier visit, Joel made for the Roman villa along a wide avenue by the lakeside. As he approached the formal entrance he noticed new leaves uncurling on branches woven through the pergola and buds swelling on the acacias and myrtle. In another month the lakeside garden would be an earthly paradise.

The porter answered his knock immediately and drew Joel into the hall. As a servant was dispatched in search of Chuza's steward, Joel was aware of the covert glances of maidservants who seemed curious about the return of the stranger and were probably hoping that Jonathan would speak to him in their presence.

They were to be disappointed for the steward recognised him immediately as Melkiah's friend and led the way swiftly to a reception room, calling for refreshments.

The steward was eager for news of his spiritual master, Jesus of Nazareth, and Joel obligingly fed him with Joash's stirring words.

Jonathan listened intently but shook his head, smiling. "The Master is not raising an army. How gladly we would fight for him, if he were! His battle is against the evil in mens' hearts and he tells us to use his own weapons of love and mercy."

Joel, knowing how scornfully pleasure-loving men of power reacted to such an approach, turned to the easier, more immediate problem. "I'm looking for Adina, Melkiah's former servant girl. I believe he mentioned her to you. Have you discovered the name of her protector?"

"His name is Marius and he was recalled to Rome a week ago."

Seeing Joel's consternation, he hastened to reassure him.
"Fortunately, he came to say farewell to my master, and requested that
we should find a place in our household for his young mistress."

Joel leaned forward. "Did Chuza agree?" He knew the answer by
the smile on Jonathan's candid face. "Is she here now? May I see her?"

Jonathan nodded. "Marius was a good man. Most Romans wouldn't
have given a thought to the future of a Jewish servant girl – particularly
one in her condition. My mistress, Johanna, has given her the task of
helping Esther. The old nurse is getting too old to chase after young
children."

"Melkiah will be greatly relieved that she has been given shelter in
your household."

Jonathan rose and pushed the amphora of wine closer to the visitor.
"I'll fetch Adina and you shall judge for yourself whether she is happy
here."

The girl who entered the room quietly a few moments later looked
very different from the fugitive Joel remembered. She wore no rich
clothes now yet her blue woollen dress was of good quality, and the
light veil which fell from the crown of her dark plaits was made of
fine linen. As she stood quietly before him, she seemed both dignified
and serene and yet there had been a flicker of anxiety in her eyes
when she had recognised Joel.

"All is well," he reassured her. "Melkiah and his family don't know
that I have come to see you. But they will be pleased to hear that you
are working in this house."

"No!" Adina had taken a step forward. "Please don't tell them." She
reacted to Joel's words as if he had raised a stick to her, and her plea
was impassioned. "I belong to their former life and I want to be
forgotten. We'll never meet again, and it is better so."

She did not need to say Asher's name for Joel to understand. "With
your permission, I'll tell no one but Melkiah. He'll be glad to know
that you are safe, and I'm sure he'll be content to leave you here."

"Does he still believe that I am a thief?"

Again Joel read her mind as she wondered whether Asher had told the truth about her.

He chose his words carefully. "Melkiah does not know what really happened but has dismissed the whole affair from his mind."

It was only when Adina's cheeks changed colour that he realised that his badly-chosen words had made the servant girl feel of no importance. Embarrassment clouded the air between them. Every question Joel wanted to ask concerned Asher, and he knew that the father of her unborn child was the one person she had no wish to discuss. He did not doubt that it had been Asher who had made her pregnant; she had not lived with the Roman officer long enough to become visibly pregnant by him so soon.

He held out a hand towards her. "Sit down, Adina." He settled the girl beside him, realising it would be easier for her to speak without having to meet his eyes. "There is something I need to know. Last time we met, you said you had seen Simeon die. Perhaps you are the only person who knows what happened."

"Asher knows."

"Yes, but Melkiah doesn't wish to distress him by making him speak of it again." Joel did not add that Melkiah had accepted Simeon's death as a tragic accident and that Joel himself was the only one who was uneasy about the incident. "Asher told us that his father fell to his death, but I'd like you to tell me exactly what you saw."

Adina half-turned towards him and he read her mystification. Although she must have known that she was not compelled to answer him, she simply couldn't understand why this stranger to the household needed to resurrect the past. He waited, making no movement or demand until, as he had hoped, the ease of his demeanour decided her.

"Simeon and his son were repairing the balustrade of the roof terrace. Asher had discovered a broken part and warned him that someone could fall." She half-smiled unhappily at the irony. "Asher had taken some tools up the staircase to the terrace and Simeon was following him carrying some stones. Just as he reached the top he lost his balance. He swayed for a moment and called something, but fell before Asher could make a move."

"Had Simeon a poor sense of balance?"

"Oh, no. Nor any fear of heights. Only the week before he'd been up a ladder pruning one of the tallest trees. Everyone said that he was as strong and fit as a man half his age."

"But on the day he died? Was there anything different about him?"

Adina was frowning and Joel knew that she was evoking the memory. "All I know is that as I watched him, I felt somehow that what I was seeing wasn't real. I realised afterwards that it was because Simeon was walking so slowly; he was ascending the stairs as if he were in a dream. His feet were dragging and his body was swaying from side to side. I remember thinking that he was too close to the edge . . ."

"Did he – or Asher – know that you were watching?"

"No. Not then. I had come to ask Asher something but when I saw their task, I decided to wait until he needed to come down for a moment."

"Where were you?"

"I'd come from the orchard. I couldn't see Simeon and Asher until I came through the gap in the hedge."

"Were you worried about Simeon falling when you saw his unsteadiness?"

She frowned. "I don't think so. I was still wondering why he was moving so slowly when he fell."

"Why didn't Asher see that his father needed help and go to take his burden from him?"

"I suppose he was still putting down his own load. When his father called out, he came to the top of the steps . . . but it was too late."

Something about the way she said the last few words alerted Joel.

"If Asher had acted more quickly . . ." he suggested.

There were tears in Adina's eyes. "He didn't act at all. His father called, and was swaying, but Asher just stood there. I ran forward, but of course I was too far away. Asher watched his father fall, and didn't move until he was lying on the ground at the foot of the stairs."

"And then?"

"Asher called out and the other servants came running. And Tamar came too. And we were all crying."

"Asher too?"

"He was stunned. When they said that Simeon was dead, he fell on the ground, and buried his head in his arms. Poor Asher! It was terrible for him."

Tears were on her cheeks now and Joel knew that she was mourning anew, both for the steward whom everyone had loved, and the son whom she had also lost.

"Later, when we were alone, Asher told me that it had been like one of those nightmares when you know what is going to happen but cannot move. It wasn't his fault, but he told me that he will never forgive himself."

Her tear-bright eyes asked sympathy for Asher, but Joel thought it wise to move away from the subject of Simeon's death.

"As you were Asher's close friend, he probably confided in you. For instance, he told you about Melkiah's leprosy but made a mistake in supposing him dead. Perhaps he said something like 'he's probably dead by now'?"

"Oh, no. He said that word had come of the Master's death. He was quite definite."

"Who could have brought such news? I thought Simeon was the only one who ever saw Melkiah, and he hadn't visited him since Chislev."

Adina shook her head helplessly. "I don't know. I didn't think about it. Too much was happening: Simeon dying so horribly; Asher saying that the Master too was dead; Tamar and her grandmother too upset to see anyone; and Asher saying that I must go to Tiberias at once so that we could live in Valerius' household together."

Joel tried to speak gently to alleviate the harshness of what he must say. "You know now that Asher lied to you more than once. He doesn't deserve your love or loyalty." Hoping that her silence meant agreement, he pursued. "When was it that you told Asher that you were with child by him?"

Adina thought back. "About a week or two before I went away." She sensed Joel's compassion and pride spurred her to resurrect the happiness that had once been hers. "Asher was pleased about the baby – once he'd thought about it. He said we would marry and have many fine sons."

"Did you ask Simeon's blessing on your plans? Or Sarah's?"

"We were going to, but Asher said we must choose just the right moment. We were happy keeping our secret to ourselves."

"Do you think Simeon would have been pleased?"

"Oh, yes. He liked me and I'm sure he guessed that we loved each other. He didn't say anything but I know he approved of our attachment."

The memory faded into sudden bleakness, and Joel felt pity for the betrayed victim of a careless youth.

Adina stood up. She was shaking and entreaty had returned to her eyes. "May I go now? I want to forget it ever happened."

"I promise I will never speak of it again," Joel assured her.

But, as he left the house, he thought of the baby who would be a permanent living reminder of the man who had treated her so heartlessly.

The return journey to Capernaum seemed endless in the fading daylight. This morning the miles had sped swiftly because of the exhilarating conversation with the two pilgrims. Now Joel's feet seemed weighted by discoveries, doubts and suspicions that he could share with no one. For Adina's sake, old sins must not be brought to the light, and the wrongs of the past must stay buried with the dead steward. Asher had not escaped punishment for his father had died, and he had the rest of his life to redeem his past foolishness.

Yet Joel's disquiet would not be dispelled. Words returned to his mind: "Go with your friend and use the light I have given you, for the lamp of the wicked shall be put out." He owed Jesus his life and would give it if necessary to fulfil his mission. If only he understood more clearly what it was! Surely he had not been sent here because of the seduction and casting off of a servant girl, when a greater evil – the greatest possible – surrounded him?

Evil men were lurking everywhere like ugly candle-snuffers waiting to extinguish the Light that was Jesus; if he, Joel, could help foil the plot to destroy the Messiah, his life would not have been in vain.

He came to a fork in the path and for a moment could not decide which route to take. It seemed symbolic.

"Lord God, send me a sign. Lead me to the evil which You would have me destroy."

He would have withdrawn his prayer if he had known that it would be answered before the sun had set by violent death . . .

Chapter 11

"What would have happened if I had never returned?"

Melkiah walked through his growing flax with a feeling of wellbeing. In a few weeks the field would be as blue as a piece of sky fallen to the ground, but in the meantime he was well content with the healthy green shoots thrusting upwards in the Spring sunshine. His feet scarcely needed prompting to take the narrow path to the lake. Although he had appreciated this sky-mirror of shining sea before his illness, now, after long years of exile, he was drawn to it irresistibly again and again. It was as if his thirst for its living water could only be quenched by being close enough to aborb it with all his five senses.

A pied kingfisher flew out of some reeds, swooped low over the water, and chose a fish for his breakfast. The simplicity of the operation made a mockery of the painstaking work of the lake's fishermen. Melkiah smiled, admiring the contrast of the bird's jet feathers against the brilliance of the gleaming white. He made no movement, unwilling to frighten away the feeding bird, needing this oasis of tranquillity to restore his spirit.

He heard young children calling to each other and saw a laughing young boy jump from an upturned boat into his mother's arms. There was something in the way that the smiling woman hugged her child that made Melkiah think of Tamar. Perhaps his neighbour and mother were right and, now that she was nearly seventeen, the time had come to make arrangements for her future. Some said that the capacity for loving was greatest at that age; he must not let his own selfishness prevent her from having the chance to become a young wife and mother.

Once father and daughter had been very close, understanding each other's hearts without a word spoken, but now he would have to ask Tamar what her wishes were. He remembered how the young Tamar had always known when something was troubling him. She had comforted him not only by her presence but by her absolute faith in him: her Abba would make everything right again for he, like Moses and Elijah, could perform wonders, if he chose.

Since his return, he had not found a way to bridge the intervening years to relate the young woman to the small girl he had once known. The two had merged as irrevocably as the river Jordan with the inland sea before him and, having missed the experiences that had shaped her, he would have to find a new way to reach out to her. His days had been busy since his return yet the years he had lost with Tamar were more important to him than the whole of his estate.

Today would be a good day to talk to her with both Joel and Asher away: the one in Tiberias, the other on his way to Chorazin to inspect a pair of oxen.

He saw several boats on the lake taking advantage of the steady breeze and was reminded of all the times he and the young Tamar had sailed over the same inviting waves. He strode towards the house, knowing now exactly where he wanted to take his daughter.

Soon after the third hour of the day had begun, he and Tamar were in their light sailing boat leaving the shore behind them. In spite of the strong breeze, there was warmth in the sun and, knowing that there was no need to hurry back, Tamar had collected a basket of food from Keturah before leaving the house.

Her usual gravity had been replaced by excited animation and her swift movements reminded Melkiah of a gazelle leaping joyously on the mountains.

"Where would you like to go?" he asked, rejoicing to see the young Tamar again.

"Everywhere!" Her arms circled her head, indicating the entire heart-shaped lake with all its hills, woods, towns and villages.

Melkiah turned the prow of the boat northwards towards the snow-covered ridge of Mount Hermon and instantly the sails filled and sent the craft easily on its way.

"Shall we go to Bethsaida?"

"Let's stay on the sea," Tamar pleaded, and Melkiah was as glad as his daughter to sail past the fishing village and keep his distance from the rest of mankind.

There was little conversation. They were content to listen to the gentle slapping of the waves against the sides of the boat and the calling of the seabirds who flew around them occasionally in the hope that they would stop idling and catch some fish.

Tamar looked from the green hills on the western side of the lake to the starker ridge of brown mountains on the east; from the shimmering sapphire-emerald surface of the water to the numerous waterfalls and streams which rushed to meet the sea so eagerly. Now and again they exchanged echoing greetings with other boats on the lake and the slight contact merely enhanced the unity of the two in the boat.

As Melkiah turned the small craft and tacked west again past Bethsaida, some young children on the beach there waved to the man and the girl in the passing boat. Tamar waved back smiling, reminded of Eliza, and Melkiah wondered if it were indeed the right time for her to become a wife and mother.

"I know where we can have our lunch," he said, and Tamar had guessed their destination before Melkiah had steered their boat into a small bay not far from Capernaum. The small beach was sheltered by the two steep sides of a deep cleft in the hillside and was sonorous with a cascading waterfall.

Melkiah tied their boat to a branch of an olive tree then helped Tamar to take in the sail. The landing board was not long enough for their purpose and they had to take off their sandals to wade through the swirling water, laughing at its icy temperature. As they brushed off the grit and patted their feet dry, they looked around at the strange yet familiar sight: olive trees clung precariously to the steep sides of the rocky hillside, their branches distorted and interwoven over the years by the channelled strong winds.

As one, father and daughter made their way up the torrent, jumping from one unsteady stone to the next. They had come this way many times in the past and joy swept through Tamar to be here again at last with her beloved father. Unerringly she led the way through the edge of some woodland to their old vantage point, a natural balcony overlooking the shining sea.

She was breathless by the time she threw herself down onto the mossy surface but Melkiah, after his toughening years of enforced outdoor living, showed no sign of exertion after the brief but exhilarating climb. As he said a blessing over the light basket of provisions, his voice was as steady as when he prayed morning and evening in his own home.

They ate in silence, their eyes on the barren hills across the lake. In spite of their mutual gladness at the other's presence, there was an unfamiliar shyness between them. In the old days Tamar had asked endless questions and their hours together had never been long enough for Melkiah to impart to his daughter all he wished her to know. Now she was a strange mixture of innocent child and newly-formed woman and he could no longer guess her thoughts. He regretted deeply that it was too late to guide her mind and heart to absorb the truths that made their nation the unique people that they were. She was not ignorant of their history – his mother had seen to that - but there had been no one to satisfy the thirst for spiritual knowledge that the young Tamar had once had. He wondered how long it had taken to die, and if it were possible to break the shell formed by layers of lesser, everyday concerns.

Tamar's eyes were on his still face. "Why are you sighing?"

Melkiah threw the remains of his bread to a nearby sparrow. "I was wondering if you're disappointed in me."

She was astonished. "What do you mean?"

"You thought I was a merchant and expected me to return and pour treasures into your lap. And instead all you got was a shaggy stranger in threadbare robes!"

"I received what I wanted - you!"

Melkiah smiled and touched her hand lightly. "I want the best for you. Tell me what you want most in the world and you shall have it – if it's within my power." Even as he spoke he wondered if he were testing his daughter.

Tamar looked bewildered. "There is nothing I want that I do not already possess." Her gaze went from her father to the splendour of her surroundings. "What use would I have for the objects others call treasures: gold, jewelled sashes and rare perfumes? Everything I love best is here."

Melkiah was content with her reply. He need not have feared. Was nature herself not the best teacher of wisdom? "Does that mean that you have no desire to travel, to see places you've never been before?"

Tamar considered. "I would like to go to Jerusalem. Every year all the families go south for their Passover visit so joyously. They sing psalms and laugh and call to each other, and the children run alongside their parents and skip in the meadows with the lambs. Capernaum is so quiet while they're away – it's as if most of the inhabitants have died! And each year I've longed to go . . ."

"That's a desire easily granted. We will go to Jerusalem together for the feast this year." Rejoicing at the delight in his daughter's eyes, he pursued. "Where else would you like to go?"

Tamar raised her arms and encircled the circumference of the lake. "I'd like to land at every village and every town and walk through their markets and see their fine houses."

This was an old game. They had explored many a new area when Tamar was young and both had enjoyed their adventures of discovery. Melkiah had never given in to her pleading to land at Magdala, the city of dyers, to see the colourful wool products on display next to Indian dresses, Arabian veils and sandals from Laodicea. His young daughter was too precious to expose to the corrupt inhabitants. However, he had willingly taken her to Tarichea at the southern end of the lake, where they had watched men packing preserved fish into casks to send to far-away customers who appreciated the good taste of Galilean fish.

"When spring comes, we'll sail as often as we can. And perhaps we'll ask young Asher to come with us sometimes."

"He wouldn't want to come."

The objection came so swiftly that Melkiah was surprised.

"He used to plead to join us," he pointed out.

"Yes, but he only came to be with you. He hasn't liked being on the water since the day he fell in."

"He was only three years old! I thought he'd forgotten that incident long ago."

Tamar shook her head. "No. He's never lost his fear – though he wouldn't admit it, of course. I knew it was the real reason why he wouldn't let Simeon teach him to swim. He said it was because he preferred land to sea but . . ."

Melkiah heard pity as well as affection in her voice and was swift to take his cue. "Tell me, Tamar, what would have happened if I had never returned?" Before she could read the implied words "if I had died" he added quickly, "Are you fond of Asher? Was he a good friend to you while I was away?"

"Oh, yes. He was my dear brother. I don't know what I'd have done without him."

"So, if I hadn't returned, perhaps you'd have married him?"

Tamar did not like the way the conversation was going and drank the last of her wine slowly to give herself the chance to think. At last she said. "I don't know what I'd have done. There was no one to guide me. I think Asher might have wanted it, and Granna thinks of him as a grandson. Perhaps she would have put me – and your property – in his care. But ..."

"But?"

"I don't want to marry him. He is as dear to me as a brother but I don't want to be his wife!"

Her eyes were troubled and Melkiah sought to reassure her.

"I promise you, here and now, Tamar, that you shall choose your own husband."

Tamar appreciated the promise for she knew that many betrothals were arranged without the bride being consulted – and sometimes even against her wishes.

"And may I choose when?"

"You may. As long as you make sure it's before the angels come to carry me off to join Abraham!"

Tamar laughed. "I will marry one day, Father, but not for many years yet."

Melkiah smiled, having enough knowledge of the attractions of youth to know that it would take one man only to revise her present intentions. "But before we leave the subject, tell me: is there a chance that you would consider Ezra as a husband one day?"

Tamar looked at him quickly. Had her neighbour broken his promise about waiting and spoken to her father? She did not want to discuss the ardent and over-zealous young Pharisee, yet did not wish to seem too much of a child.

She chose her words carefully. "I do not want to marry him now. Perhaps, in a year or two, I might feel differently."

Melkiah stood up, as thankful as his daughter that the discussion was over. "So that leaves just one decision for you to make: shall we walk through the woods and explore the caves or return to the boat?"

Tamar smiled her relief. "Both! I want to discover the first blue iris, and can we look for some water tortoises in the stream? Do you remember how we used to watch them swimming so fast?"

Melkiah laughed. "I can see we won't be home 'til sunset!"

The sun was setting by the time Joel approached Capernaum. He was so deep in thought that he suddenly realised that he had walked past the narrow track that led directly to Melkiah's house. He hesitated, then decided that he might as well continue on this path which marked the boundary with Zelek's property, then turn right towards his host's home.

In spite of the reflections from the pomegranate sky, the lake was curiously dull, like a tarnished mirror, and shrouds of mist were starting to form, like fallen angels assembling to witness some tragedy.

Joel's steps quickened, his eyes on the large boulder that marked the place where he would find the path to Melkiah's house.

As he reached it and turned, out of the corner of his eye he caught sight of some tasselled material protruding from the hidden side of the boulder. He retraced his steps and saw that a man was lying in the shelter of the large stone.

He recognised him immediately but there was something about the uncomfortable position that made him move swiftly. He knelt and examined him for a long moment and a chill invaded him and the mist from the lake seemed to seep into his mind.

The man was dead.

Time passed and still Joel did not move, his brain and limbs shocked into semi-paralysis. A young healthy man, not yet thirty years of age, lay face upwards with his eyes unseeing and his mouth open as if in surprise at the unexpected visitation of the angel of death. And the man who lay without life on the bare ground was Zelek's eldest son, Ezra.

Joel had little medical knowledge but looked to see if there was any obvious injury that could account for the fatality. Almost immediately he discovered a stain on the head-covering, and when he lifted it carefully he saw a blood-streaked lump on the back of the dead man's head. It was only a small wound but the moment he saw it, he knew that this head injury had been the cause of death.

Joel looked at the boulder thoughtfully, trying to imagine Ezra losing his balance and crashing onto it so disastrously. It seemed an unlikely thing to have happened, yet he went over the surface of the boulder as well as he could in the failing light. The merest trace of blood would prevent him from having to face the unthinkable alternative.

As he rose to continue his search, he tripped over something, and looked down to see a round stone. Its surface seemed to be reflecting the setting sun but Joel knew somehow that its streak of colour would not disappear with the sunset. He picked it up and identified the blood he had been looking for.

He frowned for the stone was far too small to have been used as a hand-weapon. Yet, as he held it in his hand weighing it thoughtfully, noting the way it fitted so neatly into his palm, it gave him the answer he sought. He need look no further. This stone had been used by someone with evil in his heart to take a man's life.

Ezra had been murdered.

Chapter 12

"A stranger possessed by a devil murdered my brother"

The light was fading fast as Joel stood motionless, stunned by his discovery. There seemed to be a bee trapped inside his head, preventing him from thinking clearly, and his limbs seemed incapable of taking direction.

It took a slight sound only to make him as alert as a wild animal scenting danger and a thought pierced him like an arrow: *the murderer was nearby looking for another victim.*

As he dropped behind the boulder and peered into the gloom, two men appeared on the track leading to Zelek's house. He relaxed as he recognised them as Levi and Jonah, Ezra's brothers, but, as they approached him, his relief turned to pity for they would have to see what no man should ever have to see.

Levi fell on his knees beside his dead brother with a shout of alarm while Jonah stared down at the contusion on Ezra's head with horror.

Joel knew that they did not understand and told them, "Someone attacked him and hid him behind this boulder."

Jonah became aware of the stone in Joel's hand and stared at it stupidly. "Where is the weapon? It can't have been that small pebble!"

"I'm afraid it was. Hurled from a sling, it's powerful enough to kill a bear – if used by an expert."

Levi himself resembled an enraged bear as he growled. "But only shepherds are that skilful and how could Ezra get in the way of a stone intended for a wild animal? There's no sheepfold near here."

"He could have been killed some distance away and brought here," Joel suggested.

But he gazed as doubtfully as the brothers at the deadweight of Ezra's body knowing that it could only have been moved with great difficulty. And there seemed to be no reason why anyone should undertake such onerous labour.

"It doesn't make any sense." Jonah shouted his despair and grief over his brother's still form, his fingers clutching a portion of Ezra's muddy robe. His eyes were wild, darting in all directions as if seeking someone to enlighten him.

Joel bent over the ground. "You can see from this flattened grass that he was dragged behind the boulder. He couldn't have fallen so neatly when the stone struck him." He looked round the darkening landscape. "There is only one place his attacker could have hidden." He pointed north to a clump of evergreen trees lining the path to Capernaum. "The distance is right for the injury and Ezra would have seen and heard nothing before the stone struck."

Levi glared at Joel in grief-filled anger. "It seems you know too much about the way my brother died!"

Joel was suddenly aware of the blood-red stone in his hand, and the unspoken suspicion in the eyes of the two brothers. He tried to divert their thoughts into safer channels. "Perhaps you know of someone who had a grudge against Ezra?"

"Our brother had no enemies." Levi remained hostile and implacable. "Only a stranger would have done this – a stranger possessed by a devil."

Joel stood his ground, though he felt menace in the darkness surrounding him. "I share your sorrow and anger," he said quietly. "Somehow we will find out who has committed this crime, and he shall pay for it. In the meantime, we cannot leave your brother lying here. Would you like me to fetch servants from your house?"

Jonah, the younger brother, saw a way to run from an intolerable situation. "I'll go. Father must be told."

"And Mother . . ." But Levi's voice failed him before he could give further instructions to Jonah.

Without another word, the youth ran off into the dusk, stumbling unevenly along the path towards his house where lamps were already beginning to shine.

"Give me that stone!" Levi held out his hand and Joel handed it to him willingly.

"Now your sling . . ."

Joel realised that Levi was beyond rational thought and held out his arms helplessly. "I have no sling – and if I had, I wouldn't have used it against your brother." He took off his mantle and smoothed his tunic against him to show that he carried nothing but a purse. He opened it to prove that it did not contain a leather pouch with attached cords.

Levi's eyes remained as hard as the boulder beneath which Ezra lay, whilst Joel's returned to the clump of trees he had pointed out earlier.

"It's just possible that the assailant dropped his sling over there before coming to hide Ezra's body."

Levi flinched at the last two words and released his anguish in furious words. "Go then, and search! Collect whatever you hid earlier, and then go away! I advise you to be well away from here before my father arrives."

Joel left Levi without a word, knowing that he needed to be alone with the brother he had loved. In fact, as it was now nearly dark and Joel had no lantern, it was impossible to search the ground beneath the trees properly. Any footprints would be invisible and he could do no more than run over the rough ground with his hands. In spite of his words to Levi, he did not expect to find the murder weapon. Those skilled in the use of a sling did not feel dressed without the simple device that made them feel the equal of any man or wild animal. Their slings were always tucked reassuringly into their belts.

Joel became aware of calling voices and saw swinging lights approaching from the direction of Zelek's house. He would take Levi's advice and make himself scarce before the grieving relatives came to the place where an outraged youth kept vigil over his murdered brother.

He slipped through the trees and joined the track that would take him directly to Melkiah's house. He was in need of a friend but, having touched Ezra's body, he was now ritually unclean and would not be able to eat at his host's table. This depressing thought was pierced by a loud cry of despair from behind him and his blood seemed to stop flowing in a moment of renewed anguish for Melkiah's stricken neighbour.

Later, Tamar would cling to the memory of the sun-blessed day with her father throughout all the woeful days ahead. She had believed that their joyful pleasure in each other's company was but the beginning of a season of time they would spend together. They had not returned home much before sunset and it seemed that they had scarcely had time to change their clothes before Joel had returned with the dire news.

Tamar spent the evening in Sarah's room, whether to give comfort or receive it, she did not know. One moment she would be gripping her grandmother's hand fiercely, the next she would be at the narrow window watching the silhouette of lantern-carrying servants milling around without apparent purpose, like a sky of stars gone mad.

Sarah was deeply shaken and wanted the reassurance of having all her dear ones nearby. "What is Melkiah doing, and where is Asher?"

"Father has gone to Zelek's, and Asher came home a short time ago. He knows what's happened; he met a crowd and saw Ezra being carried home on a litter. He's as shocked as we are."

Sarah could not stop trembling and Tamar fetched another shawl to wrap around her grandmother.

"Poor Zelek. He was so proud of his son. And poor Azubah. There's no sorrow greater than losing a child. I must go to her tomorrow."

Tamar looked doubtfully at the old woman who did not look strong enough to leave her chair, let alone travel to a neighbour's house. Yet her own unhappiness made it difficult for her to advise her grandmother. Ezra had loved her, wanted her to be his wife. If only she had given him the promise he had wanted . . . It was a foolish thought, she knew, for he would have died just the same – and if he had not, she would have been betrothed to a man she had no wish to marry. Yet at this moment she would gladly have sacrificed her own happiness to restore Ezra to life.

Sarah had been following her own grim thoughts. "I suppose he was killed by robbers. Ezra was always richly dressed and they would have expected to find a well-filled purse."

Later others echoed Sarah's guess when they discovered that Ezra's purse was missing from his belt. The mountainous north of Upper Galilee was inhabited by many a robber and outlaw who made a good living from the pedestrians and caravans using the busy highway route from Damascus to Ptolemais. It was not unknown for some of the bolder ones to slip into the more populated lakeside villages, particularly during the winter months when travellers were few and far between.

Ezra, with at least ten shekels in his possession from a sale made on his father's behalf, must have fallen victim to such a ruffian.

The following day, Sarah kept to her resolve to visit her bereaved neighbours and, although anxious about his mother, Melkiah made no real attempt to dissuade her. A wagon took Sarah and Tamar to the main entrance of Zelek's property and Tamar supported her grandmother's painful steps through the gate and across the courtyard. Eglah followed them carrying the traditional gifts of mourning bread, spices and anointing oils.

No one marked their approach for they were not entering a silent house. More than one voice was raised in a wail and the rhythm of the threnody told of the presence of professional mourners. Tamar knew that all the leading men of Capernaum, including her own father, would be supporting the stricken Zelek and his sons, and as they were received into the house by a distraught, barefooted servant, they heard the harsh voices of the latter's elegies:

'Alas, my son! My golden arrow has been destroyed;
My horn is broken and now I am defenceless.
My tears of sorrow will become a river
That will wash me into my own grave.
My first-born, my pride, the joy of his mother,
Has been cut down before bearing fruit.
Ezra, my helper, the son of my right hand,
How can you support your father from Sheol? . . .'
'Ezra, our brother, favoured from birth by God and men,
To whom shall we look now to lead us in the ways of the Lord?'
'Alas, my brother! You are a sapling cut down
Before achieving your full strength and height . . .'
'Lord, avenge yourself on the man
Who has killed your faithful servant . . .'

Tamar was glad to be led away from such open grief but there was no escaping the penetrating ululating of the professional women mourners from around the room where Ezra lay.

The bereaved mother, Azubah, was sitting on a low stool surrounded by her daughters, as Tamar led her grandmother through their neighbours towards her. This room, silent in itself, seemed to be a receiving room to which concerted voices beamed their keening plaints; here, the women were getting their breath back before continuing their own dirge, and tearful faces showed the reality of their shared sorrow. And in their midst, with the customary dishevelled hair, mother and daughters had the haggard look of those who have neither eaten nor slept.

Azubah looked up as Sarah reached her and Tamar was glad that her grandmother could not see the deep anguish in her friend's eyes.

"Sarah . . ." She took the blind woman's hand and held it against her cheek. "It is good of you to come."

Once the two women had visited each other often, sharing the concerns of family life, but since Sarah's blindness and Azubah's ill health they had not been able to meet.

Myrtha, the eldest daughter, brought stools for the visitors and Sarah reached out to her friend, unable to find words to express the tears in her heart.

"Of course, I came," was all she could say and Tamar, knowing that she was beyond speech, spoke her own sympathy to mother and daughters, and signed to Eglah to hand over the mourning bread and anointing oils.

It was mid-morning by the time Joel arrived at the house of mourning, in company with two synagogue elders who had come to investigate the untimely death. Having been purified, Joel had been making his way with reluctant steps to the house where he had been welcomed for Melkiah's sake, when Uzziel and Ishmael had fallen into step beside him.

If Levi had discussed his suspicion of the stranger from Judea with the elders, there was no sign of it in their attitude towards him.

Uzziel laid a hand on Joel's arm lightly and spoke in a friendly manner. "Before we go into the house to mourn the loss of a fine young man, will you show us where you found his body?"

Joel led them to the boundary stone and pointed out the flattened grass where Ezra had lain, but there was nothing else to see. Although there were many footprints nearby, made by those who had come hurrying to the spot, it was too late to discover any marks left by the only man who had been there at the moment of Ezra's death.

The three went towards the house soberly. The elders had many duties ahead of them. After examining the body of the dead man, it was up to them to discover the identity of the murderer and take him before the magistrate for justice. If, as sometimes happened, the guilty man could not be found, then they would have to make the prescribed sacrifice so that Capernaum could be proclaimed innocent of the crime. Today, once they had learned all they could from an examination of the dead man, they would give permission for his body to be made ready for burial. While the body was being embalmed, they would prepare for the funeral by composing short addresses to deliver at intervals during the burial procession, and decide who should speak the oration at the grave itself. And, in the meantime, it was their duty to oversee all the strict mourning observances – although their vigilance was scarcely necessary in the household of so strict a Pharisee.

Flanked by his remaining sons, Zelek stood to receive the latest arrivals. His clothing was plain and Joel knew that his inner garments would be torn in exactly the prescribed way. They were all barefoot and unwashed, but even if they had been allowed to groom themselves nothing could have disguised their wretchedness.

Zelek greeted the elders huskily and spoke to Joel courteously enough in a strained voice very different from his normal confident speech. Joel was relieved that Melkiah's neighbour had not been influenced by his sons' suspicions, or perhaps was prepared to keep any doubts hidden for the time being. He felt unspoken hostility from Levi and his brothers and was glad to leave their side and join Melkiah.

Zelek left the room with Uzziel and Ishmael, fresh tears running down his cheeks as he prepared to show them the body of his first-born son and the destruction of the hopes and dreams of over twenty years.

Joel sat motionless, wishing he were anywhere but in this house of mourning. He did not belong here and it was unendurable to listen to the dirges of the professional mourners and to witness the true grief of the family. He, himself, had not slept or eaten since his tragic discovery and now distress and faintness circled in his head in sombre waves.

He wondered how easy it would be to discover the identity of Ezra's murderer. Neither Melkiah nor Jairus knew of any enmity towards the young Pharisee and could only suggest that it had been the impulsive act of a passing thief. This theory was not supported by the choice of murder weapon. Violent men invariably used cudgels, having no fear of recognition as their merciless face would be the last thing their victim would ever see.

As Joel had anticipated, the day seemed endless, and the funeral itself was no easier to bear. It seemed that everyone in Capernaum had come to join in the funeral convoy as it made its way very slowly to the burial sepulchres outside the town. Grieving women were in front of Ezra's bier, which his brothers and friends carried in turn. The hired mourners and musicians came next, making sure that so important a family received good value for money, and after them stumbled more relatives weeping without restraint and calling out Ezra's name in sorrow and despair.

Joel saw that even Melkiah, who usually had his emotions well under control, had tears in his eyes. Like everyone else, he greatly pitied the family who had lost such a promising first-born son.

All listened to fulsome speeches in Ezra's praise without criticism or impatience and Joel could not help contrasting the occasion with the hasty burial of lepers he had witnessed.

He sighed, wishing that this day could be an end to the grieving rites. However, neighbours would be expected to go to the bereaved's house daily for a further five days to mourn in deep silence, broken only by the questionable comfort of listening to reminders of the Lord's just judgement.

Rain began to fall as the long procession reached the burial site, and it continued to fall during the dark days that followed. Melkiah came to hear all there was to know about the investigations into the untimely death and discussed them with Joel, though not with Tamar, realising that she could not cope with any more distress.

The officials of Capernaum had appealed for information about strangers in the town on the day of the murder, and had received the usual number of eager and imaginative descriptions. If they had believed all the eyewitness accounts, they would have had to accept that every scoundrel and murderer in the whole of Israel had been in

Capernaum on that day. However, by the time all the information had been sifted, they were left with the bare fact that no one had witnessed the murder or knew of any reason why it should have taken place.

The houses of some of the inhabitants known for past dishonesty had been searched for Ezra's missing purse. Insults and threats had been exchanged freely, innocence protested vociferously, and many a scuffle had taken place, but nothing incriminating had been discovered.

In fact the empty purse was unearthed in a hollow by the lake nearly a year later but the find caused scarcely a ripple amongst the inhabitants of Capernaum, for by then the identity of the murderer had long been established.

It had been a disclosure they had tried to forget for the criminal had not been a passing malefactor but someone who had lived in Capernaum all his life.

Chapter Thirteen

"How can we know which of us will die next?"

Tamar rose early and left the house soon after sunrise. She had not slept well and instinctively sought light to alleviate an oppression that she had not been able to throw off. Days of rain had followed Ezra's funeral but now the sun seemed to promise comfort, growth and new beginnings. Its rays made the dew seem like golden frost on every field and meadow, and it seemed that each leaf and flower was radiating sufficient liquid light to banish darkness for ever.

Tamar walked past crops reaching joyfully towards the cloudless sky, past trees singing with irrepressible choirs of birds, and the contrast to her own sorrow made it all the harder to bear. She knelt and picked a bunch of daisies and the wonder of each dew-filled corolla filled her eyes with tears. How could anything be perfect in a world where men killed each other for a few coins?

"Are you gathering herbs?"

Asher's voice startled her. Unable to speak, she shook her head, clenching her fists on the fragile stems. He did not need her words and held out his arms to her.

Tamar saw the companion who had been the dearest person in her life during the years of her father's absence, and went to him without a moment's hesitation. She felt his strength enfolding her, and rested her head against his shoulder in a way that felt familiar and comforting. Asher sensed that she had a great burden of fear and sorrow to release and was content to hold her gently while her tears fell.

"My sister . . ." he murmured. "Tell me why you're so unhappy."

His words reminded Tamar of all the occasions in her childhood when she had fled to the refuge of Asher's arms. He had always listened to her and, even when he couldn't change the circumstances, his sympathy and loving words had eased her distress and made her feel secure again.

"Are you crying for Ezra?" he prompted gently.

She nodded, raising misted eyes to his. "If only I had given him what he wanted . . ."

Asher was surprised at her words. "What did he ask of you?"

"He wanted me to be his wife, but I wouldn't even agree to a betrothal."

Asher remembered the conversation he had witnessed, and saw again the exultant way Ezra had left Tamar. He felt as confused as Tamar had been on that occasion. "But you did promise him something?"

"Only to let him ask me again in a year's time. I was sure that I would give him the same answer then, but I hoped that by then he might have found a different bride." She drew back a little and met his eyes unhappily. "I wish now that I'd given him what he wanted."

"Perhaps you should have done," Asher agreed, but when her eyes widened in renewed distress he added swiftly. "Tamar, you gave him hope. He was happy with the promise you gave him. It's time now to try and forget."

"How can any of us forget when he died so close to our house? I'm afraid to go past that boulder in case I see his body lying there. I seem to see it wherever I go . . ."

Her words reminded Asher all too clearly of the vision that haunted him day and night – his own father lying dead at his feet – and he returned to the subject of Ezra's death as the lesser evil.

"If only I'd been here that day, I might have seen something."

"You went to inspect some oxen," Tamar remembered. "Did you buy them?"

"I'd have done your father a disservice if I had. The pair were so unevenly matched, I could tell they had never worked together before." Asher had taken satisfaction in rejecting the animals, infuriated by the amused condescension of the farmer who had expected to deal with an experienced steward. "So, as I'd had a wasted journey, I decided to come home over the hills to check on the spring pastures for our flocks. We'll be able to move them soon . . ."

He could see that Tamar was not thinking about his words but had returned to her own fearful thoughts. He held out his hands towards her. "What is it? There's something worrying you beyond Ezra's death."

Tamar gripped his fingers tightly. "Don't you see? If Ezra could be struck down, so could any of us. We don't know where the murderer is hiding. Perhaps you will die . . . or Father . . . or I will. Wherever I go, I seem to hear footsteps following me, and it's the same for all of us. How can we know which of us will die next?"

Asher saw terror in her eyes and strove to be reassuring. "The murderer will have fled on the day of Ezra's death and will be far from here by now. He certainly won't have stayed in the area to risk paying for his crime. You're quite safe, my Tamar. I promise you that no one will ever harm you."

"I want *you* to be safe. I couldn't bear it if anything happened to you."

Asher put an arm around her and kissed her brow lightly. "I promise you that nothing will happen to me, either. How could it, when we watch over each other like human guardian angels?"

It was an old vow from their childhood and Tamar smiled for the first time. She indicated his working tunic and dew-soaked sandals. "You're no Shining One! But I'm content to have an angel whom I can see and touch." Her eyes were peaceful as she added. "Yes, we'll look after each other like we used to do. All will be well."

As Asher left her, well satisfied with their encounter, Tamar found that her oppression had lifted. She was even able to laugh as she saw a clutch of ducklings following their mother to the water's edge, jostling each other in their eagerness to take the prime position immediately behind her. Whatever else happened, there would always be new life and innocent pleasures.

Having been concerned about Tamar's deep depression, Melkiah was relieved when he caught sight of her later. The breeze was playing with her veil and blowing it above her head like a plume of smoke. She was smiling as she tried to catch it and her steps were light.

He himself continued to mourn his neighbour's son, but the unexpected death had made his own child even more precious to him. He knew that she had been afraid to leave their property but could not believe that any danger threatened her.

Going to meet her, he suggested. "It'll be your birthday soon. Go to Miriam and choose a rug for your room. Perhaps she'll design one specially for you."

Tamar set off readily as she hadn't spent any time with her friend since the day she had visited her with Joel. She'd seen her in the synagogue each Sabbath but they had not exchanged more than a few words and each time she had been concerned for her. Miriam reminded Tamar of an untrimmed lamp burning fitfully, with alternate flaring flame and dim light.

A Roman on horseback gazed at Tamar appraisingly as he rode past but the young Jewish girl scarcely noticed him. Normally she would have appreciated the fine horse at least, for Melkiah had taught her to befriend the animals in their stables, and there was not one that she did not recognise and greet with affection.

Today, however, her thoughts veiled her surroundings as effectively as a sea mist and she continued on her way wondering about the change in Miriam. She wanted to help her friend but it was unlikely that the older woman would confide in one so much younger than herself.

As on her last visit, Miriam greeted her gladly and displayed colours and patterns with enthusiasm, but her restlessness was very noticeable.

"Don't go," she said, when they had agreed upon a design. "Stay and talk a while."

She took Tamar to her workroom and called for raisin cakes which arrived still warm from the oven. They sat and shared the refreshments that neither of them really wanted, and Tamar was very aware of Miriam's nervous glances over her shoulder, and the movement of her slim fingers as she twisted a gold ear-ring or pushed her lustrous hair away from her face. Miriam was distracted as if trying to round up stray thoughts that needed her attention, or pondering a problem that had no solution.

Miriam, in her turn, had observed the lines of strain around Tamar's eyes and knew it would be wise to avoid the subject of Ezra's death. She began to speak of her recent visit to the lakeside town of Magdala. Although Ishmael was too strict a Pharisee to go there himself, he had sufficient business acumen to accept that his wife needed to go there from time to time to buy from the wool merchants and browse among the colourful dyes.

Tamar listened attentively to Miriam's descriptions of the pleasure town where even the rooms around the courtyards of the magnificent houses overflowed with rare plants and luxuriant greenery. Of course, the strong-smelling dyeworks were well away from the place where the wealthy people dwelt. Their trade was restricted by law to the outskirts of the town to ensure that there was no pollution of the spring water that was channelled into so many fountains.

Tamar had been imagining the bustling pagan town as Miriam spoke. "How I wish I could go there with you."

"Perhaps one day your father will allow it."

Tamar thought it unlikely, but was diverted by a sudden cacophony from the street outside. Miriam rose and Tamar followed her to the stable courtyard which was buzzing like a bee-hive stirred with a stick. A train of camels was proceeding in an orderly line, held in check by the merchant's retainers. A group of admiring children had been drawn in, as by a fisherman's drag-net, and were darting delightedly from one camel to the next. They called out to each other in shrill voices, pointing towards the out-of-reach luggage baskets, wondering aloud about the many wondrous treasures they might contain.

"It's Alexander," Miriam told Tamar. "He always collects some rugs from us on his way to Ptolemais."

She went to greet him but Ishmael was already at the side of the thickset man with the broad forehead and broader smile.

Alexander acknowledged Miriam with a deep bow and a gleam from his carob brown eyes. He admired Ishmael's wife for her beauty, intelligence and creativity, and appreciated her radiant vitality almost as much as the jewel-bright rugs she designed for him.

As Miriam began a smiling greeting, Ishmael interrupted her. "You must congratulate Alexander. His wife has given him a son."

This was no surprise as it was the merchant's custom to give his wife a new baby yearly to keep her occupied whilst he was on his travels.

His beard and bushy eyebrows quivered with the expansiveness of his smile as he confirmed. "The Most High has blessed me greatly. I have seven fine sons now, as well as five daughters." Looking round, he called a young boy to his side. "Daniel, my third eldest," he introduced, as if there could be any doubt about the paternity of the youngster with identical dark curls and round beaming face.

"I'm going to be a merchant too," the boy told them. "I want to make a great fortune – and give it all to my mother."

"*You* are your parents' fortune," Ishmael said, and turned to Alexander who stood with an affectionate hand on Daniel's shoulder. "I would give half my wealth to gain a son such as this one." The passion in his voice betrayed his anguish. "Your marriage is richly blessed because your wife is a true daughter of Abraham." And now his eyes were upon Miriam in open rejection. "A man needs a son – but there is no blessing on our marriage."

Tamar, distressed by her friend's public humiliation, stepped forward quickly and took Miriam's arm.

Alexander, sharing Tamar's distaste for Ishmael's heartless words, made a great show of greeting the unknown girl who had acted loyally, and insisted on presenting each woman with an ivory gift from one of the camel's saddlebags.

Tamar went home thoughtfully. She knew now the reason for Miriam's sadness but could see no remedy. She did not comprehend why some women were barren and others had the ability to have many children. It was understandable that Ishmael should be eager for sons to continue his business but until recently he had been a loving and indulgent husband to his beautiful wife. What could have happened to make him suddenly blame Miriam, as if she were deliberately withholding the heir he needed?

Melkiah was disappointed when Tamar returned so soberly from visiting her friend. He would have to be patient and trust time and the unfolding of spring to heal her. There was real warmth in the sun now, and the winter landscape that had greeted him on his return home in Shebat had turned almost overnight into a light-filled growth on field and meadow, hillside and garden. Orchards shimmered with delicately scented blossom, rose trees bore slim buds, and bees and butterflies flew joyfully from the white blossom of olive trees to the scarlet of pomegranate. Fields of flax had become a waving sea of blue and green, wheat stalks thrust upwards strongly, and, in the kitchen garden, lentils, peas, cucumber and melons raced from seed to flower to fruit on their diet of showers and sunshine.

Melkiah and Joel were walking between fields of wheat and barley, watching Asher talking to a worker on the far side of the field; there seemed to be some sort of argument, but when Asher pointed and spoke emphatically, the man ran to do his bidding.

Joel laughed. "Confidence carries the day!"

Melkiah smiled. "He knows what he wants, and he's usually right. He wears his father's shoes well."

"Will you confirm him as your steward?"

Melkiah sighed. "He's too young, of course. Even if he knew as much as he thinks he does, outsiders wouldn't deal with someone of his age. I'll have to find an older man until a few years have gone by."

"He won't like it."

"I'll wait until the time of mourning for his father is over, and be my own steward until then. Perhaps you'll help me guide him? He listens to you."

"He's avid to learn," Joel agreed. "I'd gladly earn my keep by becoming your steward myself, but it wouldn't be wise."

He didn't have to explain. Both men knew that Asher would resent a Judean of no experience being put in a position of authority over him.

"You are my friend. I'd never let you work for me," Melkiah protested. "Otherwise you'd be ideal and I know Asher would come to accept you and work alongside you with a good grace."

Joel did not share Melkiah's confidence but his future was so uncertain that there was no point in pursuing the matter. However great Melkiah's kindness, nothing could prevent him from feeling about as useful as an empty oil-lamp. He had decided to stay here until Ezra's murderer had been brought to justice, and then he would go to the Messiah and follow him as a disciple.

The song of a blue wagtail brought his attention back to his surroundings. Galilee must surely be the most beautiful place on earth in which to be exiled. He would learn to sail, and fish, and farm – and watch his neighbours as they watched him . . .

✡   ✡   ✡

In fact, but for an unfortunate encounter that took place later that week, Zelek's sons would have ceased to look on Joel with suspicion, cold days of mourning having extinguished their immediate reaction to finding him beside the murdered Ezra.

Joel had set out for the slopes above Capernaum, making his way through the red anemone-starred grass towards the winter sheepfolds. There was tranquillity to be found among the sheep and playful lambs, and the shepherds themselves were peaceful company with their simple philosophy and patient endurance. They knew who they were in relation to God and the knowledge gave them wisdom and inner strength that shone from them like the stars they revered as friends.

Joel's progress was being watched by Asher and Nahum, the son of Zelek's steward. Nahum was a merry lad whose irreverent speech against his elders concealed an inherent loyalty to both his father and his master. The two youths had been friends for many years and had always spoken freely to each other to release the frustration of being treated as if they still had much to learn.

Nahum nodded towards the disappearing Joel. "Where is he going so eagerly? To meet a servant girl in some hidden thicket?"

"Not he. He's going to play at being shepherd for the day."

Nahum grimaced. If fortune had offered him the chance to live in idleness, you wouldn't find him volunteering to tend animals.

"He knows a bit about sheep," Asher admitted. "Perhaps he's tired of being a dependent visitor and wants to earn his keep. They'll be counting and marking the flock for the tithe soon. Perhaps he's gone to mix the dye!"

"A staff might be of more use. They say a young lion has been spotted not far from here."

Asher smiled. "He wouldn't need such a clumsy weapon. He's expert with a sling."

His words fell into an awkward silence. Nahum realised that Asher must be regretting his words, but he could not ignore their import.

"David and Goliath," he reflected aloud. "I wonder which of us could have hit the only unprotected part of a giant's forehead. Would you like to try, my friend?"

Asher shook his head. "Not unless there was an army of giants behind me to follow through! Anyone who misses Goliath doesn't get a second chance." His eyes followed the disappearing Joel thoughtfully. "*He* would have taken on Goliath - and won. He's a better shot than any man I've ever seen."

All the laughter had left Nahum's eyes. "It was strange that he was the one to find Ezra that day . . . He was returning from Tiberias, wasn't he?"

Asher hesitated. "Yes, but . . ." His eyes evaded Nahum's.

"Tell me."

Asher shrugged, then decided to speak. "There's something that troubles me about that day. There's a path leading to Melkiah's house from the Tiberias route. If Joel had taken it, he wouldn't have gone anywhere near where Ezra was discovered. I keep wondering why a man who had already made a long journey should have ignored the shortest way home, and kept walking . . ."

"He's a stranger. Perhaps he didn't realise that there was a shorter way?"

"Our house is clearly visible from the point where the track goes down towards it. My master and Joel took it together the first day they arrived."

Asher could see that Nahum's thoughts were unhappy and decided it was time to divert him. "However, the ways of Judeans are ever beyond our understanding! When has simplicity ever described their actions? Let's forget the stranger and talk of more important things: have you seen the gap in the hawthorn hedge between our vineyards? Will you ask your father for two men to join mine tomorrow to make it secure?"

"Come with me. You can ask him now."

Asher went with his friend meditatively. He would make sure that there was no further talk of Joel, but there was nothing he could do to prevent Nahum's new knowledge and suspicion acting like leaven to spread through the whole of Zelek's family.

Chapter 14

"A life for a life"

Joel was running, fear in his heart, spurred by a thudding behind him. Weariness weighted his feet just when he needed the wings of an eagle to escape his pursuers. He did not even know where the narrow track was leading, but he stumbled down it desperately, scarcely noticing the bramble branches that tore at his hands and the uneven stones that threatened to trip him and send him crashing to the ground.

It had happened so suddenly. One moment he had been kneeling by the spring, drinking the clear water with his cupped hands, the next he had been surrounded by a group of faceless people. Faceless? He shuddered, for they had features of a sort but so distorted that they were scarcely recognisable as human. Their eyes, without brows or lashes, were almost sealed by ugly scabs, their scalps were rooted with sparse tufts of lifeless white hair, and there were no beards to conceal their grim mouths and rotting teeth. Skeletons, with the merest covering of ulcerated flesh, they had reached out white-scaled arms towards him. He had shrunk back from stumps that had once been fingers, from claws which resembled severely-pruned branches of trees, and the movement had taken him onto the downhill track that offered escape.

It was only as he began to run that the greatest horror struck him: he found that his own feet were ulcerated and that it was impossible for him to achieve more than a painful, hobbling stumble. His numb white hands felt no pain from the brambles, and his torn and threadbare tunic gave him the same, terrifying message: he too was a leper.

It was difficult to breathe. He gulped in air desperately but the pain in his chest was growing with every lurching step and he knew he could not go on much longer. Behind him, he heard the relentless pounding of maimed feet and hoarse cries that surely came from *beasts rather than men created in the image of God. Some of his pursuers threw stones and lumps of hard-packed earth which struck his back or soared past his head like vicious birds of prey.*

The path ended suddenly in a tree-bordered stream that separated the wild hillside from the fertile plain.

"If I cross it, I'll be safe," Joel realised, and desperation gave him the final burst of strength that enabled him to wade through the cleansing water. Knowing that his pursuers had stopped at the water's edge, he climbed the shallow bank thankfully and half fell through the trees that hid the meadowland.

A line of men stood facing him, and there was not a pair of eyes amongst them that did not spell death.

Ezra waited but ten paces from Joel, his brothers on either side of him. Every man held a stone in one hand and a sling in the other, and was measuring the distance to their human target with murderous efficiency.

"A life for a life," Ezra pronounced, and his words were the signal which set the ropes whirling and the stones flying.

The deadly hail struck Joel in a dozen places and he fell into the darkness of a starless night.

He woke bathed in sweat, with heavy limbs and a head that felt as if he were wearing an iron helmet. He pushed aside the light woollen covering and rose from his bed with slow movements. The night mare still held him on her back as an unwilling rider, but when he stumbled towards the window and opened his eyes to the breaking day, she went on without him into the dark, leaving him as shaken and relieved as a thrown rider.

"It was only a dream," he said out loud, and breathed in the cool, fresh air while his eyes confirmed that he had returned from hell into the paradise that was Galilee.

Only a dream, yet he had seen many such sights in his years amongst the lepers, and not only seen them, but lived with them daily and shared the anguish. And doubtless the dreamed attack by Zelek's sons was the result of an incident that had happened the day before.

Joel had been returning from visiting Jairus and had reached the narrow track that led to the road that served the southern houses of Capernaum. As he had drawn level with the place where trees and bushes grew impenetrably, not far from where Ezra's murderer had lain in wait, he had heard the sound of horse's hooves behind him.

The rider was travelling fast and, as the light was beginning to fade, Joel turned and stepped into the centre of the track to make sure that he would be seen. The path was so narrow that a man and a horse could pass each other with care and courtesy only, but to Joel's alarm the horse came straight towards him without slackening speed.

Even as he threw himself against an unyielding thorn bush, he saw the rider's face and understood that the evasion would be of no use. Levi's face was suffused with implacable hatred: the moment of vengeance had come.

The living fury of both the man and the beast with the flailing hooves was so close that Joel threw his arms across his face in useless protection. But at that very moment the horse was checked brutally and reared with a series of outraged whinnies.

In the time it took for Levi to gain complete control of his mount, Joel became aware of two men walking along the track from the direction of Melkiah's house. He recognised neither of them but knew that their presence had saved his life.

As the concerned strangers hurried towards the site of the near calamity, Levi gained sufficient command of himself to speak. "I lost control of my horse. It seems that this is a dangerous place . . ." Then, without apology, Ezra's brother had ridden away, leaving Joel shaken by his narrow escape but filled with pity for the violent Levi. He too hated Ezra's murderer and knew that if the victim had been his own brother, Daniel, he too would have been inclined to take the law into his own hands.

And thus Levi had given Joel food for nightmares but the Most High had rescued him from sudden death as surely as his Messiah had rescued him from the slow death of a leper. He knew that the only way he could ever repay such a debt was to march under the banner of Light and go wherever the true King of the Jews led him. How much easier it would have been to join a physical army and fight real battles; but this King, the Son of the Most High, insisted that souls were conquered not by violence but with love.

No wonder so many of his followers were floundering helplessly. What action could one man take to stem the wickedness he saw around him? The idea of overcoming evil with love seemed about as practical as going into battle armed with a branch of blossom.

Remembering his dream, Joel knew that he would continue to be suspected of Ezra's murder until he could find out who *had* killed him. Some people believed that the murderer had fled and was now far away, but Joel had seen enough evil in Capernaum – particularly among those who claimed to be the most righteous – to believe that it was probable that he still lived amongst them.

All Joel had to do was to discover his identity. All . . . He smiled wryly. It might be simpler to empty the lake with a conch shell.

He left the house very quietly, with a friendly wave to a servant girl scattering corn for the doves. She looked after him without surprise for both the Master and his guest seemed to be drawn irresistibly to the shining lake at all times of the day and night. The whole household was aware that Melkiah had formed a habit of spending an occasional night in a boat far out on the water, and more than one had seen him return with the peace of the moon and the stars reflected on his face.

Tamar had not slept well either but she smiled at her father as they breakfasted together. They did not speak of Joel's absence, guessing that he would be on the shore with one of the fishermen.

"I'm sure you would prefer to celebrate your seventeenth birthday simply," Melkiah said, "but I would like to provide a feast for your friends."

Tamar was aware of his keen glance and it was almost as if he were issuing a challenge. He must be well aware that, in spite of Sarah's urging, she had little contact with the other wealthy unmarried girls of Capernaum. She wondered if he were disappointed in her.

"I haven't many friends," she admitted. "Except for Miriam and Susanna."

"And some of the other fishermen's wives and daughters?"

"Yes. I know them all – and the children. I love being with them because they take such joy in life although they haven't much."

It seemed that her reply had pleased Melkiah for he was smiling as he wiped the last few crumbs from his beard. "Perhaps you've heard that the Messiah urges us to invite poor people to our feasts rather than the wealthy. Of course, the Pharisees are scandalised at the suggestion of sitting at table with unlearned men who do not know all 613 precepts of their Law!" He smiled at his daughter. "What about you? Would you like to celebrate your birthday with humble, unlearned guests?"

"Oh, *yes!*" Tamar's face was as bright as a newly-lit lamp. "There's nothing that would please me more. How many people may I ask, Father?"

"As many as you wish." Melkiah would have fed every man, woman and child in Capernaum to keep the radiance in Tamar's eyes. "Invite all the fishing families you know, and the wives and daughters of our own labourers, of course, and perhaps Jairus will suggest some other appropriate guests."

"His daughter, Mirjiam, would know. Shall I ask her to help us?"

"We have three days. Is that long enough to make all the preparations?"

"Kenturah will be busy, but I'll make sure that she has extra help. Susanna will guide me to make sure that no one is forgotten and Miriam may have some ideas about entertainment. Father, do you think we could give some gifts to the children?"

"Of course. Everything shall be as you wish."

Tamar darted about as swiftly as a swallow during the days that followed: from Miriam to Susanna and her friends on the shore; from the synagogue leader's daughter back to Kenturah at home to encourage her into new creative fancies for the feast.

It was Sarah who reminded Melkiah to hire some musicians, while suggesting that Asher too should play for the guests. She showed Melkiah her gift to Tamar, a linen tunic and matching veil, and he reassured her that it was indeed the colour of wild hyacinths.

"The pearl diadem Anne wore on our wedding day is waiting for Tamar," he remembered. "Should I give it to her now?"

Sarah shook her head. "It would not be appropriate for Tamar to greet her guests dressed like a high-ranking Jewish lady. Some of them do not even possess a respectable tunic. I suggest you keep the diadem for Tamar's own wedding day. That will be here soon enough!".

Melkiah wondered if all blind people take the opportunity to speak more candidly than they would if they could see their listener's reactions. He had told his mother that he was in no hurry for Tamar's marriage, but it was obvious that she believed that her gentle promptings would change his mind. He shook his head in fond exasperation and changed the subject.

"The rug Miriam designed for Tamar has been delivered. I wish you could see it, Mother. The colours remind me of your lakeside garden."

"Tamar will describe it to me," Sarah said serenely. "She has shared her sight with me ever since I lost my own. She helps me to 'see' so clearly that I feel no deprivation."

In fact, on the day of her seventeenth birthday, Tamar was too busy greeting her guests to have any time to describe the scene to her grandmother; but she was storing every detail in her memory to be recounted later.

The fishermen's families arrived diffidently and would have fallen into petrified shyness after the formality of being refreshed with perfumed water but for the excited children at their side.

Tamar's plain white tunic contrasted vividly with the ebony coronet of her plaited hair, and the heightened colour of her cheeks matched those of her animated young visitors. Her eyes smiled so warm a welcome that everyone who entered was immediately enfolded in her cloak of happiness.

"She looks like an angel," they murmured to each other and Melkiah, overhearing, was well content. He did his best to put his daughter's guests at their ease in such unfamiliar surroundings, and Miriam and Mirjiam, also dressed very simply, greeted each guest with equal friendliness.

Susanna, determined not to let her friend down, arrived in a tunic newly-dyed a patchy green, and scarlet flowers adorning her dark curls. Eliza's round face was beaming like the noon sun and she too wore green and had field anemones in her hair.

Tamar picked up Eliza and whispered in her ear. "I'm glad to have a walking strawberry at my party. Will you sit next to me so that I can nibble you?"

Smiling, Susanna took the young girl back from Tamar. "I wish you many years of happiness," she said formally, but her eyes were as mischievous as those of her giggling daughter.

The guests were awed when they entered the large dining-room hung with garlands of olive and myrtle and gleaming with well-polished lamps. Vases of pear and pomegranate blossom stood in every niche and quince-woven greenery adorned the tables which had been set together to make a long U-shape. Attendants were still arranging food on the linen cloths and this was the main attraction for children who had never seen more than a day's provisions in their lives before. Their eyes roved unbelievingly from platter to platter: from roast lamb and grain; vegetables cooked in oil, cucumbers, beans and lettuces; eggs, cheese and curds; to bread, scones and fruit deserts. Amphorae held honey water and fruit drinks for the children and wine for the women.

Melkiah had welcomed each guest as they had entered his house but, believing that his presence would put a constraint on the assembly, had decided not to dine with his daughter and her friends.

The room was strangely silent and Tamar could see that the display of food in unfamiliar surroundings had intimidated her guests. They sat at the tables meekly and only the children whispered, and explored with eager eyes.

A little boy decided that it must be some sort of market and cried aloud, "We've forgotten the baskets!" and the resulting laughter broke the thin shell of formality.

Having said a blessing over the food, Melkiah withdrew and the party began. That day poor families feasted as if they were rich – and not just on food but on an occasion that might never occur again.

Tamar was caught between laughter and tears. She did not know some of the women very well, and others were complete strangers to her, yet there was not one who had arrived empty-handed. Shyly they each presented her with a small gift: a posy of forget-me-nots; a handful of dried fruit; a shell hair ornament; an anklet made of wood; a small leather container; a pottery bowl, and several batches of little cakes.

Tamar had some of the barley scones in front of her now, knowing that she must forgo Kenturah's creative efforts and eat instead the fare made for her with love. She had wanted to bless her guests and instead they had given to her of the little they had.

"Did you like my present best?" Eliza demanded, a red flower falling from her curls as she looked up at Tamar.

"I shall keep it forever," Tamar assured her. "Look, I have it here beside me." She pointed to the large pebble which, with clever markings, Tobit had made into a water-turtle.

"Can it swim?" Michael, a three-year-old spoke through a mouthful of honey-cake. "Shall we put it in the lake and see?"

"I think it might swim away," Tamar told him gravely. "If I put it by the fountain, I'll always know where to find it."

The meal proceeded and the laughter and chatter were very different from anything the dining-room had ever witnessed before. It flowed up the stairs to Sarah in her room and she smiled. She would join the company when the entertainment began. Once the meal was over, Tamar's guests would be glad to sit quietly for a while and listen to some music. It would be good to hear Asher sing again.

In fact, all Sarah's powers of persuasion were needed to coax Asher to entertain the company. Normally he would not have been averse to displaying his talent to an assembly of women and girls, many of whom openly admired the handsome acting-steward. He was well aware of how intoxicating his playing and singing were on female listeners, but he was not in the mood to take this chance to bind Tamar closer to him.

Tamar herself had realised the moment Asher had entered the room that something was wrong. His expression was one that she had seen often in the past, usually when he had been forced to give up one of his plans. When Simeon had not allowed him to act like a son of the house he had reacted with anger and disappointment and had worn the same sulky, frustrated look as today.

She had had no opportunity to question him and was relieved to see Eglah lead Sarah into the room.

"Asher is here before you," she told her grandmother. "Will you ask him to sing for us?"

Sarah felt for Asher and took one of his hands. "I can't believe you need persuasion to help Tamar celebrate her special day."

"There are other musicians here."

"Not like you."

Tamar saw conflict on Asher's face. "I can't sing. My throat is rough," he said at last. "But I'll play for you and Tamar if you truly wish it."

His voice *was* strangely hoarse so Sarah settled for the half-victory. "Thank you, Asher. Go and fetch your kinnor before the dancing begins."

The guests settled expectantly, and sat very still as Asher's fingers plucked the strings of the harp-like instrument. He played with confidence and passion but there was no discernable melody and there was something strangely disturbing about the music.

Tamar found herself wishing that he would stop. In the past, his singing had made her spirits rise but this unaccompanied music spoke of disasters in the making: a giant wave submerging a boat; an earthquake flattening a settlement; a fire sweeping across a tinder-dry valley.

Tamar saw that several young women could not take their eyes off the handsome musician, but the small children were getting restless and, like Tamar, were relieved when the last note quivered into the air and faded.

The moment Asher left the company, Eliza ran to Tamar. "Will you tell me a story?"

Her trusting eyes looked up at her tall friend pleadingly and her small fingers held onto Tamar's tunic.

Tamar smiled, her anxiety over Asher temporarily forgotten. "You shall have a story from the best story-teller in Galilee." She drew her grandmother forward and the women listened as eagerly as the children as Sarah brought to life one of the traditional stories that had fascinated Tamar as a child. She wished that her grandmother could see the unblinking eyes of the motionless children with their smiles and frowns accompanying the vicissitudes of the story characters. She wanted to hug them all and keep the whole company of tiny angels beside her for ever. What joy to live in a world of innocence and starry-eyed wonder where conflict and peace-destroying passions were unknown.

She was able to forget Asher's brooding behaviour while Sarah held the company enthralled but, as the musicians struck up and some women began to dance, an overheard sentence brought her concern back.

Two fisher-girls were laughing together and Tamar caught the word "Asher" as she slipped past them. A circle of clapping children kept

Tamar in one place long enough to hear Rachel answer, "Yes, I noticed. I wonder what's wrong with "King David" today?"

Tamar knew the name Asher's musical ability and lordly air had earned, and knew too that he was aware of it and was not displeased.

"Perhaps he misses Adina," Rachel's companion suggested. "He hasn't been the same since she ran away."

"Were they betrothed?"

"No, but I saw Adina on the shore one day and she told me of their plans to marry. She was so happy, she had to share her secret with someone. She made me promise not to tell anyone, but it scarcely matters now."

"I wonder why she left him – and where do you think she went?"

The other shrugged. "I wish I knew. They've searched everywhere."

"Perhaps she found that she was with child and ran away because she was afraid?"

"No. If that had happened, they could have got married quickly. Tamar would have helped them."

"Unless she wanted Asher for herself?"

Tamar was very still but at that moment the fisher-girl glanced behind her and saw the shock in her hostess' eyes. Instantly her face became suffused and they stared at each other in equal confusion and embarrassment while the dancing flowed around them.

The impasse was broken unwittingly by Melkiah when he stopped the music and made the announcement which was to be the talk of Capernaum for many days to come.

Chapter 15

"I thought you were dead"

Melkiah spoke clearly to the throng of attentive guests. "I have a gift for all the children present." He smiled and held out an inviting hand. "Come with me and I'll show you."

Although most of the youngsters were in awe of the wealthy landowner, the promise of a present overcame their shyness and they ran to him eagerly. Seeing the over-tired youngest children clinging to their mothers, Melkiah indicated that they too should join the crowd following him from the hall.

"Where is he taking us?" Susanna asked, but Tamar had been taken by surprise at her father's words and was as intrigued as her guests.

Eliza slipped her hand into Tamar's. "Will it be a big fish or a jar of honey?"

Her eyes were round with excitement and the same eager anticipation was in the eyes of all the children as they passed through several courts and followed Melkiah under the arch that led to the stables.

Here there was no room to proceed further as the paved yard in front of them was filled with bleating lambs. They were jostling each other nervously, moving *en masse* first one way then another as a different animal inadvertently took on the role of leader. Their plaintive laments were not unlike that of babies crying and the children were instantly in harmony with them.

Melkiah's smile was warm as he looked about him and he raised his voice to be heard over the babble of voices praising the superb quality of the flock. "Each child may choose a lamb and take it home, in honour of my daughter's birthday."

Tamar was as delighted as her guests as she went to thank Melkiah and they watched together in amusement as the enthusiastic children ran into the bewildered flock and tried to isolate the lamb of their choice. Eliza was caressing a white one; Michael was trying to drag an unwilling animal towards him, and the cries and struggles of all the young – two-legged and four - added up to complete confusion.

Laughing, Melkiah decided to amend his plan.

"Leave them for now," he called out. "Come tomorrow, and bring a rope tether. Your new friend will go home with you happily then."

All the women with children left the party soon after this, stammering words of gratitude for all the blessings of the day, but the younger, unmarried girls stayed for another hour or two. It was only when the musicians stopped playing that they realised regretfully that the pleasures of this unusual evening were over.

Tamar echoed their appreciation. "Thank you, Father. I'll never forget today. While you were away, I used to dread my birthday for I knew that if you didn't appear I wouldn't see you for another long year. But today has made up for all the times I missed you so much. You've made my friends so happy!"

Melkiah looked at her face, as brightly lit as a seven-flamed candlestick, and knew that she was unaware of the enjoyment that she herself had given by receiving her guests so lovingly.

He smiled at her. "Tomorrow, you shall help your young friends choose their lambs."

"It was a wonderful idea of yours."

Both father and daughter knew that by presenting a pet lamb to a child the whole family would be helped in a way that their pride could accept.

"They are very fine lambs," Tamar mused. "Asher must have picked out the very best."

"Eventually!" There was a twinkle in Melkiah's eyes and Tamar suddenly realised how hard it must have been for her foster-brother.

"Poor Asher!" his master said. "He has much knowledge about the land, but has plenty to learn about loving his neighbour as himself!"

His tone was affectionate but Tamar was beginning to realise why Asher had looked so sulky earlier, and her heart went out to him. He had been forced to give away the pride of his flock when he already had other difficult losses to cope with, including the one of which she had just become aware. She could not bear the thought of his unhappiness on an evening when she herself felt so deeply contented.

"Is there no news of Adina?" she asked. "How she would have loved today!"

"If it is possible to find her, I will do so," Melkiah promised. "Try not to worry. I feel sure that she is safe."

Joel had told him briefly of Adina's new position in Chuza's household in Tiberias but, diverted by the aftermath of Ezra's death, they had not discussed the matter further. As far as Melkiah was concerned, it had been concluded satisfactorily, but he knew his daughter well enough to know that she would not forget her former servant-friend. Sooner or later she must be told an edited version of the situation.

It was nearly dark by the time Tamar went in search of Asher. Realisation had added compunction to her sympathy. "We asked him to sing even though he is mourning the loss of his father – and the girl he planned to marry – immediately after having to give away his best lambs."

She found him in the vineyard, picking up near-invisible stones and throwing them savagely towards the base of a nearby fig tree. The soft thuds were not sufficient to cover the incessant bleating from the flock on the other side of the house and she put a gentle, restraining hand on his arm.

"Don't worry. The children will love our lambs and tend them like new members of their families."

Asher pulled away. "We don't raise animals to be children's playthings!" He glared at Tamar who was now no longer the young woman he desired, but the daughter of the man who had wronged him. "Your father doesn't understand," he railed. "You know how we looked after the ewes in the winter, spending night after night in the sheepfold, determined to keep them safe whatever the cost. Micah was injured when a wolf attacked, as you know, but even on that occasion we only lost one animal. Our shepherds walk miles to find good pastures and everyone agrees that your father has the best flock in Capernaum."

"They are much admired," Tamar agreed, attempting to mollify him. "They are indeed worthy of the Temple."

"The tithe, yes. I don't grudge the Most High some of our lambs – do they not already belong to him? – but to give away over fifty of our best animals on a whim, to children, most of whom he's never even seen before! . . ."

"They are my friends."

Asher did not hear her. "What's the point in any of us working when our Master gives away everything we've worked so hard to raise and harvest and store – grain, oil, wine, honey? . . ."

"He has given alms freely since his return," Tamar agreed, wishing that she herself had been as generous in her father's absence. She forbore to point out that her father was free to dispose of his own goods as he wished, as she had heard the break in Asher's voice.

She touched his sleeve gently. "Asher, I'm sorry you have so many sorrows. I only learned today what Adina is to you."

He was alert instantly. "What have you heard?" In a moment he changed from an aggrieved youth to a vigilant man.

"I didn't know you loved her but I heard Rachel say that you were going to marry her. If only you'd told me sooner, perhaps between us we could have kept her safe."

Asher saw her concern and chose his words carefully. "I *was* fond of the girl, but she was over fond of me. The idea of marriage was all on her side! Since her disappearance I have reproached myself for not loving her more."

Tamar had seen how other young girls had openly admired the handsome young steward, and wished now that she had noticed Adina's interest in time to guide her away from an unwelcome devotion.

"You mustn't blame yourself. My father believes she is safe and will be found one day. In the meantime, I want us all to be happy together."

The naive earnestness in her voice made Asher smile for the first time that day. Tamar's body might be that of a lovely young woman, but her mind was still that of the little girl who had played happily at his side.

Tamar saw his smile and was relieved. "Sad things have happened since my father's return but I want us all to make a new beginning. Promise me that you will be content, Asher."

He put his own hand over hers. "I promise."

But what she asked was like asking a river not to flow into the sea, and he was glad of the darkness veiling his eyes. Only when all his plans had been carried through would he be content, and by then the

134

desirable daughter of the house would be at his side sharing their fruit.

He had sufficient caution to know that he must build slowly on the relationship that had been restored on the day he had comforted her after Ezra's death. If she wanted a loving brother, then that was what he would be – for the time being.

He was smiling as she returned to the house but both light and darkness were swirling in his soul. The darkness was deep when he thought of all his prime lambs being given away so needlessly, but Tamar's renewed friendship was the key that promised him everything he had ever wanted. Time would change many things, and he would ensure that the period until fulfilment would be short.

It was fortunate that Melkiah was not concerned with the approval of Capernaum's leading families, for much criticism had followed the unusual birthday celebration. Men spoke censoriously of the foolishness of inviting worthless poor people to the house of a wealthy man; well-to-do maidens felt slighted at not receiving an invitation; Pharisees and elders raged against the ludicrous charity of giving good animals to those who had not earned them. It was true that the Scriptures spoke of being merciful to the poor, but any student of the Law could tell you that this meant to give alms of the prescribed amount on the prescribed occasions.

The prophet Jesus had infuriated them over and over again by greeting the poor as his friends and by refusing to accept any invitation unless the poor would benefit in some way. Melkiah's allegiance to the one whom he accepted as the Messiah had changed him into the kind of person who should no longer be considered as one of the leading men of influence. "Wait," they counselled each other. "When Jesus is shown up as an impostor and has been destroyed, his followers will come to their senses." Melkiah would ask their pardon for his foolishness and, after he had made the required sin offering, they would reinstate him to the position he had held before he had become a leper. And by then Joel too would have been revealed as a deceiver and dealt with accordingly.

However, less than a week after the much-criticized birthday celebration, news came which made the elders view Melkiah's guest at least with different eyes.

John, a Scribe from Bethany, came to stay with Ishmael and Miriam for several days. During his visit Ishmael questioned him eagerly about the latest news from Judea. As the Sanhedrin in Jerusalem had dictated the views of the Capernaum elders about Jesus of Nazareth, Ishmael was not surprised to learn that they had driven him from the Holy City. No one knew where he was now although some said that he was wandering in Ephraim, ministering to ignorant people who knew no better than to honour him.

When the talk turned to Bethany, John brought up the subject of the most powerful man there, Lazarus of Theopolis. Not only was Lazarus one of the wealthiest men in Israel, but other colourful events that surrounded his family had been discussed endlessly in every town and village in the land. The inhabitants of Capernaum had a particular interest because of their proximity to Magdala. Here Lazarus' sister, Mary, had lived scandalously for many years until something unbelievable had happened.

Up to that time, Ishmael, like many other elders and teachers, had often used the example of Theopolis, a wealthy northern governor, as a warning. This misguided father had educated his son not only in the Sacred Scriptures but in the philosophies of Rome and Greece, and had allowed his daughters to mingle freely with other races and become familiar with their customs and diversions. Lazarus and his sister, Martha, had not been adversely influenced by their unusual freedom, but by bringing pleasure-loving Romans and Greek singers and dancers into their home he had introduced Mary to a way of life that seemed vastly more exciting than her Jewish heritage. She herself was a great beauty and had been sought after, flattered, and led beyond the innocent songs and dances to a world of unfolding delights of the senses.

When Mary had run away with her Roman lover, her mother, by then a widow, had died of sorrow, and her brother and sister had suffered shame as she went on to follow wherever her desires led her.

Finally, she had made her home in her own villa of Magdala, where she had entertained her lovers, held feasts of the finest wines and gourmet food, and hosted evening boating parties on the lake. Many an honest fisherman had had his fish frightened away by the lights and laughter of the slender pleasure craft holding Mary's inebriated guests. Mary's delicate but provocative clothes and exquisite jewellery caused virtuous women to lower their eyes after a warning glance at their accompanying husbands. Mary of Lazarus might dress like a queen but she was no better than any other harlot.

Her sudden conversion took everybody by surprise. She had gone to listen to Jesus the prophet with no other thought than to amuse herself and some friends for an idle hour. Although Jesus had not spoken to her directly, something had drawn her to listen to him again and again, until she had astounded everyone by repudiating her past and resolving to live a new life.

The Scribe John marvelled aloud to Ishmael. "I find it hard to believe that Mary is the same woman who caused so much grief to Lazarus and Martha. For years people were wary of going to their house in case the notorious Mary might be there. But now she stands beside Lazarus and Martha as they reverently welcome the man they believe to be the Messiah, and they smile upon her as if she had always been the most virtuous of Jewish women! She ministers humbly to those in need, and yet she's as alive and fulfilled as a newly-married woman. It's almost enough to make me believe that Jesus *is* who he says he is!"

Ishmael looked sharply at his visitor, who went on almost apologetically. "Miracles of healing mean nothing – Satan will lend his power to anyone who will help him lead people astray. But when lives change so totally . . . Mary has great beauty and enough money to indulge all her desires. So, what did Jesus do to her to make her content to live simply and serve him – and the poor – with such innocent joy?"

"Jesus is as handsome as a King, with a hypnotic voice," Ishmael hinted.

John shook his head. "The women who follow him do not see him as a man but as a spiritual leader to be revered." After a short silence, he mused. "Although he has been rejected officially, there are those among our leaders who speak no word against him and discuss his teaching amongst themselves. Even Rabbi Gamaliel does not condemn him and has allowed some of his own disciples to go and listen to the Galilean Rabbi."

"Who else is in favour of him?"

The Scribe hesitated, then decided that it would do no harm to reveal what had become common knowledge in Jerusalem. "Joseph the Elder from Arimathea, for one. Nicodemus, a Pharisee member of the Sanhedrin, has been repeating some of Jesus' words favourably. And there are others."

Ishmael listened attentively until a more immediate problem came to his mind. "Tell me, do you know a family in Bethany who have lost a son to leprosy? The leper's name was Joel."

John nodded. "Shallum and Abigail continue to mourn him. It is over four years since he left home, and news of his death came soon afterwards – surprisingly soon. There is another son, but Joel was the favourite and I don't believe they will ever accept that he is lost to them for ever. Martha and Mary are good to Abigail, and Lazarus invites Shallum to many a gathering at his house but . . ."

"The family are favoured by Lazarus! Are they then wealthy and of importance in Bethany?"

Ishmael was leaning forward as if to receive John's words the quicker and the Scribe smiled to himself. "They are neither rich nor poor, and would have no importance but for Lazarus' patronage. Why do you ask these questions?"

Ishmael continued to watch his visitor intently. "A young man calling himself Joel ben Shallum came here recently with Melkiah, who had himself been a leper. They both claim that Jesus of Nazareth cured their leprosy."

John had paled. Joel alive? Cured? He felt himself beginning to shake. It could not be the same man for he had died nearly four years ago . . . It was true that Shallum never saw the body of his son . . . If there had been a mistake and Joel was still alive – cured – surely he'd have gone straight home? The last thought was so surely true that he said out loud. "I wish with all my heart that our Joel *had* met the wonder-worker in time to be cured, but whoever this man is, it cannot be him."

His voice was hoarse and his eyes sad with extinguished hope but Ishmael seized on the information he needed. "You knew Joel? You could identify him?"

"I knew him well. He was often at my cousin's house."

"Listen." Ishmael told quickly of the suspicions that had arisen around Melkiah's young guest because of his refusal to talk of his home, or to return there.

John listened frowning, and stood up the moment Ishmael had finished his tale. "Tell me where to find this Joel. I need to know the truth as much as you do now. I cannot return home until I've seen him."

"I'll come with you."

But as the two men walked through the carpet shop, Miriam intercepted her husband. "Aaron and Judith of Sepphoris have just arrived. Their son is getting married and they want many carpets for the house they are building for him. Aaron asks to see you."

Ishmael scarcely hesitated. "I will come at once. Miriam, direct John to Melkiah's house." And, in the time it takes for a coin to pass from a palm to a purse, he disappeared in the direction of a good profit.

Miriam was smiling as she told the young Scribe where to go but, for the first time since meeting her, he scarcely noticed her lively eyes and attractively husky voice.

He went on his way deep in thought, but in the event had no need to remember all the directions to Melkiah's house, as he caught sight of a familiar figure before he was halfway there.

"Joel!" he called, not really believing, but the moment the other turned and retraced his steps all doubts fled.

A startled pigeon flew out of a nearby thicket as the two young men gazed at each other in simultaneous wonder.

"John?"

"Joel!"

The Scribe grasped Joel's arm. "Ishmael told me that there was a Joel from Bethany here but I couldn't believe that it was you." He was trembling. "I feel I'm talking to a ghost! I thought you were dead. Your parents mourn you yet."

Joel smiled at his old friend and clasped him warmly, but the other's words had wounded him. "You can feel that I am real. Another leper called Joel died and my family were informed in error. When I found out, I decided to leave the mistake. It was better that they should mourn all at once than die with me daily over many years. I did not know that I was to be restored to health . . ."

"But when you were, why didn't you come home immediately to turn your parents' sorrow into celebration?"

"There was nothing I'd have liked better but it was not possible."

A strong breeze was tugging at the robes of both men and filling the air with the mingled scent of hawthorn, fennel and thyme.

"Let's walk along the shore," Joel suggested. "I want you to tell me all about my family, and I will tell you why I have acted as I have done. It hasn't been easy . . ."

"I will tell you everything, but you must come back with me and see for yourself. The whole of Bethany will rejoice."

"It was foolish of me to believe that I could keep my identity secret for ever. I realise now that I will have to return, but it cannot be quite yet. What you tell me will help me make my decision. In the meantime, I beg you to keep your knowledge of my existence here a secret from my family. They would not understand how I could stay away."

John wanted to protest but, seeing the strain in Joel's face, was prepared to help his friend. Later, after a long conversation, he was far from convinced that Joel was right but agreed to keep silent for a month or two.

"And then," he threatened, "if you haven't arrived to make your parents alive again, I will personally come here, bind you, and deliver you to them as a parcel on the back of a mule!"

"I will come between Passover and Pentecost," Joel promised. "You have relieved my mind of my chief worry and I believe now that it may be possible to return from the dead without doing too much damage."

After John had left him, he mused wryly. "So, in the weeks left to me before showing my parents that their elder son is still alive, all I have to do is to clear my name by discovering Ezra's murderer."

It seemed a daunting task, but Joel had an idea and a suspicion which he hoped would prove to be unfounded, yet could lead him to the truth.

He would have lost all his confidence had he known that danger threatened every member of Melkiah's family and that death itself was very close.

Chapter 16

"A barren woman is the curse of God"

After the Scribe John had returned to Bethany, the attitude of the leading men of Capernaum towards Melkiah's guest changed dramatically. John had not betrayed his friend's confidences so, although curiosity about Joel's reasons for staying away from his own home remained, it was sufficient to know that he was no impostor and that his family was in favour with the powerful Lazarus of Theopolis.

All of a sudden Joel was greeted with smiles and respectful bows, while the elders in charge of the investigation into Ezra's death discussed the case with him as freely as if he himself had never been under suspicion. They shared their scant knowledge with him, which amounted to nothing more than the names of a dozen imaginary villains who had been seen in various locations in Capernaum on the day of the crime. It was true that a few local people had been accused by their neighbours but, after investigations, the law officers were not surprised to find that their names had been given to avenge private grievances.

In fact, soon after the elders took Joel into their confidence, they announced their official finding: the murderer had left Capernaum on the day of the murder. They would, therefore, make the prescribed offering in reparation and declare their town innocent of the crime.

Joel would have liked to have concurred with this verdict but was convinced that the murderer was still in their midst.

As far as the elders were concerned, the affair was at an end, and it was only when Tamar had an unexpected visitor that Joel discovered one of the matters to which they had turned their mischievous attention.

He was walking on the roof terrace overlooking the main gate, his bare head lifted to the warmth of the sun that was opening rosebuds and forming embryo fruit on the trees. It was a day to bless an ex-leper as he saw his own new life reflected in every garden, field and orchard.

He caught sight of a woman hurrying towards the house and recognised the spirited Miriam. Even from a distance he could tell that she was in some distress for her hand brushed at her cheeks impatiently and she stumbled more than once.

Joel moved back into the shelter of a fig tree which had been trained against the wall of the house to provide shelter from the scorching summer sun. Knowing that Tamar had set off in the direction of the vineyard, Joel walked along the roof terrace and, after a moment or two, saw Eglah conducting the visitor past the vegetable garden towards the bare vines. Before turning away, he saw the two friends meet and go to sit on the corner of the old well.

His mother would have said, "It's too beautiful a day for sorrow," but Joel had discovered that misfortune did not wait politely for an appropriately drab day to appear.

Tamar received Miriam with bewildered compassion. She clasped her friend's hand tightly, but her sympathy only released a torrent of weeping that even a loving arm could not check. There were red veins in Miriam's large eyes and her lips were swollen and dry. Her veil was carelessly fastened and when it blew into her face she tore it off impatiently, revealing tangled hair.

"I'm sorry," she gasped at last, rubbing away her tears. "I didn't mean to distress you, but I didn't know who else to turn to . . ."

"Please tell me what's wrong."

Miriam's eyes were suddenly hard. "Ishmael says he's going to give me a writ of divorce." She saw Tamar's disbelief and gave a twisted smile. "I didn't believe it either."

"But *why?*"

"It seems that I cannot give Ishmael the heir he needs."

"I thought he loved you," Tamar said helplessly.

"I thought so too." Miriam tried to be fair. "I believe he still does, but Sadoc and Uzziel have just returned from Jerusalem where they consulted the Doctors of the Law on Ishmael's behalf. They were told that a barren woman is the curse of God upon a house, so it is his duty to divorce me and marry again in order not to deprive himself of having children."

142

"But why should he believe them? Has he consulted Jairus and the elders of our own synagogue?"

"Jairus has counselled patience, I know, but most of the elders are against me because of my Philistine ancestry."

Tamar was at a loss. "But you're still young enough to bear a child."

"Ishmael says that as I haven't conceived in twelve years of marriage, I'm hardly likely to bear children now that I'm so much older."

"Older!" Tamar gazed at the friend she believed to be at the perfect age for beauty and assurance. "If Ishmael loves you," she pursued. "Surely he will wait, rather than lose you? Why don't you go to the Temple together and pray?"

"Do you think we haven't? Year after year, sacrifice after sacrifice, prayer after prayer . . . No. Ishmael's patience has finally run out and now the thought of an heir is far more important to him than I am."

Two butterflies fluttered round the sleeve of Tamar's tunic, attracted by the bright colour, but she scarcely noticed them; her eyes were upon her stricken friend. "What can I do? What can anyone do?"

"I wondered if Melkiah? . . . Ishmael might listen to him."

Tamar shook her head doubtfully, knowing that there was no friendship between Ishmael and her father because of his allegiance to Jesus of Nazareth. His intervention would surely only harden Ishmael in his resolve to follow the advice that suited him.

Her troubled gaze caught sight of Joel and she wondered suddenly if his new standing in the community could be put to good use.

"Perhaps Joel could help?"

Miriam considered Tamar's suggestion wearily. She had not really believed that Melkiah's advice would help in any way and desperation only had brought her to his house. She had given no thought to Joel, who was after all scarcely more than a stranger, but, like Tamar, she was well aware of his altered status.

"How could I ask him?" she murmured.

Tamar, who had felt increasingly helpless ever since her friend's arrival, was glad to see a way to help her. "I will ask him for you."

She rose quickly and walked to the house without a backward glance. She knew herself well enough to know that when there was a difficult task ahead, the only way to tackle it was to do it immediately. As she climbed the outside staircase to the terrace, she realised that it would have been better to take Miriam indoors first and offer her some refreshment, but it was too late to turn back now.

Joel smiled at Tamar's approach and waited to see if she would mention her friend's arrival.

Tamar sat beside him on a wooden seat in the rooftop garden where the perfume of jasmin drew attention to each delicate star blossom as bright as the snow capping Mount Hermon. Its beauty made the sight of Miriam sitting forlornly by the old well all the more poignant.

Tamar looked away shyly from Joel's enquiring eyes and began her tale. She had already decided to spare her friend the added distress of having to tell a near-stranger the reason for the threatened divorce.

With her eyes on a family of ants moving purposefully across the shade-patterned ground of the terrace walk, she explained the situation.

Joel's immediate reaction was surprise, not that Ishmael should be proposing such action, but that Miriam should have confided in one who was scarcely more than a child. Also, knowing how hard it must be for Tamar to speak of such matters, he was pleasantly surprised that she had accepted her friend's problem as her own and was taking some positive action. More than once he had thought her aptly named ("Tamar" meaning "palm tree") as she too kept her gaze on the sun and stars she loved so that she would not have to face the lesser beauty of the world around her.

He became aware that the growing silence was increasing her embarrassment and knew that he must give her an answer. Beyond her, he saw a sailing boat on the sparkling crystal of the lake and wished fervently that he was in it.

Lowering his eyes to meet the trust in hers, he smiled his consent. "I don't know how I can help, but I'll come and speak with Miriam."

He followed her down the open staircase with the reluctance of an unarmed man going to face an enemy. Miriam was not an enemy, of course, but the situation was an enemy that could not be vanquished easily.

Walking alongside Tamar, he realised that he was probably the least qualified person in the whole of Galilee to tackle the task, the thought of which caused him to slacken his pace and made her turn to him anxiously.

Miriam saw his reluctance and stood up as they approached, her face half-hidden by the veil she had replaced in Tamar's absence.

Tamar hastened to reassure her. "I have explained your problem to Joel."

Miriam's eyes met Joel's candidly. "I'm sorry to involve you. Tamar suggested that you might help."

"I wish I could, but even in my home town I had no influence. So why should a man like your husband by swayed by anything I have to say?"

"Perhaps your association with Lazarus of Theopolis . . . ?" Miriam suggested, then decided to be frank. "I have no one else to speak for me. I'm not really expecting you to change Ishmael's mind for he is quite determined. But how can I agree to let him go without even trying to dissuade him?"

They all knew that the question was academic for Miriam would be considered a divorced woman from the moment that the writ had been put into her hands.

Seeing her struggle for control, Joel spoke quickly. "Tell me: if Ishmael should repudiate you, have you any idea whom he would choose to give him the heir he wants?"

Tamar had not thought to ask this and glanced swiftly at her friend.

Miriam met their sympathetic gaze resolutely. "Oh, yes. His new bride would be Selida, eldest daughter of Amos who died last year." She half-smiled at their lack of comprehension. "Let me explain. Now that both of Selida's parents are dead, she lives in her brother's household. You probably know him – Sadoc, the Pharisee."

A picture of a proud, greedy man flashed into Joel's mind and he nodded.

"An unmarried sister is untapped wealth to Sadoc. He wants to make an advantageous marriage for her – and who better than a fellow Pharisee, the wealthy owner of a carpet business?"

"Was Sadoc one of the elders who went to Jerusalem to consult the Sanhedrin about Ishmael's position?"

Joel did not need Miriam's nod of affirmation. Too many of the Scribes and Pharisees devoted their lives to interpreting the Law of God in a way that suited their own desires.

"How do you know about Selida?" Tamar pursued. "Surely Ishmael couldn't be so cruel as to name her before you?"

"He spoke of her last year when she went to live in her brother's house. We actually laughed together about Sadoc offering a good dowry to find a good husband for her." There were unshed tears in her eyes, but Miriam continued her explanation steadily enough. "Ishmael has not told me that she is the one he has chosen, but I heard him and Sadoc talking about her last week. Then, this morning, he told me that she is coming to look over our workshops today."

"And you very sensibly ran away," Joel reassured. He wanted to ask if the Pharisee's sister was beautiful but decided that the question was tactless. In any case, with the appreciation of a healthy man newly restored to life, he was well aware of all the loveliest young women in Capernaum and knew none by the name of Selida.

Tamar's thoughts were following the same track. "How could Ishmael possibly turn from you to *her*? She's as solid as an ox and has such a sharp tongue that no man has ever offered for her. It's not long since poor Ezra incurred Sadoc's wrath by refusing to consider her as a wife."

"It's difficult to see her attraction," Miriam agreed. "Doubtless it's her presumed fertility. Her mother had fifteen children before she died."

Workers in the nearby vineyard were glancing at the trio by the well with curiosity and Joel felt that there was little to gain by prolonging the discussion.

"If I went to your house now, would I find Ishmael alone?"

"Perhaps Sadoc and his sister will still be there. Ishmael will be angry with me for not staying to show them round." The houses of Capernaum were not visible from this side of the house, and Miriam did not regret her brief escape to this beautiful place where spring flowers would linger until they had passed on their glory to the luxuriant growth of summer.

She turned to Joel. "I'll go ahead of you, and if I do not return, it will mean that Ishmael has no other visitors. But give him time to lecture me on my disobedience!"

She took Tamar's hand and held it briefly. "I'll come again soon. Perhaps tomorrow."

"I pray that . . ."

Yes, pray for us both, Joel thought, as he followed Miriam at a distance.

Why was it that ever since his return to health every task he had been given was one for which he had been totally unfitted?

He saw fishermen baiting some wickerwork fish-traps, passed a potter skilfully shaping a clay pot, noticed a carpenter patiently smoothing some wood with a fish-scale rasp, and moved quickly out of the way as a Roman soldier rode purposefully by. He could not help envying each one of them.

"Most High Lord, I owe You my life," he admitted. "And I will serve You until the end of my days. But couldn't You find me some work that I could do well for You?"

His footsteps slowed as he passed through the market square greeting a few acquaintances, but all too soon he was before the carpet shop of Ishmael the Pharisee. He still had no idea what he was going to say to him. He ran through various openings:

"Greetings, Ishmael. I hear you plan to divorce your lovely wife who is worth ten of you . . . I am not without influence in high places and I know just the place for someone like you: how would you like life on the high seas – as a slave for the Romans? . . ."

A pleasing picture of the swarthy Pharisee chained to the oars of a galley ship, his arrogance finally subdued, helped Joel through the moments until he was alone with Ishmael in the reception room.

He accepted the proffered wine and returned the customary courtesies with outward graciousness, but disliked his hypocritical role and it was only his concern for Miriam that enabled him to meet the other's piercing eyes with guileless good-humour.

For some time they spoke of unimportant matters but when Ishmael led the conversation to Lazarus of Bethany, Joel saw a possible way to proceed. He was well aware that the Pharisee resented that he had not been told Joel's reason for staying away from his home, John having kept his friend's confidences. He wondered now if he should sacrifice his need for secrecy to win the other's good favour but, realising that the Pharisee would neither understand nor approve of his reasons, decided that his best hope lay in exaggerating his friendship with the influential Lazarus.

He began to speak of the rich man and described his magnificent home in Bethany with its extensive gardens, orchards, vineyards and olive groves. Catching Ishmael's avaricious eyes upon him, he remembered the other's chief interest and went on to speak of Lazarus' library.

"He has perhaps the finest collection of scrolls in the country – and not just our own sacred writings, but the philosophies of Greece, Rome and Persia. He has an insatiable love of learning and likes nothing better than to read his scrolls from day-break to nightfall." Although there had been only one occasion when Joel and Lazarus had exchanged three or four sentences about a scroll in his host's hand, Joel elaborated, "We had many an absorbing discussion and I learned much from him."

Ishmael, who had frowned at the reference to the forbidden philosophies of alien races, was nonetheless impressed by Joel's words. Soon perhaps the young man would be living in Bethany again, and have the ear of one of the greatest men in the country.

Joel, the reluctant diplomat, continued to build on his advantage. He held up his cup appraisingly. "This wine is perhaps the finest I've tasted in Galilee." He accepted some more, took an appreciative sip, and plunged along a hitherto untravelled road of fantasy. "Lazarus is much admired for his wisdom," he mused. "Many people come to ask his advice and he resolves their problems with the wisdom of Solomon."

Joel went on to tell of the solution to a property dispute suggested by Lazarus, then, sure of Ishmael's rapt attention, allowed his invent-iveness free rein.

"Once, a goldsmith from Jerusalem, Matthias, came to consult him. He was a wealthy man and his wife appeared to be barren. Her twin sister, also married, had several fine sons, but after twenty years of marriage the goldsmith's wife, Esther, had not provided him with a single heir. Matthias had a lawyer friend who urged him to divorce his barren wife and marry again."

Joel took a lengthy draught of his wine while both he and Ishmael wondered what advice Lazarus had given.

"Lazarus did not agree with the lawyer," Joel decided. "He said it was a spiritual problem, a question of faith. He reminded Matthias of how old Sarah had been when she conceived Isaac; of Rachel's unhappiness at her childlessness until she had borne Joseph; of the so-called barren Hannah who had eventually been blessed with Samuel; and – nearer our own time – how Elizabeth, wife of Zechariah the priest, had been over fifty years of age when she had become mother to the child who was to become John the Baptist.

"Lazarus pointed out to Matthias that many of the greatest men in our history were born to those who had the faith to wait for their arrival. The Almighty wanted to test their patience to find out if they were worthy to receive such children." Confident that his fish was safely in the net, Joel concluded. "Lazarus counselled Matthias to rededicate himself and Esther to the Lord and ask for a new blessing on their marriage."

Joel felt Ishmael's penetrating gaze upon him but dared not meet the hawk-like eyes. He let a silence develop while he decided how many children to present to the imaginary goldsmith.

Ishmael swallowed audibly. "Did Matthias take Lazarus' advice?"

Joel smiled. "He did indeed. He had to wait a further two years but then Esther presented him with twin sons. And I believe there was a daughter after that . . ."

There was a light in Ishmael's eyes now, life that had not been there the moment before, and Joel judged it was the right time to leave the subject. He was not supposed to have any knowledge of the callous action Ishmael had been advised to take, so went on to recount a further instance of Lazarus' wisdom to disguise his knowledge of the significance of the previous story.

He was well aware that the Pharisee was not listening to him and was as eager to see his visitor depart as Joel was himself to go. Thankfully, he rose to his feet, bowed to his host, and left the house, taking in deep breaths of freedom.

He did not know if his words had helped Miriam's cause but he resolved that if they had won her a breathing space, he would persuade her to approach Jesus when He returned to Capernaum. He was quite sure that the Messiah would gladly grant the requested gift of new life.

✡   ✡   ✡

Ishmael paced up and down for several hours, but the battle had been won before Joel ben Shallum had left him. Although the scribe, John, had not revealed his friend's secret, he had assured Ishmael that Joel's reason for staying away from his home town was to his credit, rather than otherwise.

Ishmael had once seen a man stoned to death, and the memory had haunted him ever since for he had never been entirely sure of his guilt. It had changed him, making him prepared to listen to others (in a conditioned and prejudiced way) and to condemn no one without definite proof.

And so he had decided to accept the word of someone he trusted, and forget Joel's imagined crimes. He congratulated himself that his decision had not been influenced by the young man's friendship with the mighty Lazarus, having come to the conclusion that a man could retain the favour of the Most High without making enemies of those wealthy people who had been deceived by the false prophet, Jesus. The deceiver's star would plunge to earth soon enough, and once he had been dealt with, his followers would resume their normal lives. The Most High would bless the man who had remained faithful to him, and meanwhile he should be indulgent with his foolish friends.

This being the case, Lazarus' words, as reported by Joel, carried as much weight as a millstone, and had pointed out to Ishmael something that he had not considered before. He had yearned for a son to inherit the wealth and position that he had gained, but perhaps the Most High wanted his thoughts to go far higher than this, and he should prepare to receive a very special child: a famous Rabbi; a future high priest; a warrior like Judas Macabee who would lead an Israelite army to overthrow Rome; or perhaps . . . even the Messiah himself. Miriam was not of pure Hebrew descent, of course, but had not King David himself descended from the Moabitess, Ruth?

Ishmael's exalted thoughts hovered over the Temple where he saw his powerful son being revered throughout the land – and on the ground underneath the lofty arches lay the broken pieces of the plan that had been destroyed that very morning.

When Selida had come in Miriam's absence to see the carpet looms, he himself had shown her round. He had never before exchanged a word with the plump girl he was considering marrying and greeted her with assessing interest.

She returned his greeting boldly but her words were over-eager and he was disappointed in her voice, which was flat and lacking in animation. Her expression was sly and greedy as she gazed about her, and when one of the weavers had stumbled against Selida and inadvertently pulled the veil from her head, she had turned on the girl in sudden fury.

Ishmael had moved out of earshot of the sharp voice berating the apologetic worker but was unable to shut out the image of the spirited, affectionate woman who was his wife whose voice was as melodious as a turtle dove in spring.

Was it not a sign from the Most High that Joel had arrived almost immediately after Selida's self-satisfied departure? He nodded, answering his own question, confirmed now in his decision. If the Lord of all the earth wished to test his faith, then he would find no lack in his servant, Ishmael.

And now, at this moment, he had not the slightest doubt that such trust and patience would be bountifully rewarded.

Chapter 17

"Why do men prefer evil to good?"

"Lord God, I don't mind being on a secret mission for You," Joel told the Most High. "If only it weren't also a secret from me . . ."

Hearing a sound in the sky, he gazed upwards half-expecting to see an angel drifting down with instructions, but saw only a swallow speeding along an invisible avenue of air.

He was sitting on the hillside far above Capernaum, hoping that a bird's eye view would suggest new directions for his investigations. His eyes were drawn to the dazzling white synagogue within a stone's throw of the shining sea of Genneserat. If only the people who met there shone with the same pure beauty. He had taken to attending the weekday services on Mondays and Thursdays, as well as the morning and evening Sabbath gatherings, and was thus earning an undeserved reputation as a devout seeker of religious teaching. Although Joel joined in the set prayers and psalms and listened to the readings from Moses and the Torah reverently, he rarely listened to the self-important interpretations that followed. His gaze would wander from the richly-garbed leaders on the platform facing the Ark where the scrolls of the Law were kept to the humble men of the congregation below. All, from the beardless youths to the oldest men with their patriarchal beards, seemed eager for instruction, yet Joel could not help wondering how many murderers, or would-be murderers, there were amongst them.

For, leaving aside the matter of Ezra's violent death, Joel was aware that a greater evil was incubating behind their shell of apparent virtue. Many of these zealous men would expect to be rewarded by God for plotting to kill the one whom they could not accept as His Messiah.

A troop of mounted men was threading its way through the bustling streets towards the road that led over the hills to Bethsaida. Joel guessed that the man leading the Roman soldiers was the Centurion

Lucius, and wondered briefly if there was trouble. However, as the men numbered no more than ten, their only weapons were their dress-swords, and their pace was unhurried, doubtless their mission was peaceful.

Joel, curious to meet the rarity of a member of the occupying forces who had won the respect of the Jewish people, had sought out the Roman centurion a few days before.

Lucius had greeted Joel with equal interest, having heard many rumours about the stranger who had come home with Melkiah.

"I know you may not enter the house of a Gentile, but we could walk in my garden."

Joel agreed readily, taking immediately to the lean Roman with the intelligent eyes and humorous face.

Bees were enjoying the flowers of an acacia tree, butterflies fluttered indecisively from lily-of-the-valley to forget-me-not intoxicated by so much choice; doves cooed contentedly from their dovecote. A little black lizard was the sole occupant of a stone seat until the two men reached it.

"Will you tell me of your encounter with Jesus the prophet?"

Joel spoke first, guessing that the other probably wanted to ask him the same question.

"It happened the year before last," Lucius told him readily. "Manaen, one of my servants, had been ill for some time with a bone disease. He suffered much and was virtually paralysed by the time the wonder-worker came here. I had received instructions that should Jesus of Nazareth hold meetings in my district, I was to make sure that no sedition was preached."

Somewhere in the garden a well-pulley squeaked and water splashed, but Lucius' thoughts were on the living water of truth that he had drunk so eagerly. "I listened to him for hours," he remembered, "and knew that here was a Man to whom the whole world should listen. I came to believe that he is truly divine and can do all things.

"When I met him in the street one day, I dared speak to him. I wouldn't have done so but for Manaen's desperate need. When I told Jesus about my servant, he didn't hesitate and said that he would come and cure him! I couldn't allow that, of course. The Jewish doctors had refused to enter the house of a pagan, so it certainly wouldn't be right to allow the Son of God to do so. I told him that his command would be sufficient to heal Manaen."

"And he gave it, and the disease left your servant," Joel prompted.

"Yes. Some of the elders spoke up on my behalf, but I know that he would have agreed without their words. He smiled at me and commended me for my faith – but who couldn't have faith in such a one?"

"Some of the elders?"

Lucius sighed. "Yes. They are on good terms with me because they know that I believe in their God and respect their religion. In many places, our soldiers make sport of all their observances, but I have forbidden my men to do so. Although it is not possible for me to share the treasures of your heritage, I believe that your God is my God too."

Joel looked at the bent head of the strong soldier and marvelled. Jairus had told him how Lucius had dug deeply into his own purse to help build the synagogue some years before. He who was excluded from the ceremonies of the chosen people, was content to help others pursue their select road to holiness.

A wealthy centurion was unusual. He wondered what fortune of war had given him sufficient means to live here in comfort and from where his contentment came. He knew that this Roman did not spend his off-duty hours in the brothels of Tiberius or Magdala.

Lucius looked up with sudden eagerness. "I have listened to Jesus on every possible occasion since the day he cured Manaen, but he hasn't been here since last summer. You met him a few months ago. Tell me what you saw."

Joel shut his eyes against the bright sunshine and through the dark spots stabbing his lids pictured again the sapphire eyes that had looked into his own.

"I saw a kind and compassionate Man whose eyes were full of pain. One who was bewildered and hurt beyond bearing."

In the silence that followed, softened only by the waves breaking on the shingly beach, the thoughts of both men were on the tragedy of the Man-God who was not recognised or accepted by the people on whose behalf he had come.

"Yes. I have seen the change in him from year to year. Why do men prefer evil to good?"

"Why do men kill?" Joel did not wait for an answer. "You have lived among the inhabitants of Capernaum longer than I have. Do you believe that the murderer of Ezra, son of Zelek, is still with us?"

"I made my own investigations but came up with nothing," Lucius admitted. "There are certainly men living here who are capable of killing in certain circumstances: the "righteous" execution of a blasphemer, for instance; or a murder of revenge for the death of a relative. But people of all nationalities and vices pass through here, and I'm inclined to think that one of these came upon Ezra and killed him for his purse."

"With a stone and sling?"

"A brigand brought up as a shepherd, wanting to make an easier living?"

Joel could see that Lucius shared his own unease about the unsolved crime and, although they continued to discuss the subject, knew that he was unlikely to discover anything of further value.

Now, sitting on the hillside with a skylark singing joyfully overhead, Joel could no longer see Lucius leading the small troop of Romans and he rose to his feet and made his way down towards the lake.

He heard the distant sound of shepherds' pipes and saw some youngsters clapping their hands in time to the lilting music, and laughing at a lamb who was gambolling ecstatically as if in response. Seagulls were following a vessel that was low in the water and heading for the shore. Joel did not recognise the fishing boat but directed his own steps to the path that would by-pass the busiest streets and take him to the section of beach where the fishermen lived.

He waved to Jether but, his head lowered over the bowl he was creating and his feet busy spinning the wheel evenly, the potter was unaware of Joel's passing.

The fish-laden boat had beached by the time Joel reached the sand and shingle along the water's edge. The sunlight was like diamond fish leaping over the surface of the glittering sea, but Tobit and others were helping their neighbour unload a more tangible catch. Joel strode to the boat and without a word joined in the chain helping to carry the laden baskets to the shed where they would be sorted and taken to the market or salted for transport to Judea.

There was no jealousy amongst the fishermen. They rejoiced in every good catch and needed no personal gain to help each other unhesitatingly. It was sufficiently heartening to handle the evidence of the bounty that lived in the lake.

At last all the fish had been transferred and Tobit had time to smile at his friend. "I'm just about to go out myself. Would you like to come?"

"Please."

The wind was very light and the boat made hardly any wake as it moved away slowly. Joel had helped to hoist the sail and now he coiled rope competently while checking the wind direction from the fluttering flag on the mast; he had learnt that a sudden change could cause the boom to swing over unexpectedly.

Tobit smiled as he gave him the tiller. The two men worked as a good team, Joel preferring to handle the boat, Tobit to see to the fishing. In spite of much practice, Joel found it extremely difficult to cast the circular weighted net over the side of the boat with Tobit's proficiency, and even when he succeeded in getting the net to spread out over the waves, the fish were not deceived and swam away with contemptuous smiles. He was of more use when he and Tobit worked in partnership with another boat with a drag-net suspended between the two crafts. It needed the strength of four men to lift and empty the pulsating net into the boat-baskets or to tow it ashore in the event of a really successful catch.

The boat was not moving very fast and gulls flew past them mockingly, showing how easily they used the slightest wind; but the men were not offended, Tobit because he had acquired patience as a fisherman, Joel because he was in no hurry to go anywhere.

Some children were playing on the shore, crawling underneath an upturned boat to hide from friends, but there was no sign of Eliza.

"She's always wandering off these days," Tobit remarked. "Twice we've caught her leading her lamb towards the pastures beyond the houses. She thinks she can do as she pleases now that she's nearly four and a shepherdess!"

Joel saw the pride and affection on his face and smiled.

A movement on the lake caught his eye. "Why aren't those men using a sail?" The craft was skimming through the waves at a good rate, and as it drew nearer Joel recognised two fishermen brothers at the oars.

"They're practising for the Spring Races. Men compete from all the villages around the lake – not the Romans, of course, only our own people."

"Who is likely to win?"

"Up 'til three years ago, no one could beat Simon of Jonah. He's very strong and no one can handle a boat better than he can. I never thought he'd find something he'd love more than his boat, but Jesus the prophet came and called him, and he went. So, it's anyone's race now."

"Will you enter?"

"Probably. I haven't the strength or the stamina to come first, but Susanna will not believe it and keeps reminding me that David beat Goliath!"

"Presumably you have teams as well?"

Tobit nodded. "One from each village or town. We miss Simon and James since they went away, but there's no lack of volunteers to represent Capernaum. I shan't be needed."

A gust of wind caused the boat to heel slightly and Joel tightened his grip on the tiller. "Where are we heading?"

Tobit pointed northwards. "My neighbour has just returned from there. Let's see if the other half of the shoal are still searching for their missing relatives." He studied the sky thoughtfully. "The weather is changing but there should be enough time before the wind starts to work against us."

Tamar was deep in thought as she walked home. Miriam had been like an overflowing fountain of sparkling water, her bright eyes shedding crystals of relief and joy.

Joel had not told either of them what he had said to Ishmael, insisting that he had not even mentioned Miriam's name, but the fact remained that the Pharisee had changed from the time of their conversation. Ishmael had begged his wife's pardon for causing her distress, said that he would wait patiently for the son he knew she would bear him, and had even presented her with a fine silver girdle in token of her new favour in his eyes.

Tamar marvelled at the way in which Miriam had been able to throw away her anguish as if it had never been, forgive Ishmael instantly without a single reproach, and pour all her love and gratitude upon a man who surely did not deserve it. Even so, she had rejoiced to see her friend's new contentment, and had witnessed Miriam's mingled tears and laughter with smiling sympathy.

Tamar's elation at the success of Joel's intervention had left her the moment she was on her way home. Miriam had been immensely grateful to Joel and full of curiosity about why he had not returned to his own home. "I do not believe he has done anything dishonourable," she declared. "I can only think that he is avoiding someone. It cannot be his parents, so perhaps it is his wife . . ."

"His wife!" Tamar was shocked. "I'm sure he's not married, and even if he were, why should he avoid his wife? Surely he'd want to be with her?"

"Perhaps his parents arranged the marriage and he never liked their choice, or perhaps she was unfaithful to him. In either case, it would explain why he won't go home. Don't you think it's possible?"

Tamar was bewildered. "I know he misses his home and his parents but he doesn't act like an unhappy man. He's always good-humoured and, although he's restless, I can't believe that he's hiding a secret sorrow – particularly an unloved wife!"

However, in spite of her words, Miriam's suggestion continued to circle in her mind, gathering momentum with each lap, so that by the time Tamar was in sight of her home, an idle speculation had turned from a possibility to a probability, and finally to a near-certainty.

She felt such sorrow for the plight of the guest whom she had not welcomed, but no longer resented, that she entered the gate without rejoicing in the delicate blue flowers of the acacia tree that graced the courtyard.

She climbed the steps onto the terrace and pulled her veil lower to shield her eyes from the sun which was daily becoming more dazzling. She had walked nearly two sides of the house, past the orchard, the shore, the vineyard and the vegetable garden, before she spotted her grandmother.

Every Spring Sarah would choose a day to wander among the herbs that she herself had set out so long ago. Now, guided by Asher, she

158

was walking slowly between the highly aromatic plants that she needed no sight to identify.

Asher was breaking off sprigs of rosemary, marjoram, cummin and thyme and handing them to Sarah who already had a small bunch of greenery in her hands. Even from here, Tamar could see her grand-mother's pleasure and, wanting to share it, ran down the nearest stairs to join the two people who had made her childhood so secure.

Asher smiled at Tamar and held a spray of pungent fennel under her nostrils. "You're like a walking herb yourself in your amethyst tunic," he told her, adding to Sarah. "Tamar grows more beautiful every year."

"I haven't looked upon her face for many years," Sarah said serenely. "But I see her clearly in my mind's eye – and you too, Asher. Good-looking children turn into handsome adults. May you both be granted the further blessings of health and wealth."

"We are what you made us," Tamar told her. "And did you not teach us that real wealth is to be surrounded by loving people?"

Even as she spoke, she realised the possible harm the indulgent old woman may have caused Asher. When Melkiah had disappeared so mysteriously, she had brought up the steward's son to believe that he was the son of the house in all but name and that there was nothing that he could not attain. Perhaps she had even promised him his foster-sister? It might be wise to clarify her own last words.

"Asher has always been the most loving of brothers, and I wish you could see what a fine young man he's turning into." Her tone was warm but there was affectionate mockery in her smile as she added. "However, no one would mistake him for a wealthy man yet!"

Very conscious of his earth-stained tunic, Asher retorted. "It could be that a labourer is of more worth than a wealthy man."

He turned to go and, although his voice had been good-humoured, Tamar felt that he had not liked the reminder of his semi-servant status. She knew that he was discontented and wondered why some people always wanted more than they were destined to possess.

She held Sarah's arm firmly as they walked between the beaten-earth path among the herbs to a wooden bench under the shade of a carob tree. They sat together and breathed in air which surely could not have been more fragrant in the Garden of Eden. Dappled sun reached them through the emerald leaves overhead, pigeons strolled unafraid at their feet, and her spirit was caught up in the pervading peace.

"I'll dry some herbs and make you a pillow," she offered, seeing her grandmother breathing in the spicy air appreciatively.

"Make yourself one too," Sarah suggested. "It will give you sweet dreams."

"Perhaps I will." Since Ezra's death, Tamar had had many disturbed nights and longed to sleep peacefully again. "Adina made me one but its scent is very faint now." She looked from the wilting herbs in her grandmother's hand to the bushes of healthy growth before her, mentally choosing the sprigs she would need. "Do you think we'll ever see Adina again? If only I knew what had happened to her . . ."

"Would you be content to know that she is safe?"

There was something in Sarah's voice that made Tamar look at her companion's face.

"You know something! Oh, tell me what you've heard."

Sarah put her bouquet beside her on the bench and pressed her fingers together tightly. "I didn't find out until yesterday evening when your father came to my room. It was when I said that Adina must be dead by now as we had heard nothing, that he told me that he'd discovered her whereabouts and that she is safe and well."

"May the Lord be praised! But where is she? Why doesn't she come home?"

"It seems that Adina was ambitious for now she is working in the house of King Herod's steward in Tiberias."

The news was so unexpected that Tamar could scarcely understand her grandmother's words. "She's working in a *Roman* household? How could she bear to live among them and be away from her own people – from us? And, how did it all happen?"

Sarah shook her head. "There's some mystery about that. Apparently she left here because she had been offered a better position in a wealthy house in Tiberias."

"How could it be better? She was happy here!"

"She did seem to be," Sarah agreed. "Anyway, whatever the reason, it didn't work out for her the way she had expected. So when Melkiah and Joel saw her by chance the day they went to Tiberias, they were able to help her. They found her a position in Chuza's house through their contact with Jonathan, his steward."

Tamar's frown deepened. "I don't understand. Why didn't Father bring her straight back here? And why, *why*, didn't he tell us? He knows how worried we've been – and all the time he knew that she was safe! Why, Granna, why?"

"Perhaps because he knew we would be distressed to hear what had happened to her. I suppose he hoped we'd forget, and come to accept that we would never hear from her again."

"How *could* he have thought that! She was my friend, and I love her. Where is Father now? I'll ask him to bring her home today."

Tamar rose eagerly, already anticipating the matching delight in Adina's dark, sparkling eyes at their reunion, but Sarah groped for her grand-daughter's hand.

"Wait. Don't you realise that it is Adina's choice to stay away from us? She wants to stay in Tiberias."

"With strangers? With *Romans?*"

"Although Chuza and Johanna are not of our race, they are friendly to Jesus since the day he cured Johanna. Jonathan too is a disciple of his, so Adina will not lack spiritual guidance."

"But here she was among her own people and we were good to her. I thought she loved us."

"Perhaps she loved one person too much . . ."

Realisation struck Tamar suddenly. "Asher! Of course. He said she was over fond of him. She ran away when she found out that he did not care. So that's why she cannot return here."

Sarah held Tamar's hand to her cheek and kissed it. "We can rejoice that she is alive and in good hands."

"Yes . . . But we must tell Asher that she is safe. He's been reproaching himself in case harm has come to her because of him."

Sarah agreed. "Poor Asher. He has enough grief with his father dead. My son asked me not to tell anyone except you, but he doesn't understand about Asher. Will you go to him and put his mind at rest."

"I'll go now. He will be relieved – and I will try to be content that Adina has been found."

Tamar came upon Asher on the edge of a field of flax rippled by the breeze into an inland sea of forget-me-not. Her spirit smiled at the beauty before her but Asher's thoughts were more prosaic. "The wind is rising and I'm sure there's rain on the way. I don't want the crop damaged before we can harvest it."

"There's always rain in Nisan. It'll be good for it. Asher, I have good news: Adina is safe."

She had his full attention now but kept her story brief. "Father saw her in Tiberias. She's working in the household of Chuza, King Herod's steward."

"What did she say to your father?"

Tamar shook her head. "I don't know. You could ask Grandmother. Father told her last night."

Asher frowned. "Your father wasn't in Tiberias yesterday."

"No. He found Adina long ago, the day he and Joel sailed to Tiberias together." She saw the hard line of his mouth and touched his hand gently. "I'm sorry. He should have told you but he didn't understand your special concern."

Asher was almost unaware of Tamar. He had never expected Adina to be discovered in Tiberias. He could not have foreseen Melkiah's return, or that the Master would ever visit such a pagan place. However, as all this had happened several months ago and there had been no change in Melkiah's attitude to him, presumably Adina had not betrayed him. He hoped it would not be necessary to take any further action.

"Granna says Adina will never come home, but I want to see her again at least once. Do you think Father would take me?"

"You must not go to such a place." Asher's voice held concern. "If you give me your word that you will not ask him, I will bring Adina to you one day."

"Do you promise?"

"Yes, but you must be patient." He sought a way to divert her. "As Joel knew that Adina was safe, I wonder why he said nothing to ease your mind?"

"It must have been Father's decision."

"He's made more than one strange decision since his return," Asher mused. "There's something secretive in Joel too. Sometimes I wonder if their encounter with Jesus of Nazareth was entirely to their advantage."

"How can you say that! Father is everything I want him to be, and Joel too is good and kind."

"Kindness can become foolishness if taken too far. Tamar, it is right that you should respect and defend your father – whether he is right or wrong – but be wary of Joel of Shallum. Do not be taken in by his apparent goodness."

Tamar felt strangely confused at the thought of her father's friend. "It is true that he has his secrets and I don't always understand him, but there is no darkness in his eyes."

Asher looked at her thoughtfully for a moment, then pointed to a path overhung with evergreen branches. "Imagine that you are a traveller passing through a tunnel of dark undergrowth. Your way becomes more and more overgrown and eventually disappears altogether. You are lost. Then you see a light shining ahead and hurry towards it gladly. Too late, you find that it is a lamp hung on a branch by robbers to lure travellers to their doom."

A chill came over Tamar. A dark cloud as large as a mountain had covered the sun.

"All lights are not good," Asher warned. "Some are false and lead to destruction. Be wary, my innocent one." He looked out over the sea and now his concern was for the approaching storm. "Look how all the boats are hurrying for the shore. There's real danger for any that are out too far." Seeing her instant anxiety for the fishermen, he touched her arm to regain her attention. "Make sure that you are in the house before the rain comes."

"I will. I wonder where Joel is? I hope he's not on the lake."

Seeing her solicitude, Asher realised that his warning words had had no impact on the trusting girl before him.

"I hope he *is* . . ." he said savagely, but not until Tamar was well on her way to the house.

Chapter 18

"She's vanished"

The wind had risen very suddenly. This was not the first storm Joel had witnessed since his arrival in Galilee but he had never expected to experience one in quite such a vulnerable position.

He knew how dangerous the lake could be when western winds swirled through the gorges into the low-lying bowl of water, rapidly turning the surface of the sapphire silk into a fury of water-mountains. Caught without warning when their small boats were swamped by torrents of water, fishermen died as helplessly as the Egyptians of long ago under the waters of the Red Sea.

Joel was elated rather than afraid. They had lowered and tied the sail before it could be shred to ribbons by the forceful wind, but their garments flapped and pulled around them as if eager to fly from their owners and go with the wind to the misted hills of Gergesa.

Tobit was shouting something over the roar of the gale, backing up his inaudible words by pointing eastwards. Joel nodded and adjusted the tiller, needing all his strength to combat the elements. Spray showered over him from waves which were breaking into the boat on every side and Tobit baled out with a fury that matched the raging sea.

Dark clouds were tearing across the sky like unleashed hounds, having reduced the sun to a faint silver target for golden arrows of lightning. Their small boat was being tossed about as randomly as a piece of driftwood, one moment plunging down into a dark trough, the next rushing up a billow of foaming water that threatened to fill the man-made craft and send it to the bottom of the sea.

In some strange way, Joel felt at one with the powerful forces as he blinked back spray repeatedly to peer at the elusive eastern shore.

Tobit had fitted the oars and was pulling with all his strength but the boat was becoming heavier moment by moment. Joel reached through the swirling knee-high water to take the old Roman helmet that Tobit used for a baler and started to bale one-handedly while keeping a grip on the tiller with great difficulty. He soon realised that for every measure he returned to the sea, the waves returned ten times more.

The wind was shrieking through his ears, the lake was as black as the ink in a scribe's horn, and the pounding of the waves against the boat had a force that seemed to be urged on by the roaring mountains. They were making no headway and Joel decided that they had as much chance of reaching land as Jonah when he had been thrown into the raging sea.

At least Jonah had had a friendly whale to rescue him, he remembered, and, as if summoned, Joel looked up to see a giant shape filling the horizon.

The approaching wave towered like the Hermon range and both men knew at that moment that there was nothing on earth they could do to escape its destructive power. The battle was over. It was time to remember the friends who had gone to Sheol, for they would be seeing them very soon.

"Jesus!" Joel shouted, but he did not have time to complete his prayer.

"I'd forgotten how spectacular our lake storms can be," Melkiah commented. "What wild music our Kinnor made today!"

The lake, often called Kinneret after it's harp-like shape, was tranquil again, shining placidly in the reflected light of the unveiled sun.

Tamar, beside her father on the roof terrace, gazed anxiously towards the distant fishermen's dwellings.

"I hope that all the boats had time to reach home before the storm broke." She could see tiny figures gathered in irregular patterns around their boats, like ants preparing to shoulder their prize and carry it homewards.

"The wind arose very suddenly," Melkiah admitted. "But the fishermen are not inexperienced and take no unnecessary risks. I expect the only damage will be to any boats that hadn't been pulled high enough up the beach. Nathanael will be busy in his boat repair shed for the next few days."

He could see that he had not allayed Tamar's fears. "Why don't you go and see your friend Susanna? She will reassure you."

"Yes, I will. I'll ask Kenturah if she has any scones for Eliza."

Tamar raced away without a backward glance, sure-footed and energetic, and seeing her plait rising and falling with each step, Melkiah smiled. A child or a woman? In spite of her graceful beauty, she seemed very young to him and he was glad. He had missed so much of her childhood and it seemed to him that she too was aware of it and was reluctant to be a woman until they had made up for their lost years as father and child.

Water-diamonds glinted everywhere as Tamar made her way towards the lake. Rain dripped off leaves and steamed in the hot sunshine and a strong smell of dampened dust came from the puddled path at her feet. The lake's storm indigo had been transformed by the sun into sheets of glittering metal, like a million swords laid on the surface of the sea, but as she reached the shore she could see a border of yellow where the waves lapped the shingle.

She caught her breath as she approached Tobit's dwelling and saw the cluster of women around Susanna, and the sober face of the neighbour supporting her. Her legs trembled as she took the last paces towards her friend.

"What has happened?"

"Tobit went fishing just before the storm broke," Susanna's neighbour explained. "He hasn't returned yet."

"Where did he go?" Tamar's arm gestured uncertainly towards the lake.

Annaleah pointed north. "My husband got such a good catch, Tobit thought he'd try his luck there too."

Susanna was staring over the empty sea with frightened eyes and Annaleah's arm tightened around her. "I keep telling her that Tobit is safe. He will have beached his boat the moment the wind changed."

Tamar touched her friend's arm imploringly. "Don't look so scared. It must have happened as Annaleah says. Surely this isn't the first time Tobit has been caught in a storm?"

Susanna met Tamar's eyes and seemed to find reassurance there. "That's true," she said with only a slight tremor in her voice. "Once the wind blew him nearly to Hippo and it took him all day to tack back, and on another occasion the boat was damaged and he had to walk home."

Glad to see new hope in her friend's eyes, Tamar asked. "Where are Abital and Eliza?"

"Abital has gone to visit a friend. She won't be worrying as Tobit hadn't intended to go fishing today." Frowning, Susanna looked towards the house, finding it impossible to think clearly. "I don't know where Eliza is."

"I'll find her," Tamar said quickly. "I've brought her some of Kenturah's honey and raisin scones. They will bring her home quickly enough!"

Eliza was not far away. She was scolding her lamb for sampling the cucumbers Tobit was growing in his small patch of ground, while the friendly animal seemed to be assuring her that he could listen and eat at the same time.

When Tamar produced the freshly-made scones, Eliza took her hand eagerly and together they ran to reassure Susanna. The lamb, Snowy, followed, bleating excitedly.

"May I have a scone now, Mummy?" Eliza pleaded, her round eyes more daisy-like than ever with their curved lashes. "What are you looking at?" she asked, becoming aware that her mother's gaze was fixed on the horizon.

Susanna drew her young daughter into her embrace but her eyes dropped no further than the boats putting out to sea. "They're going all over the lake," she murmured thankfully.

Eliza pulled away so that she too could see. "Has Abba gone fishing too? Where is he?"

For a moment Susanna could not answer her daughter but Eliza's need gave her the courage she required.

"He went fishing earlier – before the storm. We're not quite sure where his boat is now, so his friends are going to look for him."

"And then they'll all come home together?"

"Just the boat that finds him. I expect the others will stay on the lake to fish."

"My daddy will have the most fish," Eliza told Tamar. "He's the very best fisherman!"

Two burly men, soaked with spray, beached their boat and called to Susanna. "Has your Tobit returned yet?"

When she shook her head, the two men exchanged glances and one of them took a hesitant step nearer, his wet sandal sliding on the slimy shingle.

"Don't worry. I'm sure they will have had time to reach land before the wind became too strong. I expect they've been driven far onto the eastern shore."

"They? I thought Tobit went alone."

"No. He had a friend of his from Judea with him – that leper who came back with Melkiah."

"Joel?" Susanna and Tamar spoke simultaneously.

"That's right." Unwilling to become involved any further, the man turned back to his friend and a moment later they had left the beach.

Tamar felt strange, as she did sometimes when she had been too long in the burning sun of high summer. She could not understand her sudden weakness. She knew her father would be concerned to learn that his friend had sailed into danger, but there was no reason for her own nervous reaction.

"Are you all right?"

"Of course." But her mouth was dry and her voice low. Trying to give an appearance of composure, she smiled at Eliza. "Shall we give Mummy some of Keturah's scones?"

Eliza's eyes gleamed as she picked out two floury rounds from the basket and pressed them into Susanna's hands. She looked towards Tamar. "And you must have one too." A small grubby finger counted out the remaining scones. "One more for me and one for Snowy. That leaves three for Abba and Joel. Will they come soon?"

Susanna gave her attention to her daughter but could not meet her trusting eyes. "Why don't you go to your look-out and watch for them? Then you can tell us the moment they come in sight?"

"Yes, I will." She put her small arms around her mother's body, her head just reaching Susanna's waist and hugged her. Then, as if sensing that Tamar too needed consolation, she ran to embrace her.

Tamar bent down and kissed the uplifted face and brushed back wind-tangled curls. "Lambs don't like scones," she told her. "Perhaps you can find Snowy some clover instead?"

Eliza nodded. Followed by her four-legged friend, she set off for the brow of a nearby hillock overlooking the lake, one of her favourite haunts. From this vantage point she was a princess looking over her own lapis lazuli sea and all the boats on the lake belonged to her. She could summon them home whenever she wished.

"We will wait until Abba has a boat full of fish and then we will call him," she told Snowy who made no objection, his mouth being full of tender clover.

One by one the boats returned, without news of Tobit. Visibility on the lake was good now and even distant boats could be seen over the tranquil water. Several battered boats had been spotted on the perimeter of the lake but none of them belonged to the fishermen of Capernaum. Some large pieces of floating wreckage had been spotted but it seemed unlikely that any boat could have been totally destroyed so quickly.

Tamar could not bear to see her friend's growing anxiety and kept her own in check by finding practical things to do. She ran home and spoke to Melkiah who sent out both of his own boats to join the search and came to question Tobit's friends as one by one they returned to the beach.

Eliza remained alone on the hilltop and Tamar took her food and drink, and later found her fast asleep in the waning sun. She covered her tenderly, deeply grateful for the ignorance that was protecting the little girl from her mother's growing anguish.

"Give me your faith," she murmured to the sleeping child before walking away slowly, repeating to herself. "Tobit and Joel are safe. They *will* return."

However, there was no sign of the familiar fishing-boat and there was no sound but the mournful cry of seagulls swooping over the surface of the darkening sea.

"Wait here," Joel suggested. "Take some rest while I fetch help."

Tobit, leaning against a branch with his eyes half-closed, straightened immediately. "No. Susanna will be worrying. We haven't far to go now."

He stepped forward and stumbled along the uneven animal track under the trees, his gait that of a man too weary to choose his footfalls.

Joel too was exhausted but all his concern was for his friend. Tobit was holding his left arm across his chest awkwardly, his face drawn with pain, and the long trek around the lakeside was increasing his agony with every jolting step. Both men knew that Tobit's arm was broken and Joel could not help dwelling on the possible calamity beyond the present injury. Fishermen need strong arms to carry on their trade and there was no certainty that Tobit's arm would ever regain its full strength. Joel hoped fervently that the physician in Capernaum was skilled at setting broken bones. There were already sufficient cripples in Israel bearing witness to the inept ones.

There was blood on his own sandal but he was scarcely aware of the wound in his foot or the aching of his bruised ribs. His eyes pierced the way ahead, longing desperately to spot the brow of the hill that hid Capernaum from their sight. As the path widened, he put a supportive arm around his friend, careful not to add to his pain.

"Soon you'll have three women waiting on you – if you count Eliza."

Tobit managed a smile. "She'll insist on being counted! I won't lack for attention with her around!"

He lapsed back into his former exhausted silence then but Joel could see that the reminder of home had given the fisherman the added strength he needed to complete the journey. He thought gladly of the loving reception ahead of them, and beyond it to hours of much-needed rest.

He did not know that by the time they reached home, they would no longer be the centre of attention, and all thought of sleep would have to be postponed indefinitely.

They could see people grouped into circles, leaving them only to form ever-new patterns, like participants in some strange dance, but they were too far away to be able to hear their urgent discussions.

They walked towards them, too weary to hurry, their eyes alone expressing their relief, and Tobit was glad beyond measure when he recognised the slight figure of his wife. She cried out when she turned and caught sight of them and broke away from her neighbour to run to him.

Joel stepped aside tactfully and his eyes went past her to identify Abital, stumbling in Susanna's wake, and, beyond her, Tamar and her father.

Melkiah spoke for both of them. "We're so glad that you're safe. Where have you been all this time?"

Before Joel could reply, he heard an urgent shout from Tobit.

"His arm is broken," he explained, but then realised that Tobit's distress had not been caused by Susanna's fierce embrace. His friend's pain and tiredness had been set aside in the shock of the news he had just been given.

Joel was beside his friend in a moment. "What is it?"

Susanna's face was wet with tears and Tobit's good arm held her tightly. His eyes were searching the darkening horizon in desperation.

"It's Eliza," he said. "She's been missing for hours. They've searched everywhere and she's vanished as completely as the sun from the sky."

Chapter 19

"There is nothing anyone can do"

The sun was sinking into the lake. It was as if flame-coloured ropes had been laid across the surface of the sea and were being twisted so that every fibre could reflect its own brilliant shade. However, now that the two missing fishermen had returned, no one was interested in the lake with its robe of glory. All were gathered within earshot of the family beset with one misfortune after another.

Melkiah, realising that their presence was merely adding to the confusion, strode some paces away and called: "Anyone who wants to help, come this way."

The crowd responded immediately, eager to know how they could assist their friends.

Melkiah recognised an energetic youth and spoke to him first. "Harim, Tobit has been wounded. Will you fetch the physician as quickly as possible?" His keen eyes identified a fisherman and a farmer, who between them were familiar with the whole district surrounding Capernaum, and he named them aloud.

As they came to his side, he directed the assembly. "Will you tell Bani and Malachi where you have already looked for the missing child and they will send you to the places that have yet to be searched. Perhaps those who have to return to their houses will bring some lamps?"

"Son, you must go and rest."

Abital was plucking at Tobit's stained tunic but he resisted her with the last bit of his strength. "How can I possibly rest with Eliza missing? I'm sure I'll be able to find her. I know all her secret places."

It was obvious that Tobit was in great physical pain, so weary he could scarcely stand unaided, but his voice held the determination of a man who would die in the attempt to regain his priceless treasure.

Joel went to his side. "You're needed here. We'll search everywhere you suggest but it's important that Eliza should see you when she returns."

172

Tamar backed up Joel, pointing to the wooded slope with its wide view over the water where the young girl had kept her long vigil.

"She fell asleep waiting for you so we left her there, hoping you would have come back before it was time to wake her."

"When I went to fetch her, she'd gone," Susanna explained. "I wasn't worried for there were a hundred places she could have been." She clung to Tamar's hand fiercely. "But now we've looked in every one . . . "

Men and women were leaving the beach directed by Melkiah, Bani and Malachi and already the first lamps were bobbing jerkily in the dusk like giant fireflies.

Joel appealed to his friend. "Tell me where to search."

Thoughts ran round in Tobit's brain like a flock of sheep that refused to be rounded up and, knowing that he was beyond rational speech, Susanna took charge.

"There are enough people searching," she told Joel. "Come home with us. You're exhausted too."

Tamar, who had admired the way Joel had put aside his tiredness out of love for his friends, added her persuasion. "You will be of more help when you've had some refreshment and had your injuries bound."

Melkiah joined them as Abital brought a second oil-lamp into the main dwelling room. Tobit sat rigidly, one arm cradled in the other, his face haggard, his eyes wild. Melkiah went to sit beside him and listened intently to his confused suggestions of Eliza's whereabouts, and reassured him that each place was being searched.

Susanna and Tamar brought wine to the two survivors of the storm but found they were so worried that they had to be coaxed to drink.

"One of your friends will bring Eliza back soon," Melkiah encouraged. "While we're waiting, won't you tell us what happened?"

Joel, seizing the opportunity to distract Tobit from his suffering, hurried to obey.

"When the wind sprang up suddenly, we were beyond Bethsaida, heading north-east. We thought we'd be able to beach the boat before the sea become too violent, but the waves became like mountains in less time that it takes to unship a pair of oars and we could no longer tell which direction to take. Part of the mast broke off, the bow slewed, and a fair amount of the lake came into the boat to join us. Tobit rowed with the strength of Samson, and all I could do was to bale."

"And pray?"

"There wasn't time to pray." But Joel remembered how he had murmured the Messiah's name as the giant wave had rolled towards them.

Susanna was kneeling beside her husband, touching fingers clenched in pain. She was greatly comforted by his presence but her eyes spoke her shock as she listened to Joel's matter-of-fact account.

"We were already half-sinking when a wall of water left over from Noah's flood came to challenge us. We thought it would be a case of 'all Your billows have washed over me' but, rather than swallowing us, it lifted us up high like another ark and it seemed that we too were to be deposited on Mount Ararat. However, after an exhilarating ride, our water-chariot got bored with us and flung us onto the shore. To make quite sure that we stayed there, it threw about fifty thousand baths of foaming water over us . . ."

Abital disapproved of the way Joel was telling of the near-tragedy, and eyed him coldly. "The boat?" she enquired.

"It's safe," he confirmed. "Damaged, but safe."

He thought it unnecessary to tell of the way he and Tobit had sought each other fearfully the moment the wave had withdrawn sufficiently for them to breathe again. And only he knew the wonderful relief he had felt to see his half-drowned friend peering towards him, his hair and beard streaming with brown water. It was an added joy to discover Tobit's boat floating nearby: they had dragged it onto dry land and, knowing that it would need much repair before being seaworthy again, had concealed it under some bushes.

"But where have you *been* all this time?" Susanna's eyes were now on the drawn face of her husband. "The storm has been over for hours."

"We rested, waiting for it to blow itself out. We lay near the boat under some tamarisks – even though the gale seemed to be trying to tear them out by the roots. We were so tired that we went to sleep."

"With all that noise!"

"It wasn't the quietest of lullabies," Joel admitted. "But at least we weren't being tossed about on a sea of camel-humps! It seemed like Paradise to wake and find the lake as smooth as the water in a fountain."

"We knew we'd have to walk home but the track seemed to go on for ever," Tobit added, trying to smile at his wife and mother.

"Surely you could have found someone to bring you home by boat?" Melkiah objected.

"It was quite deserted where we were, and even when we reached Bethsaida there weren't any of the usual boats available. Most of them were drawn up high and others waterlogged or damaged. The northern shore took the brunt of the storm."

Joel added. "I wanted to borrow a donkey or mule-cart for Tobit but he insisted that it wouldn't take long to walk home." As he spoke, he realised that Tobit had been light-headed with pain and exhaustion and probably had no idea of how slow their progress had been.

Suddenly Harim walked through the open door, his eyes going straight to Melkiah. "I've brought Azariah."

He stepped aside and the tall physician bowed his head to enter the low doorway. He too addressed Melkiah.

"What may I do for you?" he asked, after greeting him.

Silently Melkiah indicated Tobit hunched over his broken arm and Azariah nodded and stepped to his side.

The physician was never summoned by poor people and did not know the fisherman but examined him with gentle competence. Deciding that the ill-lit position was inadequate for treating his patient, he strode to the adjoining kitchen area and called Tobit to sit under a window aperture on a bench against a smoke-darkened wall.

The women hurriedly transferred their two lamps to a nearby niche and were waved away imperiously. Azariah clapped his hands sharply and his servant appeared from outside, carrying a laden bag. He put it on the beaten-earth floor beside the physician and prepared to hand his master whatever was needed.

Azariah looked down on the disabled fisherman with sympathy. "You need strong arms, I know, but it's a simple break so it should mend well. There will be a moment's pain but once I've bound it, it won't be so uncomfortable."

He tipped some powder from a small leather bag into a cup and added some wine. "Drink this."

"I have to stay awake to see my daughter . . ."

"This is just to deaden the pain."

However, by the time the physician left the small house, Tobit was stretched out on his sleeping mat in a deep sleep.

"You, too," Melkiah commanded Joel, whose wounded foot had been tended by Abital. "You may think you're awake but you're talking in your sleep."

"It will be time enough to rest when Eliza has been found," Joel decided. "I'm sure we'll hear soon."

His confidence was rewarded, for the first news came soon after Azariah's departure. The sandal-maker's wife was too shy to enter Susanna's house in the presence of the important Melkiah and called her name timidly from outside. The young fisherman's wife ran to the doorway and drew Mary in eagerly.

"Has Eliza been found?"

"Not yet, but I think I know the way she went. Benjamin was climbing trees on the hill near Eliza and he spoke to her when she came to fetch her lamb."

Although Benjamin was only a year older than her daughter, Susanna knew that he was both observant and reliable so listened to Mary with almost joyful hope.

"They spoke of the fierceness of the storm," his mother continued. "And Benjamin told her that none of the fishing boats had been able to find Tobit's." Mary bit her lip at Susanna's reaction but went on resolutely. "He said perhaps the boat was at the bottom of the sea and that her father had had to swim to the shore."

Susanna tried to work out how her daughter would have reacted to such a suggestion. "But why didn't Eliza come to me? Where is she now?"

"Benjamin says she went to look for Tobit."

"Which way?"

"North, towards the mouth of the Jordan. She said that if he had to walk home, he would need some food, so she took him some scones."

Melkiah was already at the door. "Leave it to me. There are several different tracks and I'll make sure that they're all covered. She can't have gone far." He gave Susanna a final reassuring smile. "You'll have your daughter back within the hour."

He did not know that he would prove his own words to be true by bringing her home, nor that the sight of her would comfort no one.

✡   ✡   ✡

As Melkiah approached carrying the still form, Susanna's wail woke the sleeping Tobit. He rose awkwardly to his feet and stumbled into the adjoining room just as Melkiah was transferring Eliza into her mother's arms.

The shock restored Tobit to full consciousness and he pushed his way through the overcrowded room to his daughter's side. "She's not dead?"

"No, but she's been bitten by a snake. See her swollen arm?"

Even the poor light was sufficient to show Eliza's condition. Her pale face was streaked with perspiration and tears, her lips blue, and her dark curls looked as if they had been glued to her small scalp. As Tobit added his cry of anguish to Susanna's, Eliza's eyes opened, but there was scarcely time to see the dilated pupils before the purple lids closed again. Although she was moaning weakly, it was obvious that she had no idea where she was.

Melkiah had already left at a run to recall the physician but every laboured breath of the poisoned child had added years to the sorrowing faces of the watchers before the two men returned.

Azariah's face was grave as he examined the tiny girl who lay as unmoving as a sacrificed lamb in her mother's frantic grip. Spreading paralysis was making her colder moment by moment. Noticing the blood from a dagger cut on her wounded arm, the physician turned to Melkiah enquiringly.

"I tried to suck the poison out," he explained. "But I think that the snake must have bitten her many hours before I reached her."

Azariah nodded. "You were too late."

The words that each of them had dreaded had come at last, forcing them to face the unacceptable: Eliza was going to die.

"There must be something you can do!"

The physician looked round the ring of desperate faces and, fond though he was of his wealth, would have given a good portion of it to be able to reverse the dying process in the tiny girl.

He shook his head. "Her organs have ceased to function and there is nothing anyone can do." He spoke to Susanna, who was holding Eliza so fiercely that when the time came the angel of death would have to wrestle with her for the tiny soul. "She's not conscious of any pain. She will slip into death without any further suffering."

Azariah went away then, murmuring regretfully that he was needed elsewhere and the last faint hope disappeared with his withdrawal.

Tamar clung to her father's arm but his eyes were upon Joel.

"If only Jesus were here . . ."

Joel nodded grimly, sharing Melkiah's helplessness.

Tamar remembered that Jesus had brought Jairus' daughter, Mirjiam, back to life after Azariah had pronounced her dead, and understood the frustration that was torturing them. The two ex-lepers were convinced that if the Messiah were here his word would be enough to save Eliza.

Tobit and Susanna were huddled so closely over their daughters' still form that the dying child could no longer be seen. Outside the fisherman's dwelling, neighbours had reassembled, sharing a silent vigil that was broken only by an occasional whisper as different people came to find out what was happening.

Tamar's legs were trembling but she was incapable of any other movement. She felt as if she were Lot's wife turning into a pillar of salt and it seemed as if the others too were victims of the same spell.

She saw Abital sway and Joel reach out an arm to the old woman whose eyes never left the three who meant the world to her.

Eliza, Jesus. Eliza, Jesus. The names tumbled forward in Tamar's brain as repetitively as the waves breaking on the nearby shore. *If Jesus were here, Eliza would not die.* But he was far away, perhaps in Jerusalem, so why was the memory of His face and voice so insistent – and becoming stronger with every shallow breath she took? If only she hadn't resented her father and Joel for believing in him. Their faith had reminded her of her own wrong decision, but now it was vitally important to admit the truth that had been planted in her and had not died in spite of attempts to uproot it.

"Jesus' disciples cure people in his name."

She spoke the thought out loud, and again Melkiah and Joel exchanged glances. She looked from one to the other. "If they can do it, why can't you? You believe . . ."

"Simple believers cannnot work miracles."

It was Melkiah who had answered his daughter, but Joel had caught a spark of Tamar's wild hope. "It is the Most High himself who heals through the name of Jesus. If we were to use his name, perhaps the Almighty would have mercy on us."

And now Susanna and Tobit had raised heavy eyes, roused by the urgency of the discussion.

"Pray for Eliza," Susanna pleaded, and they did not know if she had understood their words or was asking them for the customary prayers for a dying soul. Melkiah had already sent someone to summon an elder from the synagogue, while suspecting that he would not hurry to concern himself with the mortal sickness of a poor fisherman's daughter.

Joel's eyes met Tobit's and he scarcely recognised him in defeat, wounded far more by this tragedy than the disaster which had overtaken him earlier that day. It helped Joel to make a decision. Like Tamar, he felt he could not stand by and watch Eliza die without even attempting to call on the only power that could save her.

"She's scarcely breathing," Abital wailed, and the words galvanised the cured lepers into acting as one.

They went straight to the motionless form and laid their hands gently upon her. Joel waited for Melkiah to speak but his eyes were closed and Joel felt urgently that it was necessary for them to speak their faith out loud.

"Most High Lord," he began desperately. "It is you who gave life to this little one. Do not take it away before she has had time to learn that she is your child. You have promised to answer all who call upon you in their distress, so, in the name of Jesus of Nazareth – whom we believe to be your son – we ask you to restore life and health to this little girl."

"Amen", Melkiah agreed quietly.

Tamar's tears prevented her from looking at them clearly; all she could see was a blurred image of her father's hand stroking the swollen arm and Joel with his head bowed over the unconscious small figure.

Abital was the first to react when Eliza gave a sudden yawn. The grandmother shrieked so loudly that Eliza opened her eyes in wide alarm. Colour returned to her face and she gripped her mother's hand with restored strength.

"What's wrong with Granny?" Bewildered to receive no reply, she looked round the unusually crowded room, her gaze returning to

Tobit's bandaged arm. "Have you hurt yourself, Abba? Is that why Granny is upset?"

She struggled out of her mother's arms and touched her father tenderly. "I will make you better." She pulled him down for a kiss before turning to survey the bemused company again. The contradiction of wide smiles and tears was beyond her experience and her small brow wrinkled in mystification.

"Praise to the Most High and his Messiah," Melkiah murmured, and his prayer was echoed by his listeners with the truest fervour they had ever shown.

Abital was examining the site of Eliza's wound and could find no more than a faint red mark on an arm that was already returning to its normal size.

"A snake bit me," the young girl remembered, and now her eyes were fearful. She held Tobit's hand tightly. "Snowy and I went to look for you. But we walked and walked and couldn't see you anywhere. Snowy was tired and hungry so we went under a tree to rest. I saw some lily-of-the-valley flowers in a hollow and thought Snowy might like some. But a snake came out and bit me . . ."

She was trembling now and hid her face in Tobit's tunic. "I ran away but my head felt funny so I lay down. Snowy cuddled beside me."

Tobit's good arm held her close to him as Melkiah told her. "Snowy saved you for he was easy to see in the dark."

Eliza smiled. "We're all home now. Did you catch lots of fish, Abba? I'm hungry!"

Suddenly the room was filled with laughter and everyone found that they could breathe normally again and began to move about purposefully.

But as Tamar, Melkiah and Joel made their farewells and went out into the dark night past the curious neighbours on the beach, they suspected that something had happened today that would change the life of the little fishing family forever.

What they did not know was that repercussions from the miraculous healing would drive the murderer in their midst to desperation, and put their own lives into grave danger.

Chapter 20

"Do you believe all the stories about him?"

Not a single word was spoken as they made their way home. Each walked apart from the others as if alone, and Tamar guessed that her father and Joel were giving silent prayers of thanksgiving for the miracle they had just witnessed.

She herself was far from tranquil. Cicadas were keeping up their unceasing chatter among the lush vegetation alongside their path, and the sound was as soothing as the caress of the waves against the shingle, but Tamar's state of mind was more in tune with the bats darting overhead in wild figures-of-eight.

I was wrong . . . Why didn't I admit that I'd made a mistake? . . . Why did I refuse to see what was before me so clearly? . . . Why did I let others influence me into making a wrong decision? . . . Why didn't I trust my father before all others? . . . What shall I do now? . . . Is it too late to change?

They walked in single file past a field of barley which was nearly ready for harvesting. Tamar could see no more than the nearest laden heads in the light of Melkiah's lantern but the scent of the ripening crop was familiar enough to enable her to picture the whole golden sweep of sun-enriched barley. She loved the land and everything that grew upon it, and had believed that her own life could be as unchanging as the seasons. She had been content simply to exist, rejoicing in all the beauties of creation, comforted by the unfailing rhythm of nature.

When they reached home they shared a simple meal but, still overawed by the power they had witnessed, had little inclination for conversation.

Tamar went up to her grandmother's room but stopped on the threshold when she found her father telling Sarah the events of the day.

"I thank God for the blessed conclusion," he admitted, "for I feel responsible for what happened to Eliza. If I had not given her a lamb, she wouldn't have started wandering further from home in search of pasture. A few weeks ago, she wouldn't have dreamt of going to look for her father."

Sarah reached for her son's hand. "Your gift was generous and you showed great faith today. How could the Most High not reward you?" There was new purpose in the lift of her head as she made a decision. "When you go to Jerusalem for the Passover, I shall go with you. I can wait no longer to hear one so powerful that a girl is brought from the brink of death simply through the invocation of his name."

Melkiah was surprised. "Even in a padded wagon it would be an uncomfortable journey for you, Mother."

"I'm coming! Even though I cannot see, I will be able to picture all that goes on. And Tamar will describe everything to me. She's so good."

Tamar slipped away unseen. She did not feel good and she did not deserve praise. She knew that Joel was in the scroll room and that Melkiah would join him there when he had finished his conversation with Sarah. She needed to talk to her father and wanted his undivided attention.

She sat by a narrow window watching the moon rise to reveal a cloudless sky until she heard her father's sandals slapping quietly on the tiled floor as he left her grandmother's room.

He smiled as she came to meet him. "I thought you were resting. You've had an anxious day."

"I'm not tired," she said, believing her restlessness to be energy. "Father, are you going on the lake tonight? May I come with you?"

Melkiah looked out of the window thoughtfully. "It's a clear night. Yes, come with me by all means. But it'll be an hour or two before the stars are visible."

Melkiah was as grateful as Tamar for the tranquillity of the silent lake as they launched the small boat in the third watch of the night.

"There's no wind. We won't use the sail."

He began to row strongly and the boat moved out across the water leaving scarcely a ripple. The moon had laid a silver trail across the jet surface, and Melkiah took their craft along it with effortless strokes.

Tamar could not see the end of the moon path because of the haze on the eastern shore of the lake, but it seemed to her that if they continued on their present course they would move on upwards into the clouds and glide among the stars. Everything seemed possible after what she had witnessed a few hours before.

Her father had stopped rowing and was allowing the boat to drift while he lay back on the oars and gazed upwards.

"Do you remember the name of the stars?"

Tamar's eyes moved wonderingly across the vault of Heaven. It was as if the Most High had flung a handful of jewels upon the earth but they had been stayed by some invisible net. She gazed at an occasional brilliant star, identified the Pole Star, and tried to trace once-familiar patterns among the northern constellations.

"I remember many of the names you taught me but there was no one to remind me which star was which. All I can recognise now is those stars looking like a plough which you told me were part of Ursa Major, and Capella because it is so bright." She turned and looked south. "Is that Orion just above the horizon, and the twins, Castor and Pollux, high up there?"

"You've remembered well. I'll teach you again, if you like."

"I would like, but there are other things I want to ask you tonight."

They were drifting timelessly in a boat on a silver lake under a sky of diamonds. Tamar knew now that she could take as long as she liked to find the words she needed to explain her confusion. Peace enfolded them like a cloak as she began.

"Father, did you believe that Jesus was the Messiah before he healed you? And, if so, where did your faith in him come from – if you hadn't even met him?"

"A leper he had cured came to us often and told us many of his wise words. He spoke of his compassionate deeds too, and everything we heard convinced us that he is truly the Son of the Most High."

"Do you believe all the stories about him? That he walked on this sea, and that a star as bright as the moon appeared in the heavens on the night he was born? Father, how can he be the Son of God if he was born like any other baby? It would be easier to believe in him if he had appeared suddenly in the sky and fallen to earth, like one of the Greek gods."

"There are some Pharisees who would agree with you! They still contend that the true Messiah will be preceded by sensational signs in the heavens: flaming swords . . . chariots of fire . . . heavenly armies marching across the sky . . ."

"Tamar, if Jesus were solely divine, perhaps he would have come as you suggested, but it seems that he wanted to be human too. It was his plan to be born as the Man-God. As man, he walks the earth in poverty and untiring service of all those in need; as God, he can do as he wishes: walk on water; command winds, waves and fire; multiply food; raise the dead . . ."

"If he can do anything, why doesn't he destroy his enemies with blazing fire, like Elijah did?"

"Why indeed! Perhaps he is giving them more time to repent."

"I need to repent," Tamar said in a low voice. "Father, two years ago, I went to listen to Jesus. He was speaking on the shore by the fishermen's beach. His face seemed to shine like an angel and his eyes were so full of love that nobody could be afraid of him. His words were simple, yet seemed to be telling truths that I had always known. Everything he said was enthralling and I wanted to go on listening to him for ever. When he got into Simon's boat and went away, he seemed to take my heart with him."

There was a sudden splash as a fish, drawn to the surface of the lake by the moon, dived under the boat, but Tamar was reliving the past and was quite unaware of it.

"What happened next?" Melkiah prompted gently.

"As I went home, my body was on fire and the ground seemed to be shaking beneath my feet. I found it difficult to keep my balance and had to cling on to Asher's arm. It was fortunate for me that he had come to find me, though I was sorry that he was not in time to hear Jesus speak.

"I went to bed and was ill for over two weeks. I heard Jesus' voice over and over again in my head, and it made me happy. I didn't even mind being ill. Then Asher came to me and told me that it was Jesus who had caused my illness. He said that he was possessed by devils and had bewitched me with his evil powers. I didn't want to believe it but Asher consulted other people about what had happened to me and they all said the same thing." Tamar looked towards her father's alert figure. "I knew I had been enchanted, so thought it must be true that Jesus was demon-possessed. And so I never went to listen to him again, and continued to believe that he was an impostor – until you and Joel came home . . ."

"Even then you didn't want to accept the miracle of our healing."

"No. I couldn't believe that so many other people could be wrong about Jesus being a false Messiah: Asher, Zelek, Ezra, and most of the elders and men of great learning." She added rather defensively. "Even Tobit warned me to have nothing to do with him."

"What about Susanna and Miriam?"

"Susanna was impressed by him but Tobit said that it was dangerous to support a man who was making so many powerful enemies. He said that he would only believe in a Messiah who had the support of all the leaders of Israel.

"Miriam? She wanted to go and listen to Jesus but Ishmael forbade it. He certainly does not believe that Jesus of Nazareth is the Son of the living God!"

Moonlight shone softly on Tamar's face, but the rest of her was no more than a dark silhouette outlined by her veil. Melkiah studied her thoughtfully.

"Tell me: on the day you went to listen to Jesus, did you feel ill before you left home?"

Tamar was struck by realisation. "Yes! My head ached and I felt weak, but I was determined to go and hear the prophet that everyone was talking about." She looked at her father despairingly. "Jesus does not harm people, but heals them! How could I have been so foolish?" After a moment, she asked. "What can I do? Should I make a sin-offering?"

"If you wish. In the meantime, stop blaming yourself! You were badly advised and came to a wrong conclusion, but it was your faith that helped bring about Eliza's healing. I believe that the one who healed her would tell you that you were forgiven the moment you admitted your fault. Let your mind be at peace."

"Peace . . ." The joy that suddenly engulfed Tamar was even greater than that she had felt when Eliza had returned from the brink of death. Yes, the Most High had forgiven her and now she was free to follow the Messiah into the Kingdom of Love. She no longer had to wrestle with the conflicting thoughts that had tormented her ever since her father had been restored to her. Now they were in accord again and she could begin to grow and learn how to become the person the Most High wanted her to be.

"I wish Jesus were here," she murmured.

Melkiah, filled with deep thankfulness, pointed out. "Jesus is like the Pole Star. Once we can identify him, everything else falls into place. The world will never be without his presence or his power again."

It was easy to believe such shining words with the still water reflecting a choir of stars all singing "He made me." Yes, now that the Son of the Creator had come, the world would change and all evil would be turned to good.

Melkiah began to row again, intoning a psalm of praise, and for the first time Tamar found that the words expressed exactly what was in her heart.

Later, as they walked back to the house, she suggested: "Why don't you and Joel pray over Granna and take her blindness away?"

Melkiah shook his head. "I do not think it would be right. Jesus has given the power to work miracles to his apostles to use on their preaching missions but the time has not yet come for him to trust every believer with such power."

"But Eliza . . ."

"The Most High had pity on her. He saw our desperation and acted lovingly. But it would be presumptuous of us to expect him to answer us in a different situation." As they entered the house, he consoled Tamar. "Your grandmother is determined to come to Jerusalem for the Passover. We can be sure of finding Jesus there and we'll ask him then to restore her sight. She's waited so long. She'll be patient for another week or two."

Passover in Jerusalem! Travelling with the people she loved best to the most exciting place in the world. Seeing the magnificent Temple and Jesus! And her grandmother healed!

One elated thought after another kept Tamar from sleeping in the few hours until dawn. The prophesied King had come – to claim his Kingdom – and she would see miracles of love happening on every side.

She dozed only as the birds began their daily song of praise to their Creator, but she rose shortly afterwards and went to join them with a joyous heart.

She ran through the archway into the lakeside garden, laughing as dew-laden leaves shared their bounty with her. It was cool at this early hour but the pleasant warmth of Adar would soon become the strong heat of Nisan which would ripen the first fruits in time for the festival.

The sun was just rising above the horizon of the lake, spreading a shower of rose petals across the surface of the sea, and, above the misted grey and lilac curves of the distant hills, the clouds were like innocent lambs frolicking in the pink and blue sky. She wondered how such tranquillity could follow yesterday's storm.

Yet there were signs of the recent tempest in broken twigs and ragged leaves and she nearly tripped over a branch that had been torn from a pomegranate tree.

"It was rotten. It needed to come down," a voice behind her said.

She turned to smile at Asher. "Yes. Even storms do some good," she agreed. Her eyes returned to the horizon. "Look at the light on those hills! The rays are coming straight from Heaven."

Asher returned her smile but there was amusement in his dark eyes. "You used to say Heaven was here, where we live."

"It's everywhere now because the Messiah has come! Did you hear about Eliza being healed when Joel prayed in the name of Jesus?"

"I heard." Realising that Tamar needed more enthusiasm than this, Asher added. "I'm pleased for you because I know how fond you are of the little girl."

"I couldn't have borne it for Tobit and Susanna if she had died," Tamar told him, "but can't you see the real reason for my joy? You and I didn't know who Jesus was, but now we've had proof that we can believe in him as the Messiah. Doesn't it make you gloriously happy?"

Asher wandered towards the lake and Tamar followed him, rejoicing in the contrast of the red flowering rushes against the white sea pancratiums. Asher had found another fallen branch and began to tug it higher up the beach.

"I'm pleased about Eliza," he repeated, "but another miracle doesn't change anything. No one disputes that the Nazarene has strange powers. It will be time enough to rejoice when the Sanhedrin pronounce him to be the long-awaited Messiah."

Tamar had been marvelling at the crystal-clear reflections of the reeds growing at the water's edge, but Asher's words made her look into the sky. She half-expected to see a dark cloud overhead but the undimmed brilliance made her realise the real reason for the impression of a sudden shadow. Asher, her friend, her brother, had called Jesus "The Nazarene" as contemptuously as any Pharisee. He could not have shown his indifference or disbelief more clearly.

There were tears in Tamar's eyes as she watched Asher lift the rotten bough into his arms and walk away from her. She ran after him.

"Asher, please don't wait until then. You yourself have spoken of the corruption among the Rabbis and Scribes in Jerusalem. They will be the last to recognise Jesus for who he is." She held the branch to keep him still as she pleaded. "Talk to my father. Read the prophets with him, like you used to do. I want to hear them too now. Shall we learn together?"

Asher was torn, not knowing how to resist the young girl whose pleading eyes and graceful figure promised many hidden delights. To ensure that he would be the man who would eventually discover them, he ought to take this opportunity to be in her company more often. On the other hand, if he showed interest in resuming his study of the Sacred Scrolls with Melkiah, before he knew it he'd be attending the weekday meetings at the synagogue as well as the mandatory Sabbath ceremonies. He dared not admit that there were many things he'd prefer to do rather than spend time on spiritual discussions, which to him seemed to achieve less than a donkey plodding around a waterwheel.

"Joel has such faith, he will help us," Tamar urged.

Her words spurred Asher into the opposite direction. "Is he not going home soon?" he demanded.

Tamar was startled. "He lives here now!"

"They say he's returning to Bethany at Passover." He turned so suddenly that a twig from the branch he was carrying grazed Tamar's face. "You will be glad. You wanted your father to yourself."

"Yes, but . . ." She was disconcerted for Joel was somehow part of her discovery of the Messiah and she had been counting on his faith to help her own grow.

Asher dropped one end of the branch onto the ground, sending a family of ducklings scurrying for cover. "Joel's parents will be glad to see him, but they'll not want an unmarried son. They'll soon find a wife for him."

Tamar did not understand why Asher was looking at her so keenly, nor what comment he expected from her. "Joel will make a good husband," she ventured. *But we will never see him if he lives so far away.*

She started when a voice spoke from behind them.

"Would you like some help with that?"

Joel himself had come through the arch and was indicating the heavy bough as he approached.

Asher nodded. "I'm taking it to the wood store."

Tamar fell in beside Joel as he lifted the other end of the branch.

"Asher says you're going home to Bethany soon?" Her voice made it into a question.

Joel smiled good-humouredly. "It seems that everyone knows my plans before I do!"

"Will you stay in Bethany?" Tamar pursued.

"That depends."

On many things, he thought. On whether I have finished the work I have to do here; on the situation with Rhoda at home; on Jesus' answer when I ask him if he will allow me to become his disciple . . .

But Asher, seeing the affection in Tamar's eyes as she returned Joel's smile, interpreted his reply as meaning that his future lay in Tamar's keeping.

After the fallen branch had been taken to the wood store, Asher watched the others as they walked away from him, conversing easily. After the usual morning prayers led by Melkiah, they would breakfast together, and doubtless spend the rest of the day extolling the wonders of the prophet from Nazareth.

His eyes gleamed disdainfully as he turned away to fetch a saw and axe. Studying and praying were all very well for those who had nothing better to do.

Once Tamar had followed him around, admiring his growing strength, and had appreciated his skill and dedication. She had since been influenced by other people. But he, who knew her better than anyone, would continue to watch over her. He would think of a way to protect her from both Jesus of Nazareth and Joel of Shallum.

✡   ✡   ✡

As Asher had surmised, Melkiah, Joel and Tamar had spent the entire morning speaking of yesterday's miracle and all the other wonders the Messiah was achieving in bodies and souls throughout Israel.

Sarah had listened to them with great joy, and a new personal hope had been born from their combined faith. She had not expected to regain her sight and had not sought to do so while her son yet remained a leper. She had joined her own misfortune to Melkiah's like the other half of a sacrifice made to the Most High, and had been glad to offer it during her years of agony over her son's fate. But today, when Melkiah and Tamar had pressed her hands fervently as if to transfuse their own hope, she had begun to believe that a miracle could happen for her too.

She sat in her herb garden, feeling the warmth of the sun on her face and absorbing it into her being as contentedly as a butterfly with open wings. In another month it would be too hot to sit here until later in the afternoon when the tree's shade would protect her, but on this day she was in her Garden of Eden. She inhaled air fragrant with a thousand perfumes and listened to a host of birds, each singing his own song with a complete disregard for that of his rival.

Tamar and Melkiah had brought her here before going to see Jairus and Mirjiam. They would return in time for the usual Sabbath preparations and in the meantime Sarah felt peace so strong it was almost tangible. She needed no sight to appreciate the beauty around her, as she had explained to Tamar earlier.

"Be patient, my dear. The Most High knows my condition and he will heal me when I have need of my sight again. I am content to wait upon his will."

Now, listening to distant dove lullabies, she drifted into sleep and the dream she would remember all her life. She saw herself sitting on the same bench with the herbs and singing birds all around her, and there was a young man walking towards her. He was tall, with rich hair which glinted gold in the sunshine and his robes shone with the purity of a white pebble in a crystal stream. He sat beside her and took her hand and she felt him touch her closed eyelids.

And even in the dream she marvelled for how could she have seen him with her eyes shut?

"Sarah." The voice was gentle, yet commanding. "Look at me."

A longing to behold one with such a loving voice drew her eyelids open and she saw. But even as she focused upon the smiling face, and was drawn into the depths of brilliant, sapphire eyes, his form faded and seemed to turn into mist. At first she could see the trees of the vineyard through his body but then, before she had time to draw another breath, there was no one there at all.

"Jesus," she murmured, and smiled in her sleep. Now she too had seen the Messiah. He had come to promise her a miracle, and when it happened she would be able to look upon the faces of her family again.

And she would be able to tend and pick her herbs as before; walk among the vines to check their progress, and watch the jewel-bright birds whose optimistic songs had lifted her spirits so often.

A familiar musical humming overhead told her that a line of swans were passing by and she opened her eyes – and saw. Saw the rhythmic movement of their powerful wings, saw the flight formation remaining true during a change of leader, saw the bright white feathers against the sapphire pavement of the heavens.

In wonder, she lowered her gaze to the delicate leaves of the nearby acacia tree cradling their rosettes of blue petals, and on to the flowering herb bushes all around her, and finally down to the beaten earth path at her feet. A tiny beetle with a shiny green shell was approaching her sandaled feet fearlessly; a sprig of broken-off dill lay crushed on the ground, its yellow flowers shrivelling but still bright.

Was she still dreaming? Never before had she seen every detail of her surroundings with such clarity. She looked down at her hands, shocked to see their wrinkles, and smoothed the folds of her favourite green tunic, noticing how much it had faded since she had last seen it.

The truth hit her then like a sudden shower of rain. *This was no waking dream, no wishful vision. Her sight had been restored. After eight long years, she could see again!* She began to tremble, but even as the shock hit her, her eyes were gazing about her in awe.

She saw a bee hovering over the blue cummin flowers, trying to decide which to enter first; she saw a butterfly fluttering towards the walls of her house and up over the high terrace; she saw the fresh green of new growth in the vineyard; she saw a man bending over the old well unaware of a second man coming to join him; she saw the loveliest sight on earth – the lapis lazuli of the lake of life-giving water that was Gennesaret.

"Why?" she whispered. "Lord God, why have you given me this blessing now? I was going to Jerusalem to see your Messiah . . . Instead, you have sent him to me in my own garden. I don't understand, but I will praise you for this as long as I live."

With trembling legs, she stood and began to walk through her herbs towards the house, her heartbeat rapid, her open eyes filled with wonder.

And she gave no thought to the words she had spoken to Tamar but a short while before.

Chapter 21

"Danger!"

"When you walk, the Law will guide you in this world. When you lie down, it will watch over you in the grave. When you awake, it will converse with you in the life to come."

Philip, a visiting Rabbi, was expounding on the Torah and the synagogue held many attentive listeners, but Melkiah had lost his concentration. Only Eli was deaf to the teaching, having as usual fallen asleep at the Sabbath gathering. The more learned the discourse, the sooner his eyelids began to close. Philip continued to weave the traditional interpetations together in a scholarly way but Melkiah heard no more than an occasional phrase, having other things on his mind.

Firstly, he could not help wondering where Joel was. After spending the afternoon with Jairus, Melkiah had come directly to the synagogue where he had expected to meet his guest. Joel had told him that he was going to see his fisher friends on the shore and he was unlikely to have gone on anywhere else with the start of the Sabbath so near. He had never failed to attend the first evening gathering on the Sabbath so Melkiah hoped that no new calamity had arisen to keep him away now.

Another reason for Melkiah's failure to give his full consideration to the speaker was his awareness that something was going on in the women's gallery. Melkiah's seat on the platform among the other leading citizens faced the Ark where the scrolls of the Law were kept but even without turning his head he was conscious of whispering and movement among the women in the gallery above.

A swift glance showed nothing untoward to explain the unusual animation among them but, at the very moment of turning away, he caught sight of Tamar. She looked jubilant, and she was not the only woman with a wide smile on her face. It seemed that the focus of attention was upon his mother and daughter and, even as he decided this, he saw Sarah whispering something to her neighbour. That she should behave so! He averted his head, disconcerted yet intrigued.

He had returned Tobit's smile on his way to his own seat earlier and wondered now if yesterday's miracle was the reason for the women's unusual behaviour. Yet, if this were so, would not he himself be attracting some scrutiny? He had not, of course, expected any reference to Eliza's healing from his peers; the life or death of a fisherman's child held no interest for them.

It was not until the final reading from the prophets had concluded the service that he received a totally unexpected and unbelievably joyful answer to the second mystery.

As he went to rejoin Sarah and Tamar, his mother broke away from a knot of excited friends and came towards him. She walked confidently with her head held high and smiled straight into his eyes and, without a word being spoken, he knew what had happened to her.

In spite of Joel's unexplained absence, it was the most joyous Sabbath celebration since Melkiah's return home. The table was laid with the best linen, and the lamps and candlesticks shone as brightly as their flames – Sarah's restored eyesight had seen to that! Garlands of flowers and leaves decorated the room as for a festival and even the servants bringing in the plaited bread, leeks, cucumbers, roast lamb, and the best wine, sparkled with the excitement that had come upon the whole household.

Asher, who had been as stunned as any of them to meet Sarah's seeing eyes, congratulated her warmly, and won her heart anew with his dazzling smile and tender glances from his long-lashed dark eyes.

Melkiah's disquiet about Joel's absence returned when darkness fell. He dispatched Asher to question every man who had been working on his land that day, and to arrange for every cubit of the property to be searched in case his friend lay injured and helpless in some hidden corner.

As the men went in different directions, each carrying a lantern, Tamar watched with a feeling of unreality. It was almost a repetition of what had happened only two days before, but surely such a search was unnecessary now? This morning Joel had been in good spirits and they had said farewell with the casualness of friends who will meet again before an hour or two had passed. She could not believe that anything was wrong. Joel had gone somewhere unexpectedly and would return any moment, apologising for having caused any concern. Quite likely he had been walking on the hills he loved so much.

As she looked towards their dark silhouette, foreboding entered her mind and remained like a hovering vulture. Perhaps, high above the village, Joel was lying somewhere with a broken leg and, if this were the case, he would not be found for a day or two. Without definite knowledge, her father would not allow his men to go further than the permitted three-quarters of a mile on the Sabbath. So, if Joel had had an accident, he would remain alone in increasing pain until he died of exposure.

Tamar went to her grandmother's room but found it empty.

"Now she can see again, she wants to help search for Joel," Eglah told her.

Tamar threw on a light mantle, left the house, and was scarcely through the main gate before she spotted her grandmother.

"I've looked among the trees and behind the walls and hedges," Sarah said breathlessly as Tamar came to join her.

"There are men enough to search, Granna," Tamar told her, seeing that she was near exhaustion. "Let's return to the house and wait for news."

"No. I want to go right round the house. I'm fond of that young man and I've yet to look upon his face."

Tamar could see that her grandmother's legs were shaky and put her arm around her to give her some support, but even so their progress to the flower garden by the lake was slow. The fragrance of myrtle and jasmine wafted to them strongly as Sarah paused for a moment to recover her breath. Both of them peered keenly towards the expanse of dark water but they knew they would see little until the moon rose.

Wishing they could borrow the night-vision of an owl, they moved on slowly and turned the second corner past some fig trees, the old well, and the vineyard.

As they reached the herb garden, Tamar had ceased to worry about Joel and was more concerned about her grandmother.

"Please come and rest now."

Sarah resisted Tamar's entreaty and the tug on her arm and stood quite still gazing back towards the lake.

"Wait." There was something in her voice that made Tamar keep silent until her grandmother spoke again. "This afternoon, when the Messiah came to me in a dream and opened my eyes, I looked around and marvelled at many beautiful things. But, I remember now, I also saw two men, over there by the old well. One seemed to be peering into it."

"Who were they? Where did they go?"

"I don't know. I've never seen Joel, and there are few people I would recognise after all this time."

"Where did they go?" Tamar repeated.

Sarah shook her head. "I didn't watch them. I only saw them for a moment before I returned to the house."

"I expect it was just two of our labourers but if you promise to go and rest immediately, I'll ask Asher which men were working on this side of the house today."

Tamar found him with her father in the stables but when she told them what Sarah had seen earlier, Asher shrugged.

"It's unlikely to be important. No one was working anywhere near the vineyard this afternoon. Perhaps Kenturah sent Dan to the kitchen garden and he had a chat with a friend before returning with the vegetables she wanted."

"Granna says that one man was bending over the well."

"And Dan couldn't resist going over to see what he was doing," Melkiah deduced. "It's easy enough to check. Asher, go and talk to Kenturah and Dan. Tamar, come with me."

Asher sped off with the energy of youth, while father and daughter walked around the house back to the herb garden and beyond. They came to the old well and Tamar set her lantern upon the heavy wood cover.

"Why would anyone peer over this?" she wondered. "There's nothing to see."

Melkiah was examining the edge of the cover with a frown. "Unless the top had been set aside. It would be interesting to look down into the shaft for, as you know, this well was in use for hundreds of years before my father sank the new one in the courtyard." He ran his finger thoughtfully along the rim where wood met stone. "There *is* something different. Hold the lantern closer."

As Tamar complied, he became certain that his instinct was right. "This cover has been moved very recently. Can you see where a knife or tool has gouged the lichen that has kept the lid on so securely all these years?"

"Joel?" Tamar asked doubtfully.

"I can't believe that he would have removed the cover but if he saw the well open for the first time he would almost certainly have been interested enough to take a look. And if he had leant too far . . ."

"He'd have fallen in! Then, without realising what had happened, someone else put the well-cover back on . . ."

"It's more likely that he would have been pushed in deliberately," Melkiah pointed out. "Remember, Mother saw *two* men. It's unlikely that the second man neither saw Joel fall, nor heard his cry for help."

"Unless Joel was unconscious."

Or dead. But neither of them would admit those words to their minds.

Melkiah shouted to three men with lanterns who had just turned the corner and as they approached at a run said quietly to Tamar. "I know it seems unlikely that Joel is in the well but the fact remains that he's missing, and I can't think of any good reason why the well-cover should have been removed."

Tamar felt so weak that she leant against the trunk of a stout fig tree while the four men moved the thick wooden cover off the well.

"I can't see anything," one of the men muttered. "How deep is it?"

"I'll find out," Saul offered. "There are crevices between the stones. I can climb down easily."

Melkiah knew that the stripling was indeed very agile but he shook his head. "The curved slabs don't go all the way down; most of the shaft has been cut out of rock. You'll need a rope."

Another man whom Tamar could not recognise in the dark ran to get one and returned very quickly, followed by other members of the search party he had met on his way to the storeroom.

It needed the strength of all the men to take the strain of the rope while Saul was lowered into the wide stone well with a small lantern tied to his belt. The air from the shaft was cold and dank and none of the men had any desire to change places with him.

Asher came running up and, realising what was happening, added his weight to the end of the rope. A brief conversation with Melkiah elicited that he knew nothing about the well-cover being moved earlier and could think of no one who would have done such a thing.

There was a shouted exclamation from inside the well but it was too muffled to distinguish any words. The rope had gone slack so Melkiah, realising that Saul must be at the bottom of the well, leant over the edge.

"Be careful, Father," Tamar implored, but Melkiah was listening intently to the echoing message from deep below him.

"Joel *is* there," he told the others. "He's badly hurt and Saul doesn't know if he's still breathing."

The men exchanged fearful glances but Melkiah knew that there was no time to give in to despair.

"We'll need a blanket and more ropes. Saul will have to tie Joel securely if we're to get him up."

Tamar wanted to protest but realised that there was no other way. Nightmares do not go away when one cannot bear them.

It seemed an age before the injured man was drawn to the surface and placed gently on the ground beside the well. Tamar, who had been supporting Sarah who had joined them the moment she heard the news, pulled herself free and fell onto her knees beside the unconscious man.

"He's still breathing," Melkiah discovered with deep thankfulness.

However, Tamar could see little sign of life. The only visible part of the blanketed form was Joel's face and in the poor light of two oil lamps it was difficult to recognise the healthy young man she knew. Pale as a corpse, his shrivelled skin was streaked with a network of dried blood and Tamar reached out to him in consternation.

"He's as cold as ice!"

Melkiah was more concerned with the huge swelling he had discovered on the back of Joel's head and the blood clots congealing in his hair.

Sarah knelt stiffly and felt his faint pulse. "He mustn't stay outside for another moment. The cool night air is more dangerous to him than his injury." She rose to her feet with difficulty, helped by Asher, and turned to him with uncharacteristic brusqueness. "Bring a litter as quickly as possible."

When he had merged with the darkness, Melkiah turned to his mother. "Should we send for a physician?"

Sarah understood that the question referred to the Sabbath regulation that a doctor could only be sent for if life was in danger, and she nodded without hesitation.

Tamar could not take her eyes off the still face. "He's scarcely breathing! Granna, we've got to do something!"

"The litter will soon be here," Sarah told her. "Once Joel is warm again, he'll stand a chance."

Saul, who had climbed into the well so readily, helped Asher lift Joel onto the sheepskin-covered plank of wood. Their movements were gentle but even so it brought a groan from the unconscious man.

"He's in great pain!" Tamar whispered, and although her words were low, Joel opened his eyes and looked towards her.

"Joel! Can you hear me?" Melkiah walked beside the improvised stretcher as it moved off. "Who did this to you?"

Joel was in a private world of darkness and echoing voices but the urgency of the question forced an answer from him.

"I don't know . . ." The words were so faint that Melkiah read them on his lips rather than heard them. Joel's eyes closed then and only opened again just before the physician arrived.

As Saul and Asher transferred Joel still wrapped in the blanket onto his own bed, he spoke one further word.

"Danger," he said quite clearly, and then his body began to shake with the chill that had pervaded his flesh and blood and threatened to sweep him along the river of death.

Azariah did not spend long examining the swelling on the back of Joel's head. "A vicious blow, but not enough to kill him," he decided. "However, there could be worse damage elsewhere on his body."

Sarah and Melkiah watched as the tall physician ran his hands gently over Joel's body, pausing frequently as if to receive the message his fingers were giving him, his eyes half-closed, his nostrils flaring as if on the verge of some important discovery. When he lifted the legs, one by one, the unconscious man moaned and Azariah spent some time examining his back. Finally, he checked the balm-sprayed bandage on his patient's head, rearranged the warm blanket and gave his verdict to the anxious watchers.

"I cannot find any major injuries: there are no broken bones and the bruises on his ribs could well be the result of Thursday's disastrous fishing expedition. As I told you, his head wound was not caused by being dropped into the well. It will throb for a few days but it is not serious and it will heal. There could be a problem with his back: such a fall will have jarred his spine badly. Until he's fully conscious, we won't know if he will be able to walk again." He nodded to Sarah. "He's in some pain so I'll leave you something to administer when he's able to swallow."

He knew that there was no need to remind Sarah to keep the patient warm for he had discovered wrapped hot bricks in the bed, and knew too that she was more than capable of dressing his wounds.

"Thank you for coming on the Sabbath. We were afraid for his life."

Azariah returned his attention to Melkiah. "If this young man had spent another hour in the well, you would be summoning the mourners by now."

He laughed with rare humility. "I don't know why you call upon me when you seem to do very well without me. I told Sarah that she would never see again, and was certain that the fisherman's daughter would die, but in each case the impossible has happened. Doubtless Joel will come running to meet me tomorrow! I wish I could work such miracles!"

"There is only one in Israel with such power," Melkiah began, but Azariah had no intention of becoming involved in a discussion about the controversial prophet, and soon took his leave.

Melkiah, shocked by what had happened to his friend while under the protection of his hospitality, was determined that Joel should not be left alone, even for a moment. He asked the others to join him in the patient's room and they came readily, in various stages of fear, sorrow and frustrated anger.

Sarah and Tamar sat on either side of Joel's bed, like two guardian angels, while Asher leant against the wall, his eyes upon the slight rise and fall of Joel's chest under the warm blanket.

Melkiah took command. "There's no point in searching the grounds now," he began. "Joel must have been attacked many hours ago. I'll get the authorities onto it after the Sabbath." His voice indicated that this would be a formality from which he anticipated no result so that the wait until the following evening when the Sabbath ended, would be of little importance.

"What we can do, is try to discover for ourselves the identity of Joel's would-be-murderer."

Tamar pressed her hands together so firmly that her knuckles went white while Sarah reached out to caress the cheek of the unconscious man.

"In the meantime, we need to guard him." Melkiah's voice was matter-of-fact, but his eyes were formidable.

"I'll watch over him," Asher offered. "I promise you that no one will get past me!"

Melkiah almost smiled at the youth's confidence but the contrast between his energy and Joel's still form was too marked.

"We'll sort out something," he agreed, "but first let's see if we can find out of whom we should be wary. Tamar, can you think of anyone with a grudge against him?"

Tamar shook her head, startled. "He has made many friends in Capernaum. Surely no one who tries to help people has enemies?"

Melkiah's eyes met Sarah's and a slight shake of her head told him that this was not the time to disillusion the young girl.

Tamar had not missed the silent exchange and thought more deeply.

"Perhaps Sadoc . . ." she murmured. Seeing that there was no comprehension in her companions at the name of the self-important Pharisee, she realised that her friend's secret could no longer be kept. "Ishmael was going to divorce Miriam and marry Sadoc's sister," she explained. "I don't know what Joel said to Ishmael but it made him change his mind."

There was a silence while Melkiah pictured the proud Pharisee's frustration when prevented from giving his sister in marriage to his wealthy friend, and Tamar tried to imagine Sadoc creeping through the vineyard to kill the man who had thwarted him.

In her mind's eye, she could see him very clearly: people were standing back respectfully as the richly-dressed Pharisee passed by. The blue fringes were long on his deep-hemmed robe, his head-dress ornate, and the sharp nose on his haughty face seemed to be attached to the sky by some invisible thread.

She smiled inwardly at the thought, realising that nothing on earth would cause Sadoc to stoop to acting like one of the common criminals whom he despised as being less than the dust beneath his feet.

"I shouldn't have spoken. It was foolish of me."

"You're doing exactly what I asked," Melkiah reassured. "I want each of you to suggest anyone who could have even the slightest grudge against Joel, however unlikely the idea seems to you. I cannot see Sadoc acting like an assassin, but it's not impossible that he should have hired someone else to dispose of someone who had incurred his enmity. I saw him once when a neighbour had cheated him of acquiring some land he had set his heart on and his rage was out of all proportion to the offence.

Melkiah observed Sarah's compassion for their guest. "Mother, you've been out of contact with others for so long, I don't suppose that you have any suggestions?"

He saw immediately that a name had come to her – saw too that she was reluctant to speak it. He went over to her.

"Mother, it is essential that we should discover the identity of the man who wants Joel dead. Whatever name, or names, you suggest will go no further than these four walls. Please share your thoughts with us."

Sarah whispered. "Ezra was murdered."

"Do you think there's a connection? That the same man attacked Joel?"

Sarah turned her head away, and only Tamar saw the tears in her eyes. "No. I mean Zelek and his other sons have never relinquished the idea that Joel killed Ezra. I know, for Azubah speaks very freely in her grief. Perhaps they want him to be guilty as he makes no secret of his belief in the Messiah. Also . . ."

"Go on, Mother. We mustn't hold anything back from each other now."

"I heard Levi and Jonah talking of Joel when I went to visit their mother last week. They believe that he is here to marry Tamar and to become your heir."

Tamar felt hot enough to suffocate but Melkiah was nodding thoughtfully. "Zelek was keen to share my wealth. Perhaps he thinks that in time one of his other sons . . ." Although his gaze was upon his mother, his mind was considering his neighbour. "He would never condone violence, but his sons might have decided to take the law into their own hands."

Asher, as anxious as Tamar to divert Melkiah and Sarah from a marriage connection between her and Joel, spoke his suggestion with apparent diffidence.

"I wonder . . . We're thinking of people who live in this area, but remember that Joel is a stranger here and very much a man of mystery. We can't imagine him committing a crime, yet there *is* a grave reason that prevents him from returning to Bethany. If he has wronged someone, and they have since learned that he has left the leper colony, they could have followed him here to carry out the justice that he evaded by becoming a leper."

Tamar was shaking her head and Asher wished he knew if she was rejecting the suggestion that Joel was not the honourable man he appeared to be, or if she were refusing to accept the idea that he might have an avengeful enemy. He knew the answer when she reached out and smoothed the hair of the sleeping man in a protective gesture.

Suddenly, he wanted to throw Joel back into the well and be the man who was receiving all Tamar's tenderness. He stifled the thought and chose a different way to regain her attention.

"There is another possibility," he said. "Joel was wearing one of my old tunics. It could be that *I* was the intended victim . . ."

Chapter 22

"I will guard him with my life"

Asher was gratified when his words had the intended effect.

Sarah and Tamar looked towards him in horror while Melkiah gave him his immediate concerned attention.

"Tell us all you know," he commanded.

"Joel borrowed one of my old tunics soon after he came here. He wanted something to wear when he went to help the shepherds or did other outside work. I gave him the green striped one which used to be my best – so many people have seen me wearing it. If you remember, the murderer came up from behind Joel, so he could well have believed him to be me."

"He would have seen his mistake the moment his victim fell to the ground," Melkiah objected.

"Yes, but by then it would have been too late." Asher's eyes shone with excitement as he put himself in the place of the murderer. "If it *had* been me, presumably he would then have added another blow to take away my life. When he realised that Joel was a stranger to him, he must have panicked and thrown Joel into the well. He knew that if he replaced the cover Joel would be dead within a short time, and there was little chance that his crime would ever be discovered."

"It was unlikely that he would have survived the night," Melkiah agreed. "If my mother hadn't seen the two men, we wouldn't have thought of the old well, and Joel would never have been found."

Tamar moved across the bed and held Sarah's hand tightly, but even with this small comfort she found it hard to speak. "Why should anyone want to kill you?" she asked and, hearing the unsteadiness in her own voice, wondered how her father and Asher could speak in such a detached way. They were discussing the murderous attack as if it involved strangers who meant nothing to them.

Asher seemed unafraid and shrugged with apparent composure. "I've no idea," he answered Tamar. "As far as I know, I have no enemies, but who knows what evil burns in other men's hearts? Perhaps one of the workers is envious of my position and resents my authority over him."

Melkiah looked sterner than Tamar had ever seen him. "We'll find out where every man was this afternoon. Did you find Dan, Asher? What did he say?"

"He says he never left the house, and Kenturah agrees that he was with her most of the time."

Melkiah nodded then turned to Sarah. "What exactly did you see, Mother?"

"My eyes were misty when my sight returned. One of the men *was* wearing a green-striped robe, but I didn't know who he was."

"And the other man?"

Sarah shook her head. "I didn't notice anything about him. I only glanced in that direction for a moment."

Tamar saw her distress and put an arm around her. How could the joy of the day have turned into such darkness and fear? All the people she loved best in the world were in this room, and she knew now that the foreboding that had menaced them ever since Ezra's death had finally erupted into real danger.

Melkiah too was contrasting the radiant Sarah who had met him at the foot of the synagogue stairs with a stricken old lady trying to hide her tears.

"I want you to go to bed now, Mother. There's nothing you can do here. In the morning Joel will probably be conscious and in need of your nursing skills."

He coaxed her to her feet. "Asher, take her to her room and make sure that Eglah is there to help her. When you've done that, I want you to arrange a guard around the house. Put them in pairs for safety and make sure that someone patrols the roof terrace." He could see that Asher wasn't as calm as he appeared to be and regretted that Simeon was no longer there to support his son. His voice softened. "I don't want you on duty. Get some sleep. There will be much to do tomorrow."

"But Joel . . . ?"

"I will stay with him during the night."

Melkiah spoke as authoritatively as any High Priest and Asher knew better than to argue.

205

He accompanied Sarah from the room, and even in her distress she was comforted to have at her side the personable youth she had not been able to see for so many years. He smiled at her as if there were nothing wrong and she was proud of his fearlessness and wished that Simeon had lived to see the kind of man his son had become.

Melkiah went to sit in the chair that Sarah had vacated and Tamar returned to her stool.

"May I stay with you, Abba?"

Melkiah knew by her unconscious use of that name that she was too distraught to be alone and nodded. "I'll be glad of your company."

Joel was breathing heavily with his mouth slightly open. His eyes were shut and there was a bruise over one eyebrow that disappeared into his hairline. The bandage around his head was already spotted with blood and, seeing it, Tamar felt as helpless as the sleeping patient.

Yet, when she looked from him to her father and saw the muscle beside his mouth tightening in the way it always did when he was tired, she said quietly. "You cannot stay here all night. Let me watch first. I'll call you later, if you like."

"No!" The word was so emphatic that her eyes widened and Melkiah softened it with an explanation. "Joel is my guest and I alone am responsible for him. I have failed to keep him safe, but at least I can ensure that no further harm comes to him."

"Is Asher not in danger too?"

Melkiah shook his head. "I don't believe there was a mistake. Asher's build is so much slighter than Joel's. It is Joel whom we must guard."

"Not by yourself. You'll need to rest sometime."

"But for Joel I would not be alive." Knowing that Tamar was nearly paralysed by her fear and realising that she needed distraction, Melkiah went on in an easy conversational voice. "Soon after I became a leper, I was making for the colony in the Valley of Hinnom when I came to Ramah. I had long since used up the provisions Simeon had given me and had lived on wild fruit for some days. I was beginning to doubt whether I'd survive long enough to find out how to live as a leper! I came to a solitary house, saw some goats grazing on the land beside it, and decided to ask for some milk.

"A woman scattering grain came round from the side of the house followed by a flock of doves and I called out to her. She was compassionate and agreed to milk a goat and also to find some bread for me. I went a little nearer but was careful to stay the prescribed distance away.

"I did not notice the farmer and his two sons coming up behind me. The first I knew of their presence was a stone striking my shoulder. I turned round but they gave me no chance to speak. They continued to scoop up stones and throw them at me with a speed and accuracy that would have impressed even the Romans! The woman was yelling something at them but I didn't think it appropriate to join in the argument. I moved away as swiftly as a gazelle – a rather elderly one! However, just as I reached the thicket, one of the younger men, who had raced ahead of me, flung a final stone and it struck my forehead."

Tamar was aghast to hear how her father had been attacked and driven away like any despised jackal, but was beginning to realise that it took no more than unreasonable fear to turn men into murderers. She whispered, "Were you badly hurt?"

"The stone knocked me unconscious, and they left me where I fell, doubtless congratulating themselves that there would be one less beggar on the road. They knew I wouldn't last long without food or shelter."

"Such cruelty . . . Abba, why didn't the Most High protect you – and prevent the attack on Joel today?"

"He will not take away from men the freedom he has given them, even when they choose evil and cause much suffering. But he is watching – and he sends good to counteract it. He gave your grandmother back her sight so that she could tell us where to find Joel in time to save his life, and, on the day I was injured, he sent that same Joel to save me."

The colour had returned to Tamar's face and, glad to see her interest, Melkiah continued his story almost cheerfully. "Joel had heard the shouts but by the time he arrived I was lying on the ground and the farmer and his sons were back in the field. He risked his life by calling the young woman and refusing to go until he had been given food, drink and bandages for me."

He smiled at Tamar. "He appointed himself my guardian angel and he never left my side after that. I wouldn't have survived without him – particularly during the winter months when so many lepers die."

Tamar realised now that both Joel and her father had suffered more horrors than she had ever dared to imagine and felt ashamed of her childish cowardice.

"Now that you've told me how much I owe to Joel, I will guard him with my life. Go and rest, Father. Your friend will be safe with me."

In spite of the resolute way she spoke, Melkiah knew that fear had not loosed its hold on her and he did not want her new courage to be tested too severely.

"I don't believe that Joel is in danger here in his room with guards all around the house. However, he may need some medical attention, so we'll watch together. I would not have him wake up and find that he is alone."

Joel was still sleeping when Melkiah and Tamar set off for the morning service in the synagogue, Sarah having chosen to remain at home to ensure the safety and comfort of the injured man.

She had ordered some fruit and milk to be brought to Joel's room, and went to sit beside his bed. In spite of the injury to their guest, she could not help rejoicing in her restored vision. This time yesterday she had been a blind old lady, unable to help anybody, but now she could watch Joel's regular breathing and see the colour returning to his face above his dark beard.

Asher came into the room, anxiety in his eyes. "Is Joel conscious yet?"

"Apparently he stirred at dawn, murmured something, then slept again. I think he'll be fully awake quite soon."

Her prediction was fulfilled almost at once.

Roused by their voices, Joel opened his eyes and looked from one to the other.

Sarah took his hand and held it reassuringly. "All is well. Would you like some milk?"

"He'd probably prefer wine!" Asher commented.

"I *am* thirsty." Joel had wanted to add "milk will do very well" but his three words had taken a surprising effort. He gestured towards the pitcher instead and tried to rise, but the movement sent such a lance of pain piercing through his back that he became very still.

"Don't try to move." Sarah poured a cup of milk and helped him to lift his head slightly. "Sip a little at a time." She smiled at him. "Your strength will soon return."

"You can see!" For a moment Joel's pain was forgotten.

"That was one of yesterday's great blessings," Sarah told him. "The other was finding you in time to save your life. Obviously, the Most High wanted you to stay in this world."

"I am in full agreement with him! But will you tell me how I came to be here, and what is wrong with me?"

Asher came over to the bed as Sarah put the cup down.

"What is the last thing you remember?"

The milk had eased the hoarseness in Joel's throat and he found he could speak more easily. "I walked through the vineyard and was on my way to the shore when I saw the cover of the old well had been taken off. I went to see what was happening . . . I don't remember anything after the moment when I peered down into its depths."

"Somebody struck your head and dropped you into the well," Asher told him, more bluntly than Sarah would have done. "Perhaps you saw him?"

Joel met Asher's keen gaze. "If I had, perhaps *he'd* be the one in the well now!"

"Do you remember anything?" Sarah urged.

"I remember lying in the dark on what seemed to be a very lumpy pallet. When I realised that I was in the well, I presumed that I had leant too far and had fallen in. And, as it was so dark, I knew that the well-cover had been replaced without anyone realising what had happened. Unlike Jeremiah, I didn't expect to be rescued . . ."

Sarah began to dwell on the horror Joel must have experienced, lying injured and alone in a living tomb, but Asher had no time for compassion.

"Have you any idea who your would-be murderer is?"

Joel tried a cautious movement but drew in his breath sharply at the renewed surge of pain. It seemed that physical action was out of the question for the time being. He put his mind to Asher's enquiry.

"I've trodden on the toes of more than one person since I've been here. Line up all the men with bruised toes and take your pick . . .

Perhaps you can suggest someone, Asher? You've lived here all your life, and you know the inhabitants of Capernaum better than I do."

Asher smiled. "It's easier to suggest men who should be murdered. I could name quite a few."

"Go away, Asher," Sarah said. "Joel isn't well enough for all this talk."

Asher heard the displeasure in her voice and thought it wise to make his peace with her. "I expect you'd like to wander among your flowers again. If you want to go now, I'll sit with Joel. I promise I won't say a single word to him!"

Sarah saw tension in her patient's still form and knew that he needed a peaceful attendant.

"I don't trust your silence. I shall stay here until my son returns from the synagogue."

By the time Melkiah replaced Sarah at Joel's bedside, he seemed glad of his host's presence and able to converse without visible effort. He had felt stronger after taking some food and claimed he was on the way to recovery apart from being unable to move.

Azariah returned once the Sabbath was over and was pleased to find Joel alert and in good spirits. Further, after a careful examination of his back, he decided that there was no serious injury to his spine.

"You have torn a muscle or two, but they will mend."

As he left the house two officials from the synagogue arrived, grimly determined to track down a murderer.

After Joel had told his story, they went away to examine the well and to question anyone who had been anywhere near Melkiah's property the previous day.

"Apparently you had a soft fall into the well because of all the rubbish that had been thrown into it after the water source had dried," Melkiah explained.

"Someone should have told my body that before it hit the bottom! I've been envying Jeremiah: at least his enemies lowered him into his well."

There was no complaint in Joel's voice but Melkiah had seen a hint of distress in his eyes and would have given much to know who had attacked his friend so brutally. Joel had shaken his head when Melkiah repeated the names suggested during his period of unconsciousness the previous day and now he tried to direct Melkiah along a different thought track.

"The man with the most enemies today is Jesus of Nazareth," he pointed out. "All who speak up for him take upon themselves the fanatical hatred of those who will not be satisfied until he is destroyed – together with all his followers."

Melkiah nodded. Reports were coming all the time of Israelites who had been forbidden the synagogue for accepting Jesus as the Messiah. Others had been threatened, lost their livelihood, or suddenly found themselves social outcasts.

"There are those who say that John the Baptist only fell into Herod's hands because of the malice of certain Pharisees who persuaded one of his disciples to betray him," Melkiah mused. He gazed at Joel thoughtfully. "Do you believe then that you were attacked for using Jesus' power to heal Eliza? If so, why wasn't I a victim too?"

"Perhaps because you had the sense to be somewhere else at the time! Doubtless your turn would have come later – there was plenty of room for two in the well!"

As their conversation continued, Melkiah tried to analyse Joel's attitude. Somehow his suggestions were not really serious; it was as if he had no intention of trying to find out the identity of the man who had tried to kill him. There could be only one explanation.

"I believe you know who it was who attacked you."

In the silence that fell between them, they heard Tamar's voice nearby calling out to her grandmother. Her footsteps were approaching.

"It would be too dangerous for me to know," Joel said quietly. He changed his position slightly and could not suppress a grunt of pain. "As you see, I'm hardly in a condition to put up much of a fight!"

"Uzziel and Elihu want to speak to you again before they go," Tamar told her father as she entered the room. "I'll sit with Joel for a while."

Melkiah saw with pity that Tamar wore the look of a woman who had been struck by someone she had believed to be her friend. No one could live on this earth without one day facing the knowledge that there are evil men, but the moment of realisation is as sudden and devastating as being turned out of the Garden of Eden. No father could protect his daughter from this moment but he could hate the man who had caused it. His face was formidable as he went in search of the investigators.

Joel too was grieved to see the difference one day had made to Tamar. Yesterday she had been a trusting child, brimming over with the joy of a future full of faith, both for herself and for the whole world. Now, she had fallen into such darkness of disillusionment that she moved from place to place with the weariness of a desert traveller who had discovered that all oases were mirages.

She could hardly keep her eyes open and although she settled herself in a vigilant pose she looked more than ready for her bed. Joel knew that she had shared last night's vigil and was too tired for conversation.

He yawned and half-closed his eyes. "Forgive me, but I feel very sleepy."

His words had the opposite effect. She sat up straighter and spoke resolutely. "Yes. Rest now. I will guard you."

He found it hard not to smile, wondering how exactly she would defend him from a murderer, and Tamar too was asking herself the same thing. As a child, she had thrilled at the stories of women who had acted boldly to save their nation: Jael killing Sisera with a tent peg, and Judith cutting off the head of Holifernes. It was true that their enemies had been asleep at the time but even so she knew that she had not that kind of courage. What would she do if a violent man should suddenly burst into this room . . . ?

She looked around for a possible weapon and saw none – unless the evildoer would obligingly kneel down for her to crown him with the water jug! Although she smiled at the thought, there were tears in her eyes and she resolved to borrow Granna's stick for her next watch.

Joel appeared to be asleep and the corners of his mouth were lifted slightly as if a smile were not far away. She was moved by his trust in her and, knowing what she owed to him, she was glad that he was alive.

Yet, in spite of all their care, it might be wiser for him to leave as soon as he was well enough to travel. Would he be safe from his enemies in Bethany? How overjoyed his parents would be to see him again.

And Rhoda. He had murmured that name in his fever last night and although her father had heard too he had offered no explanation.

Now she began to wonder who Rhoda was and whether she would be able to protect Joel.

The thought of him leaving them was strange. Why did she feel that the shield that would keep them all safe was the unbroken ring of all those she loved: her father, grandmother, Asher, and Joel himself? The world had become such a frightening place that their only hope seemed to lie in staying together.

Joel had been watching her through half-closed eyes.

"Don't be so fearful. You'll be safe again soon."

She was startled to find him awake and aware of what she was thinking. She did not want to discuss the evil that still threatened them and begged, "Will you tell me about your home?"

Joel smiled and began to talk of his parents: of their house high on a hillside within sight of Jerusalem; of their fields and olive grove; of Daniel, his younger brother.

"And Rhoda?" she ventured. "You spoke her name last night. Who is she?"

The wood pigeons were calling outside in long soft notes but neither Joel nor Tamar heard them. Their eyes met and Joel knew that the time had come for her to know something of the truth.

"She is the reason I've stayed away," he admitted. "She is my brother's wife."

Chapter 23

"Did you think that I was the murderer?"

Tamar looked steadily at Joel wondering how such an open face could conceal so many secrets. She knew he had yearned to see his parents again but had not suspected that a girl also held a central place in his thoughts.

"Do you love Rhoda?" she asked. "Did you want her to be your wife?"

There was no distress on Joel's face as he answered Tamar. "My parents chose her to be my bride. We were to be married but then I contracted leprosy and had to go away. Later, I heard that Daniel had married her in my place."

"An added grief for you to bear," Tamar murmured, knowing how inadequate any sympathy would be. "But, once you were cured, wouldn't the joy of seeing your parents again have made up for the sorrow of seeing Rhoda married to someone else?"

"You don't understand. I have stayed away for Daniel's sake."

A memory returned to him. Daniel saying bitterly: "Why is it that you have everything? You are the elder son and our father's heir; you are clever enough to be a Rabbi – and call Lazarus of Theopolis your friend; you are our mother's favourite – and all the young women of Bethany sigh after you; and now you are to marry Rhoda, the only girl I could ever love!"

Joel had been stunned. The brothers had been on good terms from childhood and never once had he realised the resentment incubating within Daniel. It had given him an insoluble problem for his parents had arranged the match with Rhoda whom he had known and liked all his life. He had realised that her devotion to him was far greater than his to her, but, knowing little of the ways of women, had assumed that it was just the way things were.

It wasn't until Daniel's amazing outburst that he had learnt that a man too could yearn for one particular woman. And, when he had realised, he had wanted to say: "by all means, marry her" – and would have felt no loss. The problem was Rhoda herself. She professed deep love for Joel and scarcely noticed Daniel when her promised bridegroom was around.

His leprosy had proved to be a drastic solution to the problem, and the day he had learnt of his brother's marriage to Rhoda had been the happiest of his exile.

Aware of Tamar's puzzled gaze, he finished his explanation swiftly. "Daniel was jealous of Rhoda's over-fondness for me. I didn't think it fair to return until she has had time to learn to love my brother."

Tamar reflected on his words, wondering if they were true. It could be that Joel couldn't bear to see the woman he loved married to someone else.

"Yet you've decided to go home at Passover?"

"I believe it's the right time now." He smiled at her. "Do you remember Ishmael's guest, John from Bethany? He told me that Rhoda had given birth to twin sons last year. He believes that the marriage is a good one and that it is a happy household once again."

"And when your parents see you! . . ."

"I long to be home," Joel admitted.

"Will you stay there, or come home with us after Passover?"

It sounded like an invitation and he was glad that her earlier hostility had finally melted. "Maybe it will depend on the unknown man of violence. If I thought that he would follow me, I'd gladly lead him away from here, but it could be that I'm not the only one at risk . . ."

He regretted his remark almost immediately. He had relaxed his guard because the newly grown-up Tamar was someone with whom he could share his thoughts, but his words had brought the fear back into her eyes. And if she should repeat them to others, they could well bring about the very evil he most feared.

Sarah was walking in the orchard, a good distance away from the side of the house where men were gathered around the old well. A bee flew away disappointed to find that the fragrant blossom had turned into a cluster of tiny apples, and she marvelled at its translucent wings and followed its flight to the foot of the boundary wall where red anemones blazed like a deep hem on a festival robe. In spite of her anxiety, she could not help rejoicing in the radiant world that had been restored to her so unexpectedly.

In the distance she saw Asher going towards a worker with a pruning knife in his hand and guessed that he had discovered a diseased branch. She watched him for a moment, wondering why the sight troubled her. Perhaps because it was a reminder that this was not the Garden of Eden, but a flawed imitation where serpents lurked.

Joel woke with a start to find Asher bending over him. He looked beyond him to find that Tamar had gone and that the room held the shadows of early evening.

Asher had seen the momentary alarm in Joel's eyes and seemed amused.

"Did you think that I was the murderer, come to finish the deed that I started?"

Joel managed a half-smile as he countered. "Melkiah tells me that you are the fearful one – that you believe that you were the intended victim."

Asher paced round the bed but his eyes never left Joel's. "Do you think I am in danger?"

"Only you can answer that. Perhaps when I leave here, your lives will become peaceful again."

"So you're going to run away and leave us to the mercy of a murderer?"

"If he's my enemy, he will follow me."

Asher took out a knife and began to whittle a piece of wood. "You don't look in a very good shape to turn and fight a violent man."

Joel agreed and admired the deft way Asher's knife was slicing accurate curls off the small piece of sycamore. "What are you making?"

Asher shrugged. "I'm just keeping my knife sharp. I think we should all be armed until your attacker has been found." He dropped the piece of wood and approached the bed. "Perhaps you should have the knife?"

The blade shone as brightly as a Roman centurion's sword and Joel could see the keenness of its cutting blade. He tried to sit up – and froze as a pain as sharp as any knife blade pierced his back.

"Why are you trying to move?" Tamar reproved, as she entered the room. "Asher, Granna wants you."

Her foster brother loitered, turning his knife so that reflections raced around the walls of the room. "I told your father that I would sit with Joel for a while."

"Granna wants your help and she says that only you will do. I'll keep Joel company. What are you doing with that knife?"

"I thought it might divert Joel."

But Tamar had caught sight of the piece of fallen wood and smiled. "I've watched Asher make more than one shepherd's pipe. Leave your knife here. I was thinking that I ought to have a weapon."

She took it from Asher's hand and the two men exchanged glances. The contrast between the sharp, working blade and the gentle girl was incongruous. It was as if a lamb had suddenly sprouted the tusk of a wild boar.

As Asher went to join Sarah, Joel studied Tamar with amusement.

"Pretend I'm attacking you, and show me how you would use that knife!"

Tamar accepted the challenge and went nearer the bed. She tightened her grip on the knife handle, raised her arm, looked from the lethal blade to Joel's lifted eyebrows - and let her hand fall.

"I'd use it if I had to!" But she had seen him fighting to conceal a smile. "Why do you always laugh at me?"

"I'm not laughing at you, but at the idea of you as a warrior!"

She made no response to his teasing and he met the hurt eyes of a child whom no one will take seriously.

"Believe me, Tamar, far from laughing at you, I admire you more than any woman I know. You are brave . . ."

She shook her head vehemently, but he continued to gaze at her thoughtfully as if his words had told him something that he himself had not realised. His eyes held hers so steadily that she felt like a small animal mesmerized by a stronger one. And yet the message he was imparting was far from being a predatory one and she received it with confusion and silent joy.

There was no laughter in his eyes now.

217

Within three days Joel was out of bed and moving about stiffly, scarcely needing Azariah's confirmation that his back injury had begun to heal.

In spite of Joel's protests, Tamar was glad when her father decreed that his friend should not leave the house without a companion. Melkiah pointed out that a would-be murderer would not attack with a witness nearby so that even the presence of a woman would be enough to deter him.

Joel could not take more than a few painful steps at a time so was resigned to spending most of his time in the gardens beyond the courtyard. The sun was gaining in strength as the days of Nisan advanced and as he opened himself to its healing rays he had to be content to watch others working all around him. He could hear voices from the far-off blue-green sea of flax that was being harvested to make linen and cord; he saw Sarah go by with an armful of strongly-scented camphor flowers; and even Tamar, sitting beside him in her self-appointed role as guard, was stitching away industriously.

She was as natural as a dove, he thought, enjoying her shy conversation, and was amused to find himself comparing her delicate beauty with the feathery pink fronds of a tamarisk undulating in the breeze.

He had taken no part in the endless investigations which had stirred up the town like a stick in a wild bees' nest – and had done about as much good. However, he had many a visitor, each bringing his or her own theory about the identity of his unknown enemy.

Miriam came, making no accusation, but warning Joel that Sadoc believed him to be responsible for thwarting his plans to marry his sister to the wealthy Ishmael.

Joel shrugged. "Sadoc's only danger is that his greed may someday lead him to burst like a swollen toad!"

Miriam remained troubled. "Then, do you think it was Ezra's brother, Levi, who tried to kill you? I know he's threatened you."

Joel shook his head. "The attack wasn't his style at all. Can you imagine him lurking out of sight, removing a cover, and waiting for his victim to fall into the hole? No, if he ever finds out who's murdered his brother, he'll go straight to him and attack him in open fury."

Miriam looked from Joel to Tamar. "Then who?"

"We have no idea," Tamar said, and although she was frowning, there was something in the way her eyes never left Joel's face that answered a different question for Miriam.

She had been puzzled by the change in her friend, a change not entirely consistent with all the momentous events in which she had been involved. Her distraction was not shock or fear but more as if she had discovered a secret too precious to share with anyone else. And she had no idea that she told her secret with every glance at Joel, at every mention of his name.

There was nothing in Joel's response to Tamar that indicated anything other than warm friendliness and Miriam was concerned for her friend. Those who fall into the enchantment and ecstasy that is love all too often discover that the way is paved with disillusionment, desolation and despair.

Nature's pace quickened daily: buds burst into bloom with the suddenness of mischievous children jumping out to surprise their friends; almonds began to form inside their silver-green husks; rain fell to swell the grain only to be set aside by the sun and turned to steam.

Mammals too left their winter sleepiness behind: shepherds worked from dawn to dusk – and often far into the night – arranging the mating of selected ewes, assisting lambs into the world, and finishing the spring shearing. Asher seemed to be everywhere at once supervising, and Melkiah in turn kept a discreet, fatherly eye upon him and found no fault in the young steward. Men worked rhythmically in flax tall enough to hide the shortest of them, cutting the stalks close to the ground and leaving them to dry in the sun. Others began haymaking and the scent of mown grass had a friendly tussle with the fragrance of mimosa, sometimes one filling the air, sometimes the other.

It seemed impossible to believe in evil when the rays of the sun turned the lake to topaz, when blackbirds turned the mulberry into a singing tree and when doves performed dances around rainbow fountains.

Yet not a member of the household or outside labourer walked anywhere without a wariness in their eyes that had not been there before, and the more nervous workers even went about in pairs.

Joel was now well on the road to recovery and Melkiah found it extremely difficult to keep up his watch over him. He extracted a further reluctant promise not to leave the property unaccompanied and Joel agreed only because Passover was near when everything would change.

✡   ✡   ✡

"I can't believe that this time next week we shall be on our way to Jerusalem!"

Sarah was spinning rapidly as if to make up for all her years of idleness but Tamar's thoughts were on the coming festival.

"Aren't you excited, Granna? How can you sit there so calmly when there's so much to do?"

Sarah, feeding a mass of wool onto the wooden spindle, forbore to point out that she was not the idle one. She smiled at her grand-daughter lovingly. "All the servants have their instructions: the pitchers are being filled with the wine, oil and flour we shall need for the Temple. Kenturah is ensuring that we shall not die of starvation on the way by filling baskets with enough parched corn, nuts, fruit, vegetables and honey to supply not only us, but apparently every pilgrim we shall meet on the way! As you want to do something, perhaps you'll help me assemble some medical herbs and ointments so we'll be prepared for illness or accidents on the way."

She saw Tamar's fist tighten on a ball of spun wool at the word 'accident' and sought to divert her. "I haven't been to Jerusalem for many years but I remember how each pilgrimage was as joyful as the first." She saw that she had captured Tamar's interest and smiled at her. "I know that each year you've gone to watch our pilgrims assembling in the market place."

Tamar nodded, picturing the men, women and children milling around in their bright travelling robes; hearing the harness bells of the laden pack animals mingled with the excited shouts of the children and the deep voices of men singing traditional psalms as they set off on the long journey south.

"I wanted to go with them," she began, watching Sarah's stiff fingers turning the spindle to twist the threads. "No, that isn't really true," she admitted. "Not without my own family. Each year I thought 'by next Passover Abba will be back and then we can all go together.' And now it has happened! And Joel too will be with us. Granna, is Father going to accept Zelek's offer for us to stay with him in his town house in Jerusalem, or are we going to camp with the other pilgrims in the Field of the Galileans?"

There was no doubting which Tamar wanted to do and Sarah laughed. "I expect my old bones will survive an extra day or two in a tent!"

During the evening meal Melkiah was gratified to see his daughter's thrilled anticipation at the thought of the approaching pilgrimage.

"When we camp at Naim, will we meet up with the pilgrims from Nazareth?" she asked him. "I want to find the people who saw Jesus grow up and ask them about him."

Melkiah and Joel exchanged glances and her father warned: "You must be careful. Not everyone in the prophet's home town loves him. His enemies are everywhere."

"Where is Jesus now?" Sarah asked.

Melkiah shrugged. "Ephraim? Beyond the Jordan? No one knows. They have made it impossible for him to travel and teach openly."

"But we will see him, won't we?" Tamar pleaded. "I've always longed to see the Temple, but now I want to see Jesus even more."

"I want to find him as much as you do," her father assured her. "I owe him my life and will give him whatever he asks of me. If he will not accept this house as a gift, I intend to offer him the use of it whenever he is in the area. It could be that he would prefer me to stay here and share my crops with the poor. I need to ask his advice." Melkiah saw the consternation that Asher could not hide and laughed. "You needn't worry, my boy. Regardless of who owns this property, you will always be needed. This is your home."

Asher's only reply was to drink deeply from his cup of wine.

Melkiah sighed. If only the son of his faithful Simeon had inherited his father's spiritual objectives. Of course, he was still very young and the vicissitudes of life would bring him wisdom.

Perhaps he would be influenced by Tamar's growing faith. Yet, as he looked from his daughter to Asher, he realised that they were no longer the inseparable friends of long ago, and it was to Joel that Tamar was giving all her attention.

Tamar and Joel? . . . His gaze became thoughtful and he saw his own speculation mirrored in Sarah's eyes. Yet, knowing that Joel too planned to ask the Messiah's guidance for his future, he wondered if it would include marriage to his daughter.

Sarah was not afraid to ask a question on behalf of her beloved grand-daughter.

"You will be going home to your parents soon, Joel. You have many years to catch up on, and they won't want to lose you again, but you have another home here now. Will you come back to us?"

It seemed that everyone stopped eating simultaneously to give Joel's reply their total attention.

Taken by surprise, he seemed reluctant to answer, but after a moment he smiled at Sarah and spoke in his usual easy manner. "You've all made me so welcome, I've never felt like a stranger here. I appreciate the offer, but my home is in Bethany. As for the future, I want to become Jesus' disciple and follow him, but I'll go home to my parents as often as I can."

"They will want you to marry and settle down."

"I expect they will." Joel seemed unperturbed at the suggestion. "Perhaps they know of a woman who has a yearning for an impoverished husband whom she will rarely see!"

Tamar had a portion of melon in front of her but it seemed to be made of wood. Her fingers had lost their strength and seemed to be incapable of digging out the firm flesh. She did not look at Joel. All that mattered was the fruit. Why hadn't Kenturah prepared it properly?

Sarah's gaze was on Asher now. He had listened to the conversation with keen attention and she knew that he would not be sorry when Joel was no longer part of their household. She looked from Asher to Tamar. They were both young and comely. For many years she had hoped that they would marry, but now she was no longer so certain of the wisdom of her plan. There was a ruthlessness about Asher's single-minded determination to acquire anything he had set his heart on. During her years of blindness, when she had not seen the calculation in his eyes, she had responded to his cajoling voice with great indulgence.

She knew now that if he looked upon Tamar as his promised bride, it was her fault. With her restored eye-sight, she saw only too clearly a young woman wary of a "brother" who wished to be her husband and yearning for a man who treated her as a sister . . .

Tamar was shaken out of her unhappiness about Joel's plans by some incredible news that came the day before they were to set off for Jerusalem.

It was Zelek who came to tell Melkiah the news that Doras, a zealous young Pharisee, had raced to bring from Jerusalem to Galilee.

Lazarus, one of the richest and most influential men in Israel, had died. This in itself was not unexpected as ulcers had been destroying his body slowly and painfully for some time and he had been bed-ridden for the last few weeks of his life. His sisters had been distraught, while many of the Jews coming to commiserate with them had secretly rejoiced that Jesus had not been able to prevent his sick friend's death.

"Doras was there when Jesus of Nazareth arrived – four days too late. Apparently, he asked to see where Lazarus was buried, and then ordered the servants to remove the large stone sealing the tomb!"

Zelek swallowed but could not dispel the croak that had come into his voice. "Your Messiah then called out Lazarus' name and ordered him to come out of the tomb!"

Melkiah wished that Joel and Tamar were beside him to hear this story which his neighbour was repeating to him with such a mixture of confusion and doubt.

"Lazarus *did* wake from his sleep of death!" Zelek continued with that same blend of incredulity and wonder. "He came out from his sepulchre bound with cloths and spices from head to toe! Several of the watchers fainted, but Doras watched as the servants removed the grave linens: Lazarus' ulcerated flesh came off with the bandages and there was clear, unbroken skin underneath. It was undoubtedly a miracle and his friends had a great feast of rejoicing."

"It's not the first time that Jesus has raised people from death to life," Melkiah reminded Zelek.

"There have been wild tales," his neighbour agreed, "but not until now have there been reliable witnesses present." He hesitated. "As you know, I do not share your belief that Jesus is the promised Messiah, but, out of friendship, I thought I should tell you what has been happening to him."

"Has this caused the rulers of the Temple to change their minds about Jesus? Will they accept him now?"

Zelek shook his head. "If Jesus is seeking their favour, he couldn't have acted more foolishly. After God, there is no greater power than that of the High Priest and Sanhedrin. Yet Jesus has never asked their advice, and is far from being the strong warrior who will subdue our enemies. He claims to be the Christ, the anointed of the Most High, but surely only someone in league with Satan would dare to prophesy the destruction of the Temple? If his miraculous powers were from God, he would not use them to heal individuals – and to win the admiration of ignorant and sinful people – but to destroy the Romans with fire from Heaven."

Melkiah made as if to speak but Zelek held up a hand and added almost appeasingly. "If Jesus kept our laws strictly and did not contaminate himself by approaching sinners, then perhaps our rulers might believe in him and honour him as a prophet."

"All Jesus wants is to do his Father's will," Melkiah explained quietly. "He does not seek mens' acclaim or earthly power."

There was pity in Zelek's eyes now. "You have been deceived, my friend. Yesterday, Jesus entered Jerusalem as its King."

Chapter 24

"I know the danger that overshadows this house"

A blackbird was singing exultantly in the palm tree close to the room where Melkiah and Zelek sat facing each other but neither heard its tuneful notes. Never had Melkiah been so desperate to hear the end of a story.

"I don't understand. If the rulers are still against Jesus, who has acclaimed him as King?"

"A vast crowd led by his followers. There's no doubt that Jesus himself planned it. He rode from Bethany to the Temple – wearing a rich red robe with his supporters running before him crying 'Hosanna to the Son of David!' They waved olive branches and palm fronds and paid him homage by laying their mantles on the ground to make a carpet for him. They filled the air with their wild cheering and, as he entered the town, every beggar and ne'er-do-well ran to join the procession. Young girls danced before him and threw flower petals, and some people even brought incense! A mad welcome – far beyond anything King David would have experienced when he returned from one of his war victories."

Melkiah closed his eyes in disbelief. "I can't believe it. He has said so many times that his Kingdom is not of this world." Anxiety sharpened his voice. "I can imagine the reaction of the priests and scribes. Where is Jesus now?"

Zelek, well aware of the Sanhedrin's secret plans, knew that its members were permitting Jesus no more freedom than a mouse within the reach of a cat's paws, but had no intention of sharing this knowledge with Melkiah. However, he was able to answer his last question truthfully.

"We do not know. He went to the Temple and, with self-appointed authority, accused the money changers and merchants of being thieves and swindlers. Once he'd overturned their tables and forced them to withdraw to the outer court, he went away."

"And the Temple authorities let him go?"

Once again there was compassion in Zelek's eyes, not for the one claiming to be the Christ, but for Melkiah. "For the time being. You must see that he has finally over-reached himself. I came to warn you, for I know that you believed in this man."

"Not believed. Believe."

Zelek nodded. "As you wish. But stay away from him. It is dangerous to befriend him now."

"But more and more people are recognising him as the Messiah. He seeks neither wealth nor state, yet from what you tell me it seems that he has decided that the time has come for him to accept the people's wish for him to become their acknowledged spiritual leader."

Yet even as he spoke, Melkiah realised that without the backing of the Sanhedrin, whose tentacles held the entire land in its grip, the desires of the common people would be of no avail.

He met Zelek's eyes and read conflict in them. Once he would have been in the forefront of Jesus' accusers, but his neighbour had lost all his zeal since the day of his son's murder.

"Why did you come here today?"

"I have told you nothing that you will not hear from a hundred other sources – though your contacts may not arrive here so swiftly. I wanted you to know the situation before you arrive in Jerusalem. Jesus of Nazareth, the one you call the Messiah, is doomed. He has called down destruction upon himself. Pity him, if you must, but stay away from him – if you value your own life."

A cock crowed far away but Tamar needed no reminder that dawn had arrived. She hadn't been able to sleep and had been thankful when the lightness in the sky, followed by one singing bird after another, had told her that the day of the great adventure had begun.

Although it was only the first hour, she rose and donned her newly-oiled sandals and a plain tunic suitable for travelling. Her best clothes had already been packed carefully in saddle-bags and had gone to join the growing pile of luggage sacks, rugs, food, and all the other requirements of a household on the move.

The foot pilgrims from Capernaum had set off several days before but Melkiah had decided that for Sarah's sake they should make the swifter journey using mules and covered wagons. Tamar hoped that they would catch up their friends in time to take part in the final singing procession from Mount Scopus up to the Temple.

Yesterday's news had added blazing excitement to her anticipation. Soon, so very soon, she would look upon the Christ of the Most High God and perhaps she herself would witness the great miracles of power he would work to overcome any final resistance from their stubborn leaders. She, Tamar, would see the beginning of the reign of the Promised One!

She left the silent house and walked lightly through the courtyard arch into Sarah's lakeside garden. A honeysuckle tendril showered her lightly with dew as she brushed against it on her way to breathe in the cool air blowing across the deep blue water. The scent of the jasmin reached her from the nearby pergola but as she entered the tunnel of white stars she saw a lone figure leaning against the arch at the far end. He had not seen her and she was disconcerted by the uncharacteristic sadness of his stance.

Joel. Could it be that he was reluctant to leave his Galilean home – to leave her? She wanted to go to him and touch his hand comfortingly but at that moment he caught sight of her and the light returned to his eyes.

His smile made her heart leap but she made her voice practical. "Father would say that you're putting yourself at risk by being alone."

"I'm not alone. Haven't you noticed my sentry?"

Tamar's eyes followed his outflung arm and she saw a tiny sparrow looking at them enquiringly, its dark grey head on one side. The bird's tiny throat vibrated with insistent notes and her lips twitched as Joel translated.

"He's warning of your presence and calling for reinforcements."

Even as she responded to his teasing, Tamar was all too conscious that soon she would stand here alone and Joel would be far away in Bethany.

"Please come back to us," she said simply, and just for a moment Joel's eyes were unguarded and she saw their glad response.

"I dare not. I wish I could tell you why . . . "

He was close enough to breathe in the familiar almond and medulla scent of her hair – too close – but found that it was beyond his power to withdraw from her.

Tamar, exulting in the invisible wave of love that had reached her, scarcely heard his confused words and was waiting almost without breathing for him to speak again when there was a sudden thunder of hooves and the jingling of harness bells.

Joel turned from her abruptly. "Asher is bringing the extra mules and donkeys. I'll go and help him."

A moment later Tamar was alone, bewildered and bereft. Why was Joel afraid to acknowledge what had happened to them? Didn't he know that they could find comfort and joy in each other's arms?

She remembered then the words that had shattered her: "Perhaps my parents know of a woman who has a yearning for an impoverished husband whom she will rarely see." These same words now brought a measure of hope. Melkiah had promised to visit his friend's family after Passover, and, as Joel's parents would indeed be seeking a wife for their son, was there any reason why they should not choose her?

"I wish you were coming too, Eglah."

The servant girl shook her head fearfully. "I wouldn't want to go all that way."

She had elected to be one of the servants remaining to take care of the house and Tamar thought fleetingly of Adina. How eagerly she would have accompanied the pilgrims.

Melkiah was checking the saddle of the horse he was to ride as Tamar and Eglah made their way through the waiting mules to where Asher was supervising the loading of the wagons.

The courtyard was filled with animals and people: men were fastening leather straps around evenly-distributed loads; women were adding last-moment essentials to haversacks; irrepressible youngsters were darting everywhere, avoiding the staffs of old men who grumbled that mothers no longer knew how to control their children; gulls circled overhead, curious to observe the unusual commotion.

Tamar and Eglah climbed inside the hide-covered wagon in which

Sarah was to travel, ensuring that she had sufficient cushions to make the journey comfortable.

"Where is my grandmother?" she asked Eglah. "I haven't seen her this morning."

"I expect she's with Kenturah, confirming that all her instructions have been carried out." Eglah jumped heavily out of the wagon. "Though she's already checked once – last night when she went down to order a herbal drink."

Tamar smiled. "She wanted to be sure of a good night's sleep. I wish I'd followed her example. Perhaps she gave herself too strong a dose! Go and see what's happening, Eglah."

As the girl disappeared, Melkiah put his arm round his daughter. "Are you ready?"

"Ready for anything, Abba!"

But her words were disproved the moment Eglah reappeared. She stumbled towards them awkwardly and grasped Melkiah's sleeve like a life-line.

"Come quickly! Your mother is dying . . . "

For a moment they were too stunned to move, then Asher, who had heard the words, ran up to them, fear in his eyes. "What has happened?"

Eglah told the three of them jerkily as they hurried after her into the house and up the stairs.

"She's been sick all night. She's very weak. She's scarcely breathing."

Sarah almost smiled when they burst into her room with matching anxiety on their faces, but she could not disguise her haggard face. The room smelt of the vomit that had overflowed the earthenware container and her soiled bedding was in a state of great confusion.

Melkiah rested his fingers lightly against Sarah's hot forehead. "Mother! Why didn't you call for help?"

Sarah's voice was faint and cracked but again she tried to smile. "Thought it would soon be over ... didn't want to trouble anyone ... then, too weak to move." She closed her eyes but not before they'd all seen tears of weakness in them.

Tamar turned to Eglah. "Bring hot water and fresh bedding. And take that away."

She knelt beside the bed. "Granna? What can I do for you?"

Sarah opened her eyes. "1 need nothing now. The worst is over. I'm sorry to delay your departure. Go now. Eglah will look after me."

"No!" Melkiah, Tamar and Asher spoke simultaneously.

"Do you really think we'd go and leave you in such a state?" Melkiah demanded. "What has made you so ill?"

"Something I ate. Perhaps the sauce on the fish."

"More likely to be one of your herbal concoctions! You always were inclined to make them too strong."

"Perhaps," Sarah conceded, no longer able to keep her eyes open. "Please go. Don't spoil your Passover."

"We want to stay with you," Asher told the still figure as Eglah returned carrying towels and perfumed hot water, and made preparations to tend her sick mistress.

The would-be pilgrims withdrew for a conference into Sarah's sitting-room where they were joined by an anxious Joel.

"I must stay," Melkiah decided, "but there's no reason why the rest of you shouldn't go to Jerusalem. Joel and Asher will take good care of you, Tamar, and I will follow as soon as Mother is better."

Tamar shook her head determinedly. "How could I possibly leave here while I'm so anxious about Granna? I'll wait with you."

Neither of them referred to Eglah's words but they were well aware that her fear that Sarah was dying could prove to be true. The same thought must have been in Asher's mind for he too emphatically refused to leave the one who had cared for him when he was a child.

Melkiah turned to Joel. "Will you, at least, make the pilgrimage as planned?"

"Yes, I'll go."

The promptness of his reply took them by surprise, but Melkiah pursued after only the slightest hesitation.

"Perhaps you would take Tamar with you? She's been looking forward to the Festival. I believe our pilgrims are almost ready to depart. Will you lead them in my place?"

Before Tamar had time to weigh the joy and sorrow of the suggestion, Joel said. "Forgive me, but I'd travel faster alone. I'm sorry to leave you all but I promised my friend, John, that I would come to Bethany at Passover. If I set off immediately, I could be there in time to celebrate the Feast with my own family."

Tamar spoke quickly before she had had time to feel the arrow that had pierced her. "I've told you, Father. I want to stay with Granna. No one who loves her could go away when she is so ill."

She saw Joel's discomfiture by his heightened colour, but Melkiah was saying good-bye to his friend without the slightest condemnation. Tamar heard the words 'Supplementary Passover' and guessed they were making provisional plans for when Sarah had recovered.

Joel went into the old woman's sickroom while Melkiah gave orders to Asher.

"There's no reason why anyone else should fail to keep their Passover in Jerusalem. Remove our luggage and send the rest of them on their way at once. Saddle Maccabee for Joel. He's the best horse for a swift journey."

Asher obeyed with alacrity and father and daughter were left alone with their brooding thoughts. Joel had made no secret of the fact that he was determined to discover the identity of the murderer in their midst, so neither of them could understand why he was withdrawing so suddenly with nothing resolved.

Tamar, remembering Joel's eyes when he had murmured, "I dare not. I wish I could tell you why . . .", was wondering what he had meant. What did he really want? And why didn't he dare to stay with her?

Joel leant over Sarah's bed. Her skin was the colour of a woman in her shroud but her tired eyes were fixed on him.

"I'm not really deserting you," he whispered. "I know the danger that overshadows this house and I shan't be far away. Do you trust me?"

Sarah nodded and he realised that their shared knowledge made her understand his unspoken message.

"You will be safe now," he said, and left her.

He knew what he had to do – and prayed that his words would prove to be true.

Tamar refused to leave her grandmother's side even though by the end of the day she was no longer so anxious about her health. Sarah was still weak but had been able to sip some honey water and no longer looked as if she were on her way to join Abraham.

Tamar stayed with her for her own comfort: alone on the slope of deep disappointment, she would have rolled into the chasm of despair. By now the others would be setting up their first camp on their way to Jerusalem. This pilgrimage was the most important event of their year so by now they would have forgotten about Sarah's illness and would be anticipating the spiritual joys ahead. And every hour Joel was travelling further away from the place of his enforced exile – further away from her – going to others who would receive him with all the love they had stored for him in his long absence.

Her father had promised her that they would visit him when they went to Jerusalem to keep the supplementary Passover, permitted to those who had been unable to keep the decreed date. Was it possible that by then Joel would be content to be back where he belonged and that they would have no more importance for him than any other visiting friends?

Then, there was their visit to the Temple. She wondered if Jesus the Messiah would still be there, or whether they would have missed the official proclamation of him as the true King of Israel.

"I'm sorry," Sarah whispered from her sick bed. "You should have left me. You're missing so much."

Tamar had not yet got used to looking into eyes with such clear vision. Not only had her grandmother's physical sight been restored, she seemed to have the ability to read souls with perception and compassion. In the past, she and Asher had sometimes tried to evade that penetrating look, but now Tamar smiled in an attempt to disguise her frustration.

"I'll not leave this house until I see you on your feet again."

"I'll be able to eat by tomorrow. I'll soon regain my strength."

But even though Sarah was able to take a little barley cooked in milk the following day, she remained too weak to move.

"You'd think she'd been poisoned," Kenturah grumbled, adding quickly. "It was certainly nothing I gave her."

"Her sleeping draught was too strong. Herbs should be used sparingly," Nike agreed, throwing a handful into the broth she was making.

Melkiah was deeply concerned about his mother and as he sat beside her he tried to discover the source of the fear and deep unhappiness that was preventing her strength from returning.

"Are you worried about Joel? Do you think he's in danger on the road?"

"I wish the danger *had* gone with him. That young man is well able to look after himself."

Sarah's remark was uncharacteristically heartless but to Tamar's surprise her father did not question it.

He nodded. "We must all take great care."

And, as he bent and kissed Sarah, Tamar noticed a muscle tightening at one side of his mouth.

"I can't understand," she burst out to Asher the following morning when she found him among the vines which were beginning to blossom. "Why are father and Granna so afraid? Most of the people we know are on their way to Jerusalem. They may be facing dangers on the road but there's no one here but us now. Is it you they're worried about? I keep thinking of your idea that you were the intended victim when Joel was attacked. It could be true . . ."

"Tears of concern for me?" asked Asher, well pleased. "Do you care so much for me?"

Tamar pulled at her bracelet so hard that it made a red mark against her wrist. "Nothing must happen to you! I couldn't bear it."

Asher put a warm arm around her. "I promise you, I shall always be here for you." He saw how tightly her lips were pressed together and touched them gently with his fingers. "You must be composed for your father's sake. He hasn't been the same since someone tried to murder his friend. He sees assassins in wind-blown branches and reads treachery in innocent faces. Your grandmother is worried about him, I know."

Yes, she thought, Father has looked grim since it happened. It's true he sees danger everywhere.

"Poor Abba. We must help him."

"Yes, we will watch over him – and peace will come to this house again."

That night, it seemed that peace was spilling over the lake from the sky like a silent waterfall, with stars spreading out to admire their reflections in the pearl and silver sea; it was as if all the treasuries of Heaven had been opened to release their entire contents onto the lake.

However, the eyes of the watcher concealed on the shore were not on the shimmering luminescence and although he was listening intently his ears were not tuned to the murmuring of surf.

He could hear the flap of sandals and knew that two people were approaching and was sure of their identity even before they came out of the shadow of the palm tree at the end of the path.

The watcher was a bowshot away from the portion of the beach where master and servant approached the waiting boat but even so he took care to stay hidden behind the branches of a willow tree. He had watched earlier as the servant had prepared the boat so was not surprised to see the pair heading towards it now.

The older man seemed to have difficulty in walking but the younger man supported him with a strong arm. He helped him into the boat, put the oars into his hands, and prepared to push the boat away from the beach. His master murmured something and half rose unsteadily, but the young servant spoke to him reassuringly and the man in the boat nodded and sat down again.

The craft was launched and the man at the oars began to row wearily but competently. A patch of moonlight like a small ghost followed his slow progress but the watching servant had seen enough. He turned and walked away swiftly making for home and his bed.

The unseen watcher continued to follow the progress of the boat with troubled eyes. It was low in the water and it seemed to him that the stern was subsiding with every stroke.

Suddenly he remembered the hammering he had witnessed earlier when the servant had prepared the vessel for his master. He had assumed that he was making some necessary repair.

Now, too late, he realised that he had witnessed one man deliberately sending another to his death.

Chapter 25

"You are a liar and a murderer"

Tamar was on the roof terrace, huddled under a canopy of jasmin as if seeking protection. She was alone – as alone as if she were the last person left alive in the world.

The sun blazed down but in spite of its heat a shiver ran through her. There would be no warmth for her ever again. She could tell by the sun's position that it was not yet noon and marvelled dully. Was it really only hours since Imri and Dan had come to her with their fears? Surely she had been here for days, looking towards the lake, standing quite motionless until her legs had trembled too much to support her.

She had seen tears in Imri's eyes. "The Master is missing! His bed has not been slept in, and he's nowhere in the house. And Dan tells me that the boat is no longer on the shore."

Tamar had not understood their concern. "My father often goes out on the lake on starlit nights."

"And returns well before dawn to have some sleep before day-break," Imri pointed out gently. "He told Asher that he would go for no more than an hour as he wanted to be well rested before the Passover begins this evening."

"Perhaps he went ashore and fell asleep?"

"Perhaps. But even so he would have woken and returned long before now."

Tamar was angry. "You look for trouble where none exists! There is much to do before the Feast. Imri, go and lay out your Master's best clothes, and make sure that no word of this nonsense reaches my grandmother. Dan, you will come to me the moment you see my father's boat."

They had gone at her bidding, and Tamar sorted out her own clothes for the celebration. Her breathing was quick and shallow: if she were to breathe deeply, as if to calm herself, she would be admitting that there was something wrong. Her thoughts sped around inside her head like darting swallows but she knew she could not bear it if they stopped. With a clear head, fear would come, the fear of losing forever the person who had given her life . . .

It wasn't true. The servants were cruel to have invented a disaster, particularly now at this time when there had been one sorrow and anxiety after another.

She had come to the roof to wait for her father's return and when she had seen some swans flying over the shining lake like arrows speeding towards their target, she had believed that they were showing her the direction to watch.

She had cried, "Abba, where are you? Come quickly, for I cannot bear this pain."

The sky was getting darker and she could no longer hear any birdsong. It seemed appropriate for without her father there could be no light, no warmth, no joy. She looked towards the lake which was turning gradually to the colour of sulphur-streaked amethyst.

"Will there be a storm? Abba, come quickly, while it is still safe."

She heard footsteps running up the roof stairs and looked towards them in sudden wild hope. She relaxed, prepared to smile. In a moment she would be released from this nightmare and would be able to live again.

"Where is he?" she demanded, as Asher appeared.

He stared at her for a moment, almost as if he did not understand her words, then shook his head.

"There's no news yet, but you must come down from the roof. Have you ever seen such a sky? Something strange is happening. The sun is being eclipsed moment by moment. It's so dark that the servants are lighting the lamps."

He held out his hand to her. "Come down."

Tamar became aware then that the darkness around her was physical, not just her own personal desolation, and bewilderment encircled the confusion inside her mind. She did not understand, but nothing mattered anyway if her father were not coming home.

"I'm staying here. I will come down when Abba returns."

Soon after, a trembling Eglah brought her a warm cloak and a lighted lamp.

"The world is ending," she whispered. "Midday, and it's as dark as midnight in winter! The judgement foretold by the prophets is upon us!"

Asher too showed fear when he returned to share her vigil. The sky was now so dark that the stars could be seen and he gripped her arm painfully.

"It's as if Satan and his demons have left Gehenna and conquered the Light. We cannot live without the sun."

Tamar made no reply. It required all her effort to breathe in and out.

Words tumbled in her brain like the Greek acrobats she had once seen entertaining the crowd. *The world is ending. We cannot live without the sun. I cannot live without Abba. How can I look for him when it is so dark? I must wait for the sun to rise. But it's daytime now and the light has gone. Joel has gone too. We're all going to die.*

"Yet Jesus, the Son of God, is on the earth!"

She said these last words aloud, in the triumphant voice of a child finding a friend in a game of hide-and-seek. "The world cannot end because he is with us. And even if my father *is* dead, Jesus will bring him back to life."

Agree with me, Asher, for if you don't, all hope is gone for ever.

Asher understood very well what she was asking of him, but building on false hope would not help the young girl he intended to marry.

"It could be that this darkness has come upon the earth because Jesus of Nazareth is dead. After his presumptuous entry into Jerusalem as King, our leaders would have had no choice but to silence him. Perhaps the Most High is punishing Israel for allowing herself to be deceived."

Jesus of Nazareth dead . . . The Messiah dead . . . The Most High punishing Israel? . . .

She pulled away from Asher as if he were one of Satan's demons.

"If they *have* killed Jesus, then the Lord God is punishing us for killing his Son!" It couldn't be true, and yet what other explanation could there be for this catastrophic eclipse of the sun?

She picked up the lamp and stumbled from the roof, leaving Asher alone in the darkness he deserved for his unjust words. She ran slowly and awkwardly like one in a nightmare who cannot go quite fast enough to evade the terror behind. She ran and fell, and climbed and stumbled, until at last she fell into Sarah's waiting arms.

✡   ✡   ✡

In the middle of the afternoon the mysterious darkness rolled back, like a dark curtain being pulled aside, and confused birds which had returned to huddle in their nests emerged singing to fly through gentian-blue sky.

Servants resumed their duties, smiling their relief, but careful to remain grave in the presence of the two mistresses who sat together so silently waiting for the Master's return.

Evening came and all over the country slaughtered lambs were being consumed joyfully in the traditional Passover ritual. But Sarah and Tamar sat unmoving like statues depicting grief and despair, and waved away any suggestion of food.

Surely a hundred years had gone by since yesterday when Melkiah had been at the supper table, heartened by his mother's returning strength, and promising Tamar to make up for her disappointment over the postponed pilgrimage. There had been affection in his voice, humour in his eyes, and she had returned his smile oh so carelessly. Why had she not gazed at that beloved face and imprinted it on her memory so that she would be able to recall it at will throughout the long years ahead?

News would come soon. A man and a boat could not vanish completely on such a tranquil lake.

He will return soon. We will hear him any moment.

But Tamar's prediction was proved wrong and in fact she had to endure endless night hours of trying to hold back the torrent that threatened to sweep her to destruction.

The sun was high in the sky before news came – news that she did not want to hear.

Sarah was still on her sick bed when Tamar went to receive the messenger.

"I'm Nathanael. You know my nephew, Tobit," he said, and she had to lean forward to hear words muffled by a thick, white beard. His back was bent and all she could see of his eyes was his shaggy eyebrows.

"Word came," he muttered. "A body has been washed ashore not far from Hippo."

Tamar found she could speak, for of course this news had nothing to do with her.

"Who is it?"

"No one knows. They say your father didn't return from the lake last night. Tobit says we could go and see . . ."

"Tobit? I thought he was in Jerusalem. Didn't he go with the other pilgrims?"

"No. His arm is still giving him trouble. Would you like us to go to Hippo?"

"Yes! How long will it take?"

The old man considered. "There's no wind so we'll need to use the oars. My nephew can't row because of his arm but I can manage. Perhaps there'll be a wind to help our return journey."

Tobit's uncle didn't look as if he had the strength to lift an oar, let alone use it.

"Asher can come with you. He can row."

But Asher could not be found and Nathanael was impatient to begin the journey. As Tamar sent him on his way, she stammered, "If . . . You'll bring him back?"

Nathanael nodded and the moment he left Tamar turned on Eglah who had witnessed the encounter.

"You are not to say a word of this to my grandmother! This may have nothing to do with your Master. Time enough when they return."

Time enough . . . What was time? Something that happened undiscerned while waiting . . . something that led inevitably to joy or sorrow? Too much time to wait if the former; not enough if the latter. Yet, perhaps time did not exist at all for every moment seemed to stand still, arrested like a rose petal crystallised in honey.

She could not return to Sarah without relaying the latest news, so kept the long vigil on a stone seat in the garden overlooking the empty lake.

No fishing boats had gone out as most of the fishermen were still in Jerusalem, and she had seen nothing since Tobit's boat had disappeared from her sight with the two men in it.

People came and spoke to her but she did not hear them. She

could not converse, nor move from this position until her father came home. This time yesterday he had been alive. And Jesus? Had that strange darkness signified his death? Perhaps Joel too was dead, pursued and destroyed by his enemy.

So much evil everywhere. Had her father been another victim? Had someone attacked him and sent him to his death? But no, he had been alone in the boat. *Abba, why didn't I go with you?*

"You must drink, Tamar."

Asher was beside her, holding a cup of date wine, his eyes upon her pale face. "It will give you strength.

I will be strong when I see him again.

But she sipped the drink to please Asher, grateful for the solicitude in his eyes. He too must be suffering, threatened with the loss of his second father. She reached out and pulled him beside her, holding onto his hand with the tightness of desperation.

Asher put his free arm around her and held her close.

"Tamar," he murmured. "Whatever happens, I'll look after you. It'll be as it was before your father came home. You, me, and your grandmother, living together contentedly. Life will go on and I will take care of everything. Don't be afraid. I'll always watch over you. 1 love you and you belong to me."

"Before Father came home." she thought. "Were we content? I don't remember . . . Simeon died and Asher mourned him . . . he wants to marry me . . . Joel is far away. I will never see him again if Abba is dead."

Asher had been reading her thoughts. "We need no one but each other. Let me look after you?"

It was almost a question and now both his arms were around her tightly and his face close to hers. He was too close. She was a fish struggling in a net, desperate to breathe, pushing him away.

"Leave me alone!"

Seeing the wildness in her eyes and the trembling of her lips, Asher overcame his initial annoyance and decided to be patient. He would stay out of sight, if that was what she wished, but he did not expect Melkiah to return alive and when she needed support he would be there.

Most of the estate workers had gone to Jerusalem but, at Sarah's request, he had sent the most able-bodied of those remaining to search for their missing Master. If Tamar's worst fears were realised and Tobit's boat brought back the body of her dead father, then it would not be long before they all discovered that he, Asher, was to be their new Master. He would possess everything, control everything, from the house and land, to the workers and servants – to the young mistress who would need comforting.

Once, when Tamar was a child, Simeon had told her of the day he had climbed Mount Hermon. Near the summit he had spotted among the ice forming at the side of a stream, a single white star flower. It had been inside a sphere of ice, frozen in its perfection, protected from all danger.

Now Tamar felt that she was that star flower with a solid wall of ice around her. She could think and breathe – though breathing had never seemed so difficult – but there was no way she could communicate with others who lived outside her ice world.

She hadn't eaten for over twenty-four hours and there was a sharp pain in her stomach, but it was nothing compared to the pain that lay in wait for her outside her block of ice.

There were petals on the bench beside her and the air was heavy with the scent of oleander; ever after she would associate that perfume with today's vigil.

She narrowed her aching eyes, searching the perimeter of the shore over and over again, trying to discover her father's whereabouts by the desperation of her love and need. She remembered how Eliza had been found and wondered if her father too were lying alone and injured in some hidden place.

Something rustled in a nearby bush. An animal? A human being? Was the man of violence lurking nearby? He had murdered Ezra; had intended to make Joel disappear forever; had perhaps lain in wait for her father and destroyed him too. If his boat had followed Melkiah's, he could have killed the unsuspecting man and dropped his body into deep water...

"The body Tobit has gone to see is not my father's", she told herself. "Nothing has happened to him. He is safe. He will come back to me."

The creature in the bush moved again. *The killer is here. It's my turn now.* She didn't care, didn't even turn her head. She didn't want to live. If Abba were in Sheol, she would bless the one who sent her to join him.

She caught sight of a boat far out on the lake and rose, shading her eyes. There was a breeze now and the square sail had been unfurled to take full advantage of it.

She stumbled from the garden onto the adjoining beach, trembling so much that she was forced to sink onto the pebbly shingle and crouch there, waiting for the veils of darkness to clear from her vision.

The boat would take a long time to reach her. *Come no closer. As long as you stay on the lake my father is alive!*

Asher had come to join her by the time she could see the men in the boat clearly: Tobit with his bandaged arm at the tiller, and his uncle adjusting the sail confidently, transformed from a feeble landlubber into a proficient sailor.

By now it was the first watch of the night and dusk was spreading an indigo cloak over the blue-grey surface of the sea. The boat, still some distance away, had come prepared and a ruby lamp swung gleaming from the prow. The breeze had stiffened and dark clouds raced across the sky, ensuring that when the sun had disappeared there would be complete darkness.

Tamar tried to rise and Asher supported her until her cramped limbs responded and she was standing beside him. In the failing light she saw her own fear and apprehension mirrored on his face, and put her hand into his. She felt its familiar roughness, was aware of the warmth of his body alongside hers, and leant closer to him.

His arm supported her as the boat finally beached a cable's length from where they stood, and it was only then that they could see that Tobit and Nathanael had not returned alone.

A body lay stretched on the wooden seat along the stern, a body they recognised, a body as still as death.

"I'm sorry," Tobit said, as he followed his uncle out of the boat.

Tamar lifted her arms as if to push away the shadows which were shrouding the sight of her father lying before her as if in sleep. His body was moving up and down with the rocking of the small sailing boat but his eyes were closed, his face as white as a ghost, and his limbs had been arranged into an uncomfortable neatness.

Tamar wanted to go to him but found herself sinking back onto the shingle, waiting for her surroundings to stop swirling around her.

Asher left her and took a step towards the boat but Tobit stood in his way accusingly.

"It's your fault he died! Nathanael saw you escorting him along the path and said he could scarcely walk. Why did you let him go onto the lake when he wasn't well?"

Asher was shaken but not prepared to accept any blame for the tragic death.

"He was unsteady because he had drunk too much wine," he explained. "I kept trying to persuade him not to go, but he insisted that an hour or two on the lake would clear his head. In the end, I decided to let him go. After all, the water was calm and even if he had lost an oar he wouldn't have come to any harm."

Asher looked from the body in the boat to the girl at his feet. "I'm sorry, Tamar. I didn't know what was to happen. I would have done anything to keep him safe for you."

"You are a liar and a murderer, Asher!"

The words came from the darkness behind them and suddenly Joel was there, brushing past them to turn on the young steward.

"Melkiah was not drunk, but drugged with the wine which *you* provided. It was *you* who suggested that he should go on the lake, and *you* who insisted when he protested that he had no strength to row. And it was you who sent him to his death in the boat which you had deliberately damaged earlier!"

Even in the dim light of the fading day, Joel could see that Asher was shocked into near-terror by the sudden reappearance of a man he had believed to be in Jerusalem. He saw Asher's wide-eyed stare, the involuntary confused movements of his hands, the way he turned his head sharply like an animal in a trap. However, even in his consternation, he did not make the mistake of speaking too soon. He remained very still, waiting for his thoughts to clear, and Joel saw the exact moment when Asher decided that the other's presence did not mean that all was lost.

He even smiled. "Doubtless you have your reasons for trying to discredit me, but there's no truth in your wild ideas. And you will find that no one will believe you."

It was then that the dead man in the boat spoke.

"Then perhaps they will believe *me*?"

Chapter 26

"The lamp of the wicked shall be put out"

Melkiah unfolded his long legs unhurriedly and stood up, his hair and beard blowing in the wind, his open eyes fixed piercingly upon the son of his late steward.

He took three steps along the centre of the rocking boat and climbed out while Nathanael held the prow steady. He waved away Tobit's outstretched arm and stood on the shore upright and strong – and undeniably alive.

Tamar was rising to her feet, energy flooding into her in the miraculous company of her father and Joel, but their presence had the opposite effect on Asher.

He seemed to be measuring the combined strength of the silently-accusing men around him before seizing his only chance of escape. He splashed into the sea, tugged the boat violently from Nathanael's hold, pushed it into deeper water and threw himself into it.

A strong gust of wind blew at that exact moment as if to aid the fugitive and, by the time Tamar had reached her father's side, Asher had set his course and was sailing away from them over the dark waves.

"We can catch him easily," Joel said, but Melkiah put a restraining arm on his shoulder.

"Let him go."

By now there was a distant roaring behind the hills and trees were beginning to toss and sway.

"There's going to be a storm," Tobit prophesied, and his uncle nodded agreement.

"Leviathan is stirring under the lake. See how he's pushing up the waves!"

Melkiah had his arm reassuringly around Tamar as they stood in a group peering through the gloom to watch Asher's boat making erratic progress in the gusting wind. They saw it heel over, water spraying into the boat with the force of a spouting whale, the prow crashing into the waves, and the wildly-flapping sail swinging so suddenly that it threatened to capsize the small craft, and yet all the time it was moving inexorably further and further from the shore.

It was now so dark that all they could see clearly was the hazy red light on the disappearing craft. The wind whipped their own tunics and mantles and blew their hair across their faces, but still they gazed across the stormy sea.

Tobit shook his head. "He's not going to make it."

At that very moment the boat capsized, blown onto its side by the sail that should have been lowered at the first sign of the coming storm.

Asher's cry travelled to them over the angry waves and they knew that he had been thrown into the sea.

"He cannot swim," Tamar whispered and although she understood little of what had been happening, she knew enough to know that by swallowing Asher the waves were sparing him from a far worse fate.

The lamp of the boat was under water and there was now no longer anything to see but an empty heaving lake under a dark sky.

Joel was the last to leave the shore, the last to look back. It was then that he heard in his mind an echo of the Messiah's prophetic words:

The lamp of the wicked shall be put out.

It was late and the women could hardly keep their eyes open but Melkiah realised that it wasn't fair to send Sarah and Tamar to their rest without giving them a few explanations.

They had changed into fresh clothes and taken some refreshment together in the near silence brought about by shock. They had been content to communicate by loving touches and eyes full of thankfulness, but now Tamar pleaded for an answer to the question which troubled her the most.

"But why did Asher try to kill you, Father? I thought he loved and honoured you."

Melkiah looked across the table to Joel. They had decided between them that it would be impossible to conceal the truth from his family.

"I think Joel knows the answer to that better than any of us, but we'll all speak of what we know."

Sarah, whose dining-couch was close to her son's, read his deep sorrow and knew that he shared her grief at what the son of their faithful steward had become.

Tamar too understood the reason for the weariness in her father's eyes but the joy of his restored presence outweighed everything, even her own sorrow over Asher's death. Her eyes kept returning to Joel. His pose was relaxed but she could see from the way his fingers gripped his cup of wine that he was not entirely free from tension. All the laughter had gone from his face but even so the sight of it gave her quiet joy. His direct clear gaze came from the light within him and to her it was a crystal stream in which she could bathe. She was deeply glad that he was with her and not in Jerusalem.

Joel smiled at her as if he had read her thoughts, and began speaking.

"Perhaps none of this would have happened if Melkiah had not become a leper. When he went away it must have set the young Asher wondering who the new Master of the property would be. It wouldn't have taken him long to realise that whoever married the daughter of the house would take control."

"We were no more than friends – like brother and sister," Tamar protested.

"Perhaps, but as the years passed Asher came to have no doubt that it was possible for him to become your husband."

Joel didn't look at Sarah who was uncomfortably aware that her over-indulgence of the steward's son had helped to give him ambitions that could never be realised.

"It was then that Asher succumbed to a weakness that he must have berated himself for ever after: he gave in to his desire for the willing Adina.

"His father, Simeon, knew and approved of his son's attachment to the servant girl and wanted to arrange a marriage. This compelled Asher to put forward his hope of marrying Tamar. Simeon, ever faithful to his absent Master's best interests, was horrified at his presumption and they quarrelled violently.

"And then, with the matter still unresolved between them, Simeon fell to his death."

Joel's honest eyes evaded Melkiah's. His friend had told him to tell all he knew to the women, but it was better that his suspicion that Asher had deliberately allowed his father to fall – and had perhaps even planned it – should remain unspoken. In the eyes of their people, patricide was one of the worst crimes, and he would not attribute to Asher something that was only conjecture on his part.

"Asher lost no time in sending Adina away," Joel continued. "And was then confident that there were now no obstacles in his plan to marry Tamar and become Master here."

Melkiah smiled wryly. "Until I returned!"

"Yes. Even so, all was not lost. As Tamar's husband he would eventually acquire all he desired. However, he soon discovered that you did not see him as the obvious choice for this honour: Ezra too had his eye on his neighbour's daughter."

A memory returned to Tamar: she was standing with Ezra at the water's edge, her hand on a willow branch, and he had been too close, too ardent.

"At the end of a year, may I ask you again?"

She had agreed in order to end the conversation. Had that misunderstanding been the cause of his death?

Joel saw her misery and dealt with the tragedy as briefly as possible.

"Obviously Asher believed that Tamar would marry Ezra and took the chance to dispose of his rival when he saw him alone."

"But Asher was in Chorazin that day. He didn't come back until after Ezra was dead!"

"If he had returned earlier, unseen, there would have been nothing easier that to go into hiding for a few hours in order to reappear later, as if just completing a wasted journey."

Sarah was wishing that she could obliterate the past as if it never had been. She looked twenty years older than she had a few weeks ago, the effect of being forced to accept that Asher's handsome exterior had hidden a spirit open to evil.

"But why did he attack *you?*" she asked Joel.

This was difficult to explain without adding to Tamar's embarrassment, but there was no hiding the fact that she had been the key to the treasure Asher coveted. He spoke to Tamar directly.

"All was well while you remained unconvinced about the identity of Jesus of Nazareth and looked on me as no more than your father's guest. Then Eliza was bitten by a deadly snake and healed by prayer in the name of Jesus . . .

"Asher alone did not rejoice at the miracle. All he could see was that you had come under the influence of the Messiah and had joined your father and myself in an alliance that could only end in disaster for him."

Joel remembered how he had recognised the expression on Asher's face: thus had his brother Daniel looked upon him for being the elder son, heir to a double share of their father's property, with the right to marry the lovely Rhoda.

"Once again Asher acted boldly and lost no time in luring me to my death. Knowing my insatiable curiosity, he simply removed the cover of the old well . . . The plan was a good one and I'd doubtless have lain there for centuries but for something Asher could never have anticipated: Sarah's blindness being cured miraculously – just in time to glimpse two men by the well."

"If only you'd seen Asher as he attacked you," Tamar lamented.

"I did."

Joel almost laughed at the way her eyes widened and answered her question before she could ask it. "My only hope was to convince him that I hadn't!"

"You tried to tell us that you were in danger when we took you out of the well," she remembered.

"No! I was warning you that *Asher* was a danger! Lying in the well, I finally realised that his obsession had turned to a madness that would stop at nothing to attain what he had decided to possess."

Joel remembered how determined Tamar had been to guard him and smiled at her before turning to Sarah.

"I believe that you were beginning to suspect the truth?"

Sarah nodded. "When I saw him in the orchard, I realised that he looked just like the figure I had seen that day at the well . . . I couldn't believe such evil of him and yet there were other signs I refused to admit. All I could do was to make sure that he did not take a turn in 'guarding' you when you were so helpless."

Joel bowed. "You saved my life for the second time. I knew then that it would be wise to make him believe that I had no designs on Tamar and that I would not be returning here after Passover."

A rainbow gleamed in Tamar's mind but she turned to her father.

"Did you suspect Asher too?"

Melkiah shook his head. "Joel is about to tell you of my stupidity. But for him I'd be adorning the bottom of the lake by now."

Joel made a gesture of denial. "You couldn't have imagined the lengths Asher would go to in order to satisfy his greed and ambition. But I saw his face when you spoke of offering your property to Jesus and knew that you had signed your own death warrant. Of course, he needed time to plan a way of disposing of you and his immediate priority was to prevent you from meeting up with the Messiah in Jerusalem."

"I suppose that's where my 'illness' comes in," Sarah said. "I knew by my symptoms that someone must have added something to my bed-time drink. I'd heard Asher talking to Eglah outside my room just before she brought it to me but it didn't make sense to suspect him, for I couldn't see why he should wish me any harm."

"He didn't. I'm sure he was genuinely fond of you," Joel assured her. "But he knew that Melkiah would not leave you if you were ill. He intended you no lasting harm."

"A dead son isn't lasting harm?"

Melkiah was close enough to feel the trembling she could not control and held her firmly against him.

"I'm alive, Mother, and intend to stay on this earth for my full three score years and ten!"

Tamar could not help wishing that Joel were as close to her, comforting her in the same way, and was glad that her unbound hair concealed her flushed cheeks as she asked him.

"Why did you leave us when Granna was ill?"

"I didn't go far but it was important that Asher should believe that I had gone. I rode south to Tarichea, stabled the horse, and walked back here to watch the house. I took Tobit and Susanna into my confidence and they have been providing for my needs ever since.

"On Thursday evening, I followed Asher and saw him prepare the boat for use that night. I was some distance away and heard him hammering but thought he was undertaking some necessary repair – rather than spiking the keel of the boat in several places so that it would sink once in deep water."

Joel looked at Melkiah apologetically. "*I* was the fool! I was looking for a different kind of danger. I thought he would get into the boat with you and make his move when you were far from land . . . "

"What would you have done if it had happened that way?"

The question came from Sarah.

"I had a boat hidden in the willows. I'd have followed and Asher could have done nothing with a witness following in his wake."

She nodded and asked her son. "How did he manage to drug you?"

Melkiah admitted ruefully. "I don't remember much of that evening. I had only one cup of wine with Asher when we were sharing our disappointment about missing Passover in Jerusalem. I felt as I once had as a youth when I'd had too much new wine and Asher suggested that some fresh air would clear my head. He walked me to the shore and put me on the boat . . . "

Joel took up the tale. "He was so confident that he didn't even wait to see you go far – or perhaps he didn't want to be seen in the vicinity. I saw your boat getting lower and lower as it filled with water and realised the truth almost too late . . . "

"You came in time," Melkiah said.

The men exchanged affectionate glances, neither wanting to relive the few desperate moments when Joel had had to drag the half-unconscious weight of his friend from a sinking boat into his own unstable craft.

"As this happened on Thursday night, why didn't you bring Father straight home?"

Tamar could not keep the accusation out of her voice.

Sarah, who had shared the same two days of torment, understood and told her. "They had to trap Asher, had to curb his wickedness. He was becoming more and more inhuman . . ."

Joel nodded. "He was like a man laying a road, ruthlessly cutting down everything that got in his way."

He walked to Tamar's side and put an arm around her, speaking to her as if they were alone in the room.

"Tamar, I'd have given ten years of my life to have spared you what you went through, but there was no other way. This was our only chance to prove Asher's guilt."

Joel's eyes were speaking a message that went far beyond his plea for understanding and Tamar felt faint and strong at the same time.

"Finish the story quickly," she whispered feeling the imprint of his warm arm around her even when he had returned to his own place.

"I took your father over the lake to the family who were stabling your horse and asked him to wait there until Tobit came for him. Then I came back to Capernaum and made plans with the two fishermen. We would have brought your father back yesterday but the eclipse of the sun took us by surprise. However, we realised the more time that passed, the surer Asher would become that his plan had succeeded, and I'm afraid your anxiety, and Sarah's, all helped to convince him.

"Then today, we had to wait for the fading light of evening to try and deceive Asher into thinking that he saw a dead body being brought home."

"You deceived *me!* . . ."

There was such anguish in Tamar's voice that any satisfaction Joel had felt at the success of his plan vanished completely. He looked at her helplessly until Melkiah came to the rescue.

"I am alive and I intend to remain so," he said briskly. "But you are half-dead with exhaustion – as we all are. It's time for bed."

And they rose with relief to part and in the silence of their rooms to try and absorb all that had happened. Their minds were too disturbed for sleep but they wanted this endless day to be over so that it could be buried forever with all its memories – memories as dark as that of the day before when the sun had been blotted out and it had seemed that the world had come to an end.

It was five days before they heard of the events which had taken place in Jerusalem at the same time as their own traumatic experiences.

Fortunately for minds and hearts still full of confusion and pain, they heard the good news at the same time as the bad so were spared the utter consternation suffered for three long days by other followers of Jesus of Nazareth.

The hatred and jealousy of the chief priests and leaders towards the man who claimed to be the Messiah of the Lord had finally come to a head. They had arrested him and taken him to the Roman Governor, Pontius Pilate, and had hypocritically accused him of sedition.

"He claims to be a King, a rival to the great Caesar!" they had declared.

Pilate, whose spies kept him well informed of everything the Jewish prophet had ever said, knew very well that there was no truth in the accusation. However, when they threatened to inform Caesar of his refusal to take action, the Governor wasn't prepared to risk losing his own position of power. Shrugging his weak scruples aside, he sentenced the innocent Prisoner to crucifixion, preceded by a brutal scourging.

And so Jesus, believed by his disciples to be the Son of the Most High God, had died the long-drawn-out death of unimaginable agony which had been devised as punishment for the worst of criminals.

It was Lucius the Centurion, himself a follower of Jesus, who told Melkiah and Joel of these events and they saw the shame in his eyes at being a member of the race who had destroyed the most perfect Man who had ever lived.

There was a reassuring gleam in the centurion's eyes, which promised further news to reduce the shock with which Melkiah and Joel had received his initial report.

"But Jesus is alive," he said simply. "He foretold that his enemies would kill him but promised his followers that he would come to life again on the third day. Those jackals knew of his prophecy and weren't taking any chances: they sealed his tomb so that it could not be opened without their knowledge."

Lucius was smiling now with the joy of a man who has discovered the impossible to be true.

"I believe that an earthquake rolled the great stone aside and that Jesus came out of his tomb – resurrected by the Most High into an indestructible Living Being."

The centurion went on to tell of some of Jesus' friends who had seen and talked to the Man who had been indisputably dead – his heart having being pierced by a Roman lance after his crucifixion – but Lucius had lost the attention of his listeners.

Their spirits were soaring like eagles towards the vault of Heaven in their exultation for, after all these thousands of years, Light had finally won the victory over Darkness.

"Where is He?" Joel asked, poised as if to run to the triumphant Messiah immediately.

"If I knew, I'd go there," Lucius admitted, adding. "But his disciples say that He has completed his mission on earth and will soon be returning to Heaven. It's unlikely that we'll ever see him again."

"What do soldiers do when their Commander-in-Chief disappears suddenly?" Joel mused as they walked home slowly.

Melkiah was already making new plans.

"Even though I can no longer consult Jesus, I owe him my life and from now on I consider myself but a steward in charge of his property. This house will be at the service of his disciples and I will share my crops freely with those in need."

Joel, who had been deep in his own thoughts, approved.

"And I?" he wondered aloud. "I had hoped to follow the Messiah, but what can I do for him now?"

Melkiah stopped at the main entrance to his property and waved Joel through the gate ahead of him.

"Perhaps," he suggested. "You should follow the guidance he has already offered you. Didn't he tell you to come to Capernaum with me?"

"I must go to my parents in Bethany," Joel demurred but they both knew that there was no future for him there.

Through an archway to the lake garden they could see Tamar gathering flowers and Melkiah stopped walking.

"You are the only person I would trust to use my wealth for the service of others. I want to make you my heir – and also to give you my dearest treasure."

He stopped Joel before he could speak.

"Save your words for my daughter!"

The serenity had returned to Tamar's face and her eyes were peaceful as she held out a lily to Joel.

"Look!"

An adonis butterfly was poised on one of the white petals, its brilliant wings fluttering tremulously as it sipped the nectar. Joel bent to admire the azure wings while searching for the right words to capture a girl as vulnerable and exquisite as any butterfly.

"I shall go to Bethany soon."

"Your parents will be glad."

But he had seen the disappointment in her eyes and was encouraged. He decided to follow Melkiah's directness.

"I'll come back if you want me to, but I must visit them first. I'd like to take you with me - as my future bride."

Tamar raised her eyes to his and was reassured when she found what she sought there.

"Yes!" she said. "When you go, I will come with you."

His kiss was as gentle as the brush of a butterfly wing and when she put her arms around his neck in a natural, loving gesture he pulled her close to him.

They drew apart as a rain shower over the lake created a brilliant rainbow.

Neither of them spoke but they knew that it was a sign: joy and sorrow, like good and evil, would alternate and sometimes merge; but light and love would never die.